DESERT HEART

M. LINGANE

First published in Australia by Insync Holdings Pty Ltd
PO Box 526, The Gap, Queensland, Australia 4061
ABN: 74 087 648 600
Copyright © Mark Lingane 2013
The right of Mark Lingane to be identified as the Author of the Work has been
asserted in accordance with the Copyright, Designs and Patents Act 1988.

Book cover design and typesetting by BookCoverCafe.com

Cataloguing-in-Publication (CiP) entry:
A catalogue record for this book is available from the National Library of Australia.

Desert Heart
Lingane, Mark

ISBN: 978-0-9874786-5-8 (pbk)
ISBN: 978-0-9874786-7-2 (e-bk)

As always, to Belinda and Sebastian.
And to the team as well.

CHAPTER 1

HOUSE OF LOVE

I wished David would bite me, sink his teeth into my neck, or scrape his nails down my back. Draw blood. I wished he would inflict something that inspired some kind of passion in me, that demonstrated that I could still feel, that not everything was ruined and dead.

But he didn't. He was there, on top, pumping away until his eyes crossed. He made his little noise to indicate it was all over then collapsed to the side. For three months we'd been sharing this bed and his routine hadn't changed once. His hands continued to fumble around in earnest incompetence. He went through his "love" checklist with mathematical precision, and it all came to naught. I mean, he was in his mid-forties, he should've known what he was doing by now.

But where was the passion? Where was the spontaneity? Where was the depravity?

And he worked for Google. You'd think some level of evil would be built in.

Despite my years of searching I hadn't found anyone who could ignite that long-dormant passion, and sometimes I just pretended. Sometimes I drank enough to remember and fantasize. Sometimes I tried to find solace in the fact that someone desired me. But I didn't feel desired. I didn't feel glamorous. I didn't feel loved.

Our bodies were present, which meant David and I had at least some kind of intimacy. He could even be making love to me in his mind, but he was merely a placeholder until it was time to move on. It wasn't his fault; he was just another man who was not Alex.

None of them were.

And it had ruined my life.

It was late and I stared at the ceiling. David was beginning to snore. The bed felt empty.

It had been ten years since I'd returned from Colombia and had testified against my company, which had sent me there. With all the tricks they had up their sleeves, the board managed to throw the CEO, Peter Cowley, under the bus and everyone else got away, including Simon Hinde, the deputy CEO. I believed Hinde had set up Cowley in the first place, exactly so he could throw him under the bus. Everyone suspected, but there was no evidence.

So Hinde got off and became CEO. He was smart. He always knew the right thing to say. He always had the right argument. He was a lawyer, after all. Like me.

Hinde desperately wanted to fire me because, in his eyes, I was the enemy, but he didn't because he knew he wouldn't have got away with it. I think he decided it was better to have me on his side than against him, so he gave me the profile, the tricky cases, the ones where people said, "Well done."

And so I slid into the despicable swamp of technicalities. What bugged me was that I was good at it. If I kept this up for very much longer I might become just like Hinde. And what was even worse, I might start enjoying it.

It had been ten years since the Colombian job, ten years since I had said goodbye to Alex Heart. I had promised him I'd be back, but with the trials and everything else that happened afterward it just never happened. I thought work and the success that followed would have filled the void, but late at night, when the void was looking back at me, I couldn't even find solace in the bottom of a glass. When I thought I could buy him out of my memory with the promise of great dreams and plans for the future, I learned what the price tag was. And it hadn't been worth it.

So what did I have after ten years? A nice place to live, a snoring forty year old, and a pocket full of broken dreams. It had all been an illusion.

The bed felt empty. It was time for David to go.

I kicked him. "It's late, David."

"Huh? What?"

"It's late. I think it's time for you to go."

I thought about telling him it was me, not him. But it was him. And, yes, it was also me. I had standards, and if David chose to spend his time with me, then he was desperate. And I would never go out with a desperate man.

"I'd like to talk to you about something, but not tonight. Schedule a meeting with me for noon tomorrow."

"That all sounds clinically efficient," he said.

I rolled onto my side and stared at the wall. "I'm not one for spontaneity. Not anymore."

"That's a shame, because I am."

He got up and turned on the lights. His penis had retreated to the useless piece of attached skin ... called David, ha-ha. The best thing that had come out of it was wrinkles. Thank you, I'm here all week. Try the veal. His pubic hair was graying. His body was sagging from decades of a desk job. Rounding off the masterpiece was a slightly balding scalp, poor skin, poor posture, and an overly hairy back. Where was Michelangelo when you needed him?

I wished he'd kept the lights off.

"And I've got something for you," he said.

Uh-oh.

"You know, the first time I saw you, and your great eyes, I knew there was something special about you. Even when you smile your eyes carry great sadness." He rummaged through his battered sports bag.

"I know everyone says you're a bitch," he said, "but I can see it's because you really care about things."

I laughed. What a charmer. I would have loved to correct him.

He presented a small velvet box. Double uh-oh.

"I've thought long and hard about this."

He knelt down. Really bad uh-oh. I knew this was the dream of so many girls, but not me. Not anymore.

"So on this hot August night in 2008, would you do me the honor of being my significant other?"

Aaaaaaaaaaaaaaaaaaaaaaaaaaaaaaaaaaaaaaaaaaa—breathe—*aaaaaaaaaaaaaaaaaaaaaaaaaaaaaargh!*

"David, I can't."

"Ellen, I know you carry this dark pain from the past, but I want to care for you, to satisfy you …"

Chance would be a fine thing.

"… to love you."

Oh god, I hope he doesn't burst into song.

"I'll think about it," I said. It wasn't a promise and I had no real intention of thinking about it.

Surely he knew I wasn't interested. Surely he wasn't so self-obsessed that he couldn't see beyond his own interests. He knew how busy I was. And how many times had I told him—told the whole world, in fact—that I was married to my career? Why didn't anyone listen? If David did care he would have known not to ask. Why did he have to ruin it? It could have been a nice summer romance, but he had to go and get all serious. He knew I moved around a lot. Did he expect me to settle down with him in the suburbs?

Damn! I was thinking about it.

It wasn't going to happen. Not in a million years. Maybe if I'd met him ten years ago, rather than things unfolding the way they did, maybe I could have seen myself with him. The old photos on his Facebook page from when he had hair didn't look too bad.

Perhaps it isn't his fault. Perhaps underneath the bad hair and poor dental hygiene he was a great, honest, and caring person, and I was being mean to him because of the past. Perhaps I really could feel like I once did with you-know-who, and I only needed to give some guy a chance. Perhaps.

Oh, Christ no. What was I thinking?

I looked at him. I thought of the suburbs. Oh, the humanity. I had a penthouse overlooking the bay. The bay! A penthouse! One I could lock and leave. I couldn't give that up for two-point-three children and a Californian bungalow.

Yet the part of me that was my mother kept prodding. I could hear her voice. *You're not getting any younger. He could complete you. A dutiful and hardworking wife is one of the most useful members of society.* According to my mother, a woman should devote her skills to the correct raising of children, and keep a stable and clean home, thereby giving the little dependants a springboard from which to contribute to the community.

All that constant nagging and berating would end. So there was an upside.

Maybe David couldn't do any better and I couldn't do any worse, so where we met in the middle it sort of worked out. And I was *still* thinking about it after I told myself I wouldn't.

Sigh. Perhaps it wasn't his fault.

"Screw it. Let's do it," I said. "Right now."

It was a moment of revelation, as much of a shock to me as it was to David. I had been unbelievably mean to him, and he had stayed with me through it all. Surely I wouldn't find someone like that too often.

"What? Do what?"

"Get married," I reminded him. "There's got to be a chapel around here somewhere. I know it's not Vegas, but there's got to be a market for all those vocal teen virgins. Something's got to give when the hormones start knocking."

David gave me a worried look. "Are you sure? Two minutes ago you wanted to think about it."

"I did. And this is the result. Get your pants on, boy. It's a nice day—night—for a white wedding."

We stood in front of the pastor. It was all a bit of a blur, but I felt, for some reason, a little bit happy. My parents were going to kill me over this.

"Do you, David Summers, take Ellen Martin as your wife?" intoned the pastor.

"I do." He was beaming from ear to ear.

"And do you, Ellen—"

My phone rang. "Oh Christ—oh sorry, Pastor, I didn't mean to blaspheme. It's my work phone."

"Didn't you see the sign asking for cell phones to be turned off?" the pastor asked tersely.

"Sorry, pastor, I never see those."

"Work is calling at three A.M.?" David asked.

"Welcome to management. Jesus—oh sorry. It's Hinde. This must be really important. I have to take it." There was an excited babbling coming from the other end. "Plutonium?" I said. "Who owns it? … Oil leases? … What's important about September fifteenth? … When? … *Now*?"

The magnitude of the call must have been obvious on my face as I stood there thinking things over. Unfortunately, the decision was easy to make.

"I'm sorry, David. The company's in crisis and I'm off to the Middle East. Qatar, in fact."

"Now?"

"Yes, right now."

"But, we're—"

"I know. Shit—oh sorry, pastor. Look," I said to David, "it was foolish doing it this way. It was just a crazy moment, but we're not teenagers. I'll go do this work thing, then come back and we can get married right."

I thrust the cheap bouquet into his chest, gave him a quick kiss on the cheek, and raced out the door.

CHAPTER 2

I NEED A MAN

Jessie landed lightly on the ground, but the momentum pushed her into a forward roll. She jumped up, disengaged from her parachute, and handed it over to the soldier waiting to receive her. Even though it was the middle of the night, the heat and humidity hit her straight away. A light beading of sweat appeared on her brow. The soldier pulled in her parachute and had it wrapped down to a small bundle within seconds.

Another soldier appeared from the darkness and saluted her. "You're live, and the target is hot, ma'am."

"Is the bike clean?" Jessie asked.

"Yes, we liberated it from Mesaieed. The estimate is a few hours before the authorities are informed. My guess would be you've got about two hours to acquire the target, and three hours to sunup. We need to be well away from here by then." He handed Jessie a black backpack and she slung it over her shoulder.

"Keep an eye out and let me know if we're compromised."

"Yes, ma'am." The soldier saluted again, and led her to the quad bike, which was quietly idling.

She jumped onto it and sped across the flat sandy expanse. The breeze cooled her sweat. Jessie wasn't a big fan of the Middle East—

the politics and protocols drove her crazy—but she liked the warmth. She had spent years in freezing training camps perfecting combat and endurance training, and survival techniques. The warmth was the opposite of those old inhospitable places, and reminded her of her teenage years hanging out at the beach with, like, her BFFs so 4L. As if!

The warmth lifted her spirits and made it seem like a holiday. Only another ten or twenty years and she'd get one.

Jessie wore a lightweight set of night-vision goggles, which allowed her to cross the sand at speed without lights. Within fifteen minutes she could see her first target. She turned off the engine and coasted the last hundred yards. She came to a halt in front of a huge Qatari villa that would have doubled for a four-star hotel in a small east-European country.

She jumped off the bike, ran up to the front door, and let loose a percussive barrage.

"Who knocks without?" came the inquiry from within.

"Without what?" Jessie responded.

"Without the door," the voice from beyond clarified.

"Knocking without a door? Sounds like Zen. 无. Categorical thinking is a delusion," said Jessie.

The door was flung open. "Jess!"

"Ax!" Jessie flung her arms around her brother.

Alex tried to prize himself away after the mandatory sibling hug-duration quotient.

"You're up late," she said.

"I was at a friend's wedding. Was that you in the helo?"

"You heard it?"

"I was trying out a new surveillance device and picked it up. Come in." Alex stood aside and Jessie entered the large greeting room.

"What were you surveilling? There's nothing around here."

"The chick across the bay hasn't put up curtains."

"Alex!" Jessie exclaimed. She gave him a look of disgust.

"Hey, they block all the decent Internet sites."

"You need a girlfriend, someone to treat you bad."

"That didn't work out for me. By the look of your outfit I assume you're here for work. Or have you become Catwoman? A glass of milk, perhaps?"

"You never know, you may meet someone tonight. Get a little action. I heard the place is full of people of easy virtue." She put her hands on her hips and wiggled them.

Alex frowned, as her stilted hip movements conveyed little to him. A dancer she was not. "Good grief, stop dancing or whatever it is you're doing. It's disturbing." He sighed and threw his hands in the air. "You sure you want to do this, you being a woman in a Middle Eastern country and all? We could have a quiet night in reminiscing about the old days."

"We've made plans and commitments."

"You made plans. I'm going to remind you once again that it's an ill-advised idea to party, especially loudly, in Qatar. Laws and jurisdictions are … complex out here. If you get caught behaving inappropriately you'll have to do lots of groveling."

"Come on, where's the old fighting spirit? It'll do you good. You need to get out of this morbid place and live a little."

"You sure you want to meet this guy? You'd be better off without me. You've got heaps of guys you can kick around with."

"It wouldn't be the same. I need you," Jessie said. "When was the last time you partied? You'll love it. It'll be like the old days."

"It's not my scene anymore." Alex collapsed onto a low collection of cushions. He stretched his arms out to the sides on the back of the low cushions.

"They don't see it that way."

"They're going to have to learn." Alex idly flicked his fingernails. The clicking reverberated in the large room as the two stared at each other. He sighed in resignation. "Have you got the party packs?"

She threw the pack at him and smiled.

He opened it and looked inside, then pulled out a balaclava and sighed. "*Last* time, okay?"

Jessie nodded.

"And this time I mean it."

Alex extended the telescopic pole. A sharp blade sprang from its thick end. He buried the blade in the ground. A steel cable extended from the top of the pole to a streetlight.

"Are you still seeing that Russian girl?"

"*Nyet,*" Alex replied.

"What happened with her? I thought she was nice."

"She was, but she was after something I couldn't provide." He pulled the pole until the cable was tight, and fastened it into position with several metal stakes.

"You'll end up with a Filipino wife—fat, sad, and gray. And you won't be much better."

"Ha-ha."

"Was it because of the Chicago chick?"

"She wasn't a chick." He threw a rock at the streetlight. The globe shattered and left them in relative darkness.

"You know she treated you badly. You don't owe her anything. You want me to knock her off?"

"Ellen was all right. She had her reasons."

"Maybe, but did she have to suffer the three-in-the-morning drunken calls, with you in tears, saying how much she meant to you? Or was that treat just for me?"

"I'm sorry. It was a tough time."

Alex was focusing on tying several ropes around the pole. He hoisted them up to the top of the pole then across so the three ropes hung evenly between the pole and the streetlight.

"Ax, you need to get a grip, get over her. She treated you badly and basically ruined you for anyone else. You haven't been happy with a girl since. That's not how you treat someone special, and you, my dear brother—and I hate to admit this—are special."

"Just leave it, all right?"

"Meh, your loss. I could talk about it for hours." She paused and looked over the surrounding area. "And hours." She allowed her eyes to become accustomed to the darkness. "And hours."

"You should be careful; you're a lot like her. Except meaner. And fatter. And not as good looking. Anyway, it's the past, and I'm trying to get over it. I want to move on."

Alex took out a pair of binoculars and scanned the prison complex.

"The Mubahathat have him," Jess said.

"Great. Nothing like picking on the easy guys. What's special about this guy? Is he your boyfriend?" Alex waggled his eyebrows.

"He's got a new device, the Fitzkie. We've been trying to get it for a year. It was developed by some Czech mathematical genius who was killed shortly after finishing it. It's something to do with banking. I don't know too much about it. He was using it to con one of the outer members of the Al-Thanis when it came to our attention. Don't know or care how he got it, but we want it now."

"Has he been moved from the isolation block?"

"No change to the records in the last twenty-four hours," Jess said. "He's still on minimum security until they coax Princess Whatshername to stop being embarrassed, and they prosecute him."

Jess checked the ammunition in each of her matte black pistols and placed them in their holsters, one on each thigh. They were the latest and greatest from Anderson, and the team at the research and fabrication labs, and her trigger fingers were itching for her to try them out.

"That's in our favor, at least," Alex said. "How long do we have?"

Jessie looked at her watch. "Eighteen minutes."

He zoomed in on a small, detached building. There was only one guard patrolling. It was a severe place, and most of the inmates were kept in place by the hardened lifers. That meant fewer guards were needed overall, but Alex knew that it also meant that most of the guards, especially the better ones, would be around the new prisoner in his special cell. Westerners always got the wrong kind of special attention in these places.

"Okay. We cut in through the fence at the closest point to the dunes, get over to the isolation building, take out the power, get him, then whatever, then out."

"The plan gets a bit vague toward the end," Jessie pointed out.

"I'll leave it to you to flesh it out, being the trained field operative and everything. No sword tonight?"

"Too flashy. You got any firepower?"

"Nah. You know me. Hate shooting people."

"What's that on your back?"

"Modified airsoft WE Baby Hi-Capa 3.8 custom-made tranquilizer with ten-milligram darts filled with a non-lethal tetrodotoxin solution."

"I'll feel safe if we meet a rhino." She gave her pistols a final check, sliding the barrel and checking the chamber and magazine of each before reholstering them. She glanced over at Alex and smiled. "Let's get the party started."

They ran across the expanse of sand. The heat of the night weighed down on them. At the fence Alex took out two pairs of wire cutters. He handed one pair to his sister and within seconds they had cut an opening in the fence wire. Alex kicked the cut section, opening it up for them to climb through. They scurried through and crawled into a small depression.

"It's quiet tonight, the roster said the patrol change is in twenty minutes," Alex whispered. "I can see three guards patrolling, all between twelve and three. We've got the gas bottles at three. Good coverage. It's safe to run."

They got up and sprinted the fifty yards to the isolation building.

They placed their backs against the wall, getting their breathing under control.

"You hear anything?" whispered Jessie.

Alex shook his head. It was times like these he wished he'd kept the Blackbirds camouflage suit. There were no windows in the building so he could only rely on the intel he had gathered. Earlier surveillance tied up with the roster details he had skimmed so at most there would only be four. Four well-trained guards.

They edged their way around the building until they came to the main door. It was secured with a magnetic latch.

"Over to you," hissed Jessie.

Alex reached into his cargo pants pocket and extracted a small black box. He quickly looked at the swipe panel then fiddled with the device. He pressed a button and a swipe card flicked out. He placed it over the swipe panel. Five nines appeared on the device and quickly decreased in number until a solitary figure remained. It flashed. The locked clicked.

"After you," hissed Alex.

"You bet. And don't you come charging in ruining my fun. Or I'll tell Mom."

Jessie burst in through the door, whipping out both pistols and charging down the short corridor.

"Hey, I was only kidding," Alex hissed. Her sudden dash had caught him off guard. "Wait." He limped after her, trying to put the swipe device back in his pocket.

There was only one guard in the entrance, although he was enormous. In spite of his size the man stood quickly, towering a good eighteen inches above Jess. He moved his hands to the pistol strapped to his side.

"*La!*" she shouted. She cocked the pistols to reinforce the command.

The guard slowly raised his hands. He glanced at the hallway to his left. Jessie was sure it was a distraction tactic and kept her eyes firmly on him. Another guard leaped out of the hallway, swinging an iron truncheon. Jessie managed to catch the quick movement out of the corner of her eye and twisted with the blow, minimizing the impact. It still hurt enough to make her drop her weapon.

Alex appeared behind her. The second guard went to swing the truncheon again, but Alex intercepted it, twisting the steel rod out of the man's hands and bouncing off the wall. He parried an incoming punch, swung the arm into a lock, leaving the guard's weapon open. Alex ripped it out of the holster, released the magazine, which clattered to the floor, and threw the pistol aside. He pushed the guard down the hallway, both figures disappearing into the gloom.

The first guard unclipped his pistol and whipped it out, but Jessie used a twisting movement to kick her leg out and knock the gun from his hand. She jabbed her right hand as hard as she could into his abdomen. The guard buckled in half. She kicked his leg and he went down on one knee. She kicked into his groin, but his hands were waiting. He blocked, grabbed her foot and twisted. Jessie went with the twist and jumped. She brought her other leg down onto the guard's shoulder.

She leaped and kicked into his side and the guard staggered against the wall. He lunged at her and landed a punch on her shoulder. The force knocked her onto one knee.

The guard brought in a wide blow, but Jessie dodged and punched him in his thigh. He regained his balance and charged at her. She tried to move out of the way but was too slow. He had her wrapped in his arms. The pair lurched back to the wall. Jessie jumped. Using the guard as a support, she ran up the wall, breaking free of his grip. She grabbed his head and leapt over him. Both crashed to the ground.

They scrambled to their feet. Jessie was the first up. She kicked twice into his ribcage. On the third kick the guard caught her leg and gave it a jarring punch. Jessie winced with the pain. She jumped onto him, climbing over his shoulder with her other leg, toppling him over backwards. They crashed into a chair and it broke under their combined weight.

Both were beginning to tire. The guard circled around, looking for some advantage. Jessie feigned left and punched right. The guard was expecting this and grabbed her hand. He twisted, forcing her into an armlock, but she kicked hard into his side, winding him. She stepped up onto the wall, releasing the armlock, and punched down with her left fist into his jaw. He stumbled back.

Jessie unleashed a cascade of punches and the guard struggled to defend himself. He took a couple of uncontrolled swings, which Jessie easily avoided. The guard pushed forward and thrust her toward the wall. She tripped him and pivoted on the spot, using his own momentum to smash him into the stone wall.

Alex reappeared from the hallway. He slipped his dart gun from the holster on his back and aimed at the guard, looking for a moment to bring him down without further delay. Jessie gave her staggering guard one final swing and he collapsed to the floor.

Jessie looked around, picked up her pistols and holstered them. "Where are the others?"

"I took care of them." Alex was holstering his own weapon.

"You know how I feel about that."

"We're not here as part of your anger-management therapy, Jess," Alex said.

"Mom, Alex won't let me beat up all the boys." She pitched her voice lower. "Alex, you need to share with your sister."

"You weakened them for me. And Mom didn't sound anything like that. Let's get your man. We've got about ten minutes left after this what-have-you." He indicated the man lying on the ground.

Jessie took a swipe card from one of the guards and they dashed into the cellblock. There were several unconscious guards lying around, no longer protecting the two cells. Jessie swiped the first panel. The door clicked open, revealing an empty cell. She swiped the second panel and the cell door opened. A frightened man cowered in the corner. He shied away as Alex charged into the room, grabbed the prisoner by his collar and pulled him out into the anteroom.

"Casey?" Jessie said to the man.

Casey nodded.

"Have you got the key?" she asked.

Casey nodded.

"Today is your lucky day, mainly because you'll now be able to see tomorrow. Come with me if you want to live."

"You don't need to do the stupid accent," Alex told Jessie.

"Casey, you good at running?"

Casey nodded again.

"Well, you're going to be running for your life. Follow this strong but rather dim-witted individual known as my brother. I'll be behind you. Do everything he does until we're out of the complex."

"Five," intoned Alex.

"Let's go, not a moment to lose," said Jessie.

She made her way to the outer door of the building and opened it. There was no one to be seen. She signaled for the others to follow. All three made their way outside and Jessie signaled for Alex to take the lead.

He edged his way along the wall. He looked quickly around the corner then signaled for the others to follow. He stared intently out at the fence, looking for any kind of trouble. He watched the searchlights swing backward and forward over the ground. All seemed clear. He nodded to the others and took off for the fence. Jessie and Casey followed close behind him.

Halfway to the perimeter there was a shout from the isolation building. A searchlight suddenly changed direction and swung toward them, but failed to pinpoint them. They redoubled their speed. The searchlight hunted frantically for them, but without luck. There was random gunfire as the guards tried their own luck at stopping them.

Alex reached the entry point where he and Jessie had cut their way in. They charged through. Alex indicated a point about four hundred yards away. The gunfire increased as more guards joined in the hunt. An errant bullet pierced the gas tank off to their right. It erupted and flames shot skyward. Telltale light highlighted their position briefly as they made their way along the sand dunes toward the darkness of the open sands. Dogs started barking.

"Trouble, folks, unless you can outrun a dog. *Go, go, go,*" Alex shouted. "This is going to be the longest two minutes of your life."

CHAPTER 3

JUMP

They raced toward the point Alex had indicated. The dogs were getting closer. The gunfire had ceased, due to the lack of any obvious targets. It was easier to let the dogs do the work.

Alex looked over his shoulder. In only two hundred yards the dogs had almost reached them.

"I'll catch up," he shouted.

He turned to face the dogs. There were two of them. He could see a handful of guards back at the fence. The dogs were just about on him. He had only one chance before he was down. The dogs charged at him, their teeth bared. Alex gauged the distance then smacked the dogs' heads together. They fell to the ground, immobile. He turned and sprinted to the pickup point.

"What did you do with the dogs?" Jessie asked.

"An old Bond trick. They'll live."

She gave him a look of suspicion. "I've told you that he's a bad influence. You better not have killed them."

"That's a bit rich, coming from you, Madam Nikita. Grab your rope. We've got less than a minute."

Alex took two ropes and handed one to Casey. Jessie and Alex tied their ropes around their waists. Casey stood looking at them.

Alex sighed. He grabbed the rope back and tied it around Casey's waist.

"Do as I say, right? And then you won't die. Understand?"

Casey nodded.

"And when I say jump," said Alex, "jump like your life depends on it."

He looked to the sky. He could make out the dark lights on the front of the helicopter. The looming machine was silent. The hush technology was amazing.

"Ready?" he said to Jessie and Casey.

The early air swept over them. Then the helicopter was above in a hurricane of noise.

Alex felt the rope tighten. "Jump!" he yelled.

All three leapt as high as they could. For a moment they hung suspended in mid-air with the wind pressing against them. Then inertia took over and they were snatched into the void. He felt the heady rush as he went from a standing start to over one hundred miles an hour in under two seconds.

Ferrari, eat your heart out, Alex thought as the adrenaline flushed through him.

Yes, he did miss it, but not enough to die for it. He knew that if he had stayed with the Agency then one day, as had almost happened once before, it would have ended him. To leave had been the right decision.

They bounced in the air as the elastic ropes adjusted to the various weights of the passengers. The helicopter picked up speed as they were winched up. Within seconds they were in the craft as it raced over the desert.

Once aboard Jessie pulled off her mask.

"Jess," said Alex, "you should've kept your mask on."

She shrugged and threw it into the corner. "What's the matter? You look worried."

"Didn't you feel that was a little too easy?"

"Easy? No. There were bullets, explosions, dogs and everything."

"Trust me, it was too easy." Alex turned his attention back to their guest. "You got anything to say?"

"There's a storm coming," said Casey.

Casey's dark eyes glared fiercely at Alex. His hair was a moderate length, but hung lank and heavy from the humidity. He was still in civilian clothes, which, although dirty after days in a cell, hinted at understated good taste and wealth. Even in his disheveled state Casey still looked a million dollars, Alex thought. As dashing and belligerent as any royal.

"I was thinking more along the lines of 'thank you for saving my life' but we can dispense with the pleasantries. It's the end of summer. Sandstorms are weekly out here."

"There's an *economic* storm coming."

"Well, that sounds scary."

"It will be. When it hits, the only person of value will be the one who has the key."

"Hand it over." Alex extended his hand. "Unless, of course, you don't want to live."

Casey looked at Alex. He came to some sort of internal decision. He reached into his sock and pulled out a small flat slab of polished black plastic. He handed it over to Alex.

"What's your name?"

"Casey Rockefeller."

"Really? It's a good name. Wish I'd thought of it. So, let me get this straight. You were trying to con Princess Aria. She was trying to con a hundred million off you. But that hundred million was her money, which you made look like yours. It was an amazing sleight-of-hand, and all due to this little device."

Alex held up the small black slab, which was attached to a USB plug. He marveled as he turned it in his fingers. The flashing navigation lights reflected off the device's polished sides.

"It's amazing what we can do now that real money has been replaced by the concept of it," Alex said. "We no longer need gold in Fort Knox. Head office is going to love it."

He handed the small key to Jessie. "Take it straight back to Anderson. And don't get any funny ideas."

He turned his attention back to Casey. "Where are you from?"

"New York."

"Yeah, right. Where are you really from, before New York?"

"Washington."

"Really? You know, twenty years ago you could easily tell where someone came from. Now, not so much. Your accent is very good. It would've taken a decade to get that good. Your skin is dark and tanned, hinting at a sun-chaser lifestyle, but your hands have faint scarring, meaning that you were once a laborer. So, you're middle-aged but solid and strong. You've had time to develop that accent without anyone knowing or caring. You have an authentic but amazingly recent passport."

He pointed at Casey. "You know what that says to me? You were born in the south Mediterranean area, maybe Greece, maybe a bit further south. You were born into a poor family. You learned quickly that you had a gift for manipulating people. I think you were very good looking when you were young. Then you got into trouble, maybe with the wrong lady, and you had to leave the country and change your identity. Foreign Legion comes to mind. They're very good at teaching people accents. They don't ask questions. And they give you a new passport when you leave."

Alex looked at Casey, but Casey remained silent.

"Okay," Alex said, "so you joined the Legion at seventeen, left at thirty-two. The Middle Eastern families are pretty good at sniffing out a fraud, so I think you spent ten years manipulating your way up the European families of power, building your credibility, until you could work your charms over here. And I bet the women have loved you all the way up."

Alex looked into Casey's eyes, but got nothing back.

"Or then again, maybe you are from Washington. Ultimately, we don't care. We're all members of the new world economy. So, Casey from possibly-Washington with the authentic accent, it's time to rethink your life. Your con is impressive, but these people are no longer Bedouin tribes. They're educated and sophisticated people. Hell, Princess Aria is far more educated than you. Also, she has so much money that hiring a team of hitmen to track you down— wherever you may be hiding—will be nothing to her. My advice to you is to stay with Jessie here. She'll take you to head office, where you can tell our people everything in exchange for safety. And that's the best deal you'll get, a whole lot better than what you were facing fifteen minutes ago."

Jessie tapped him on the shoulder. "Ax, it's time."

"Thanks. Pass me the incini-pack."

Jessie handed Alex a small black cardboard box. The two looked at each other. Casey's eyes darted back and forth between them, taking in all the nuances. Memorizing them.

She lunged at Alex and wrapped her arms around him. "Thanks, Ax."

"Jess, be careful of ol' Casey. I believe he's ex-Legion, which means he's trained and dangerous. Keep an eye on him."

Casey gave Alex a particularly dark look.

"He's old. I can take care of him."

"He's not old. He's the same age as me."

"My point exactly."

He rolled his eyes. "Okay, you've had your fun, now *stop* calling me. You cannot overestimate the amount of trouble we would both be in if I got caught doing this. It's your legacy now."

"I only did it because it was your birthday. You're officially the oldest survivor in our family. It's been twenty years since Mom and Dad were shot. I wanted to do something together so we could remember."

Alex sighed. "Jess, you've got to move on. I don't want to remember it anymore. It's been a burden for too long. I want a fresh start, and remembering them just drags me back into the way things used to be. I don't like that life, and I don't like who I used to be."

He paused and took her hand. "How about this? You move on from Mom and Dad, and I'll move on from Ellen."

"Deal," she said.

He looked into her eyes, searching for a clue that she was taking it seriously, but with Jessie he could never tell. The pain she used as her shield was impenetrable, even to him, and no one knew her better. Maybe she would never let go.

"Here's to the future, Commander."

Alex half-saluted her, shouted his usual goodbye—"Stay safe, Jess"—and jumped backward out of the helicopter. He turned to face the ground as the helicopter flew off into the distance, did his usual countdown, and opened the parachute.

He landed heavily and rolled forward. The ground was hard out here, and his knees gave him a painful reminder that he was not eternally youthful. He pulled in his chute quickly and crammed it into the small incini-pack. He broke the igniter off the side of the box, struck it, quickly flicked it into the box, and threw the package off into the desert. There was a brief dark glow and the remaining ash drifted away on the gentle breeze. He ripped off his mask and stuffed it into one of his pockets. He rubbed his hands all over his face, relieving the incessant itching from the coarse wool of the balaclava.

There were about two hours to daylight. If he could get home in an hour he could still get a couple of hours' sleep before he had to face the recruits for early-morning training.

CHAPTER 4

SINISTERS ARE DOING IT
FOR THEMSELVES

It was two in the morning. In spite of visibility in the sandstorm dropping to less than ten yards, Dahsa drove the Land Cruiser in excess of a hundred and twenty miles an hour along the empty Doha streets. His passenger was Lieutenant Abdul Aziz, an old war dog.

Abdul Aziz was running late because Captain Saif al-Noor had been questioning him about his recent requests to visit London. Frustration and anger rolled off him, adding to the uncomfortable feeling in the cab.

"Who is he to question me?" Abdul Aziz shouted. "Ever since Al-Noor was unjustly made captain of the new Special Tactical Forces he's been sticking his unwanted nose into my business. And why?"

Dahsa was a Nigerian that Abdul Aziz had smuggled into the country during recent excursions into Somali waters. A boat off the Somali coast had pillaged a shipment of narcotics, which was going to cost Abdul Aziz more than an arm and a leg if they failed to get to Bahrain before the Formula One season started. It had been a huge inconvenience and very nearly an embarrassment, but he had found the pirates and killed them all except for Dahsa, and got his prized cargo back on track.

Dahsa had learned that it was best never to say anything at all to a psychotic killer. Just listen. And when you saw your chance, run. Or stab him in the back. Or both.

"I feel like a volcano's erupting inside of me over the injustice of it all. Does he have any experience in leading men in battle? No. He's just a friend of the great Malik. Hah! Oh, how everyone loves the great Malik, the fool that he is."

Abdul Aziz had thought that Malik might have been different. He came from the right family—the royal family—but Malik wasn't the favorite. He wasn't ever going to be the heir apparent or emir, so surely he knew what it was like to be unfairly repressed. Abdul Aziz fumed as the car squealed around the Rayyan roundabout and headed west toward the desert on the Dukhan Road.

But in his heart Abdul Aziz knew he would never rise above his current position as lieutenant. He was an Iranian, and that was that. No matter what he did for this country he now called home, he would never be recognized. He could feel the bile, the hate, and the jealousy all running through his veins, defining every thought.

The streetlights flicked past, a thin pale line of light hovering in the sky above the median strip. Dahsa steered the Land Cruiser off the road into the dust. He drove a short distance into the wilderness where a small *majalis* was set up behind a gnarled copse of trees, the only vegetation within view. The Land Cruiser struggled through the dust and eventually found stability on the rocky surface.

Abdul Aziz knew it was going to be impossible to build anything here. Pyramids, maybe. The effort involved in getting basic amenities into any part of this country was astronomical. And when it was being done by a handful of workers from the subcontinent being paid a fistful of rats every month with no modern machinery, it became ridiculous.

The headlights flashed across the black-and-white striped tent. Dahsa turned off the lights and killed the engine. Still fuming, Abdul Aziz got out of the Cruiser, slammed the door and tried to regain his composure. The sandstorm had kept the heat and humidity at bay, and the summer had been bearable this year, but still, it was hot, windy and dusty. He wiped his hand across his brow, which had already formed a few beads of sweat. He brushed down his ceremonial uniform, dislodging the occasional pocket of sand that had collected in the ornate folds of the cloth.

There was a full moon, and the dust caused the light to diffuse the moon's glow into an eerie halo, barely discernible through the haze. The only sound he could hear was from the small generator that powered the air conditioner, refrigerator, satellite receivers, and TVs inside the tent. At the edge of his hearing he could just make out some demented youths tearing over far-off dunes. It was night and he knew the sound had probably carried for miles. The youths were no threat to the meeting.

Abdul Aziz strode into the tent.

"*Salam alaikum*," said the figure in the shadows. The voice was deep with self-importance.

Abdul Aziz thought the man always tried to sound as if he'd had a Cambridge education, without ever having paid for the privilege.

Abdul Aziz returned the greeting. "May Allāh, peace be upon him, smile upon our meeting." His voice sounded strong, decisive and authoritative. He knew this, as he had spent many years practicing and learning from the Western officers he had met and, occasionally, killed.

"I thank you for your kind wishes, Abdul Aziz. Can I offer you refreshment?" asked the shadows.

"Thank you, sir. May I be so impolite as to ask what you have?"

Out of the shadows stepped a short holy man. His shrouded figure was draped in a pure white Versace *thobe* that accentuated his fat, bloated body; he was particularly obese for a Qatari. Little could be seen of his face, however, as the cloth was loose and the breezes from the air conditioning kept the white fabric pressed across his dark features, drawing out the whiteness of his eyes: disinterested eyes, lazy eyes.

Abdul Aziz knew that this was no ordinary priest; anyone could see that. The man was a sheikh, a chosen one selected by elders of the Advisory Council, who were steeped in wisdom and could perceive inner spiritual and cultural knowledge.

But Abdul Aziz knew the man, Adnan Muanietha. He also knew that he was young to be an elder; he was inexperienced and impatient.

"Certainly," said Adnan. "I can offer you a Turkish."

Abdul Aziz waited for any other options. His throat was dry and he would have killed for a cold demonic beer from the heathen West, may they spend an eternity rotting. In fact, he had killed, although his recollection was poor. But that's because he had been out of his skull on some amphetamine cocktail, he recalled, also supplied by the infidels in the West, may their eyeballs be ripped from their sockets.

After a brief pause Abdul Aziz grunted. "I would be truly honored to receive one of your most hospitable Turkish coffees."

"Bijid!" commanded Adnan.

A diminutive Nepalese teenager hurried into the tent from outside. It was dark in here, yet the boy appeared to see perfectly. There was a clinking of china, a sloshing of water, and a brief stirring. Bijid appeared next to Abdul Aziz with a small cup made of cheap plastic. The young man was dressed in smart black slacks, a pressed white shirt, and a maroon waistcoat. He also had body odor bad enough to mature cheese.

As usual, thought Abdul Aziz, the Turkish is awful. None of these subcontinental workers could ever get the hang of it.

"How is your son? Is his health well?" Abdul Aziz asked Adnan.

"My son is well. His studies progress. He's nearly finished his time at university."

"Is he still in America?"

"Yes, but he shouldn't stay too long. We don't need him to go native."

Both men nodded in silent agreement.

Abdul Aziz took a long sip of the piping hot coffee. His tastebuds screamed in disgust. "And may I ask how your second son is fairing in London?"

"He too has nearly completed his time at the heathen places of education," Adnan Muanietha said.

"And how is your youngest son?"

"He has his ups and downs. But after the last incident he has focused on what he needs to do, and he won't be asked to leave the school."

"Not that they would ask anyway," Abdul Aziz highlighted.

"This is true," agreed Adnan. "The boy who was supplying the drugs was given forty lashes, and is in jail. Ten years."

"Praise Allāh, for justice has been served."

"Praise Allāh, peace be upon him," replied Adnan, a little uncertainly.

"How are your camels?"

"Ah, I have some excellent news in this regard. I have found a magnificent source of some of the finest camels I've ever seen. In Australia, of all places."

"Australia?" Abdul Aziz was surprised. But wasn't Australia similar to Qatar in that it was mostly desert? So maybe it was not so much of a surprise. Those infidel trainers who kept speaking of the beach, sea and surf must be lying.

"Yes, and a bargain at half a million riyal each."

"How many did you buy?" Abdul Aziz asked.

"Only fourteen."

"Starting slowly, I see. What did you do with the old stock? They would make excellent food for the hungry and poor. It would give them some greater incentive in believing in the cause."

"Oh, no. They're far too good to be given to the poor. I'll just burn them."

"After killing them."

"Yes ... probably. After killing them." Then Adnan hastily added, "In fact, sacrificing them to Allāh. For the greater good."

"Allāh, peace be upon him, has truly smiled upon you. Fortune and good tidings are falling from the sky. This is a gift from the heavens. You must be grateful to Allāh, peace be upon him."

Abdul Aziz took another swig of the thick coffee and swallowed in desperation. Good grief, it was awful stuff. He wondered if the host was drinking it as well, or whether it was just a torture Adnan meted out to unsuspecting guests. The stuff was normally difficult to drink or consume, having the taste and consistency of ancient mud, but this swill was truly beyond description or tolerance.

Abdul Aziz coughed. "How is your wife?" he spluttered.

"Fine. And yours?" said the host.

"Fine."

If he starts talking about his prized cats or flea-ridden goats, I may have to kill him, Abdul Aziz thought. This was ridiculous. How could the infidels in the West offer one brief line of greeting and never be offended? One simple stupid word and they dived straight into business. In ten minutes of conversation all he and Adnan Muanietha had discussed were their children and the wellbeing of the sheikh's livestock. What did this have to do with the reason he was here?

"I see you've finished your Turkish," said the sheikh. "Would you like another?"

God, no! I hate the poorly made insipid filth, he thought. Why can't the man have an espresso or cappuccino machine?

"You are truly a man of fairness and wisdom," he said. "I thank you for your kind offering, and feel humble in your generosity."

Bijid appeared once again with the elaborate gold urn. Abdul Aziz watched him, noticing that he walked a little oddly. He surmised that Bijid was also performing other services for the host.

"Now, Abdul Aziz," Adnan started.

"Yes, sir, I await your words of wisdom."

Adnan Muanietha held up his hand to indicate that Abdul Aziz should stop interrupting.

"I have funded many of your endeavors, including your recent one to Somalia, without ever inquiring into what they were, and I've even given you a place to stay, when needed, in my own house and treated you like my own family."

"Yes, sir. Your generosity has met no bounds."

And in his own mind he continued: *I loved that rat-infested hole in the ground you wouldn't give to your servants, and how it obviously inconvenienced your very existence.*

"I see." There was an uncomfortable pause. "I thought you were not fond of Malik."

"Not fond!" said Abdul Aziz. "Don't get me started. I've worked for that man for years, and he's overlooked me time and time again. I stood before him requesting the respect and position I've earned, yet he denies me. And when he finally relents he tells me that *they*—the coward can't even say it's *his* choice—say the decision has been made. Procedure has been followed. And who is the stellar soldier that procedures chose?"

Abdul Aziz's hand swept dramatically around the tent. He glanced left and right, feigning a search for the mysterious soldier. "Saif al-Noor, a West Point graduate. A man with letters after his name. Letters!"

He folded his arms in disgust. "How does such a man survive in the hellfire of war?"

Abdul Aziz struggled to compose himself. He pulled at his cuffs to focus his attention. "But Saif al-Noor has been chosen by the great Malik, and I must be accountable to a college student recovering from spring break. But we shall see what kind of soldier he is when he takes his place on the field. Then, instead of asking if this is a dagger he sees before him, it will be a dagger behind him … in his back. Which he won't be able to see." Abdul Aziz paused to collect his nerves.

"I too would hold the very blade if it was for your own good," said the host.

Abdul Aziz filed that comment under Very Suspicious.

"But this is how life out here goes." Abdul Aziz sighed. "Our wise and noble leader has decreed it to be so. And this will not be the first time nepotism and politics have won out over service and loyalty. And after all I've done for these selfish madmen, with their forged and worthless credentials. The world is failing, and it's being led into ruin by fools like Malik al-Thani and his inbred family."

Abdul Aziz looked directly at his host. "So, not fond? I *loathe* the man."

Adnan was clapping. "Very impressive. Of course, I would never doubt your passion. I love the vitriol and spittle. Tell me, Abdul Aziz, were you at Malik's wedding last night?"

"Er ... yes."

"Who did he marry?" Adnan asked. His voice was flat and emotionless. "Speak up, special guest of Malik. Tell me who he married."

"He married Elissa." Abdul Aziz sighed. This was about to get difficult.

Abdul Aziz realized he could no longer hear the sounds of the distant quad bikes. He had stopped paying attention during his outburst, and now he couldn't recall if the bikes had been getting louder, thus closer. As it was August, Adnan's sons may have returned for their vacation. They could be the ones out there.

But there's no need to worry, he reminded himself, as the sons were all cowards. Except when they were in their Land Cruisers. Or when they had guns.

But there was no excuse for a military man like himself letting down his guard. There were enemies inside and out.

"And you, with your vitriol and amazingly long diatribe against Malik, let it happen. You know what she means to me," the host was shouting.

"Surely you don't need a third wife."

"Do not dare tell me what I do or do not need, servant," Adnan screamed.

Adnan knew only too well what he needed, and what he needed was Elissa. His thoughts flicked to her. She was young and modern. He imagined her skin: pure, pale and unblemished, the skin of royalty. Although she would have to cover herself once she was married to him. Then she would be for him alone to see, to caress, to run his hand over her stomach, over the curve of her hips and around her thighs, and in between to …

She would be his to pleasure him in the way only the third wife could. He had seen what all those modern Western women did on redtube.com.* She would have to do all the things he instructed her to do or suffer the consequences.

Adnan stepped back into the darkness to hide his desire, which was beginning to stick out through his robes. His eyes dilated and lost focus as his hand went to his crotch.

"Greater men have not survived calling me a servant," Abdul Aziz said. "I suggest you rethink how to address me." He paused, allowing the statement to settle into Adnan's slowmoving thought processes. "Let me explain. It was all very sudden. We … I was only given the briefest time to prepare and attend. My wife and Malik's wife are always together. It would've been politically foolish not to attend."

Abdul Aziz interrupted Adnan's fantasy by saying, "By the way she acts it's obvious she loves the fool. They're rarely apart. Literally. He's always touching her inappropriately. I even saw the couple holding hands once in public. Really. What has happened to standards?"

"She loves him?" Adnan howled. "She is a woman. She knows nothing. She will do as she's instructed."

"Many humble apologies," said Abdul Aziz, not meaning it for a minute. "Allow me to fix this situation."

---

* I know you're dying to look, but don't.

"You *will* fix this situation. I instruct you to do so." Adnan noted the look on Abdul Aziz's face and hastily added, "Please, now tell me of your plan."

"Malik is a very powerful man. He comes from a very powerful family."

"*I* am a very powerful man," Adnan said. "*I* come from a very powerful family. I've had to endure marrying simpletons and producing retarded offspring to ensure this. The shame and suffering I've had to endure to get my basic rights should not be suffered by any man of nobility."

Abdul Aziz tried to suppress the myriad of images relating to his host and the many painful ways Adnan could be killed.

"No one doubts it, sir," he said. "You continually remind me of your hardships, most graciously. Let us remain less emotional about this issue. Obviously we should do what we can, but we cannot all be leaders. Too many cooks and all that."

"I would never follow such a man," said Adnan. "He has no sense of tradition. The old emir was far more one of us. He made sure we all got what we deserved, and we all deserved the best."

"I hear your astute point, and agree with your wise observation, but I'm only following Malik to serve my own objectives. As I said, we can't all be leaders, and not all leaders should be followed obediently. You'll find many, soldiers who are happy to kneel before such leaders, content in their obedience. But everything gets worn away, and when these misguided men are old and of no use, Malik will cast them aside, and leave them to walk as the Bedouin, lost and mumbling in the desert until the sands take them in a lonely and pointless death, finishing them in the same way they lived their life. Without reward. Without recognition. Without respect."

Abdul Aziz let the last sentence rest, with the word "respect" reverberating in Adnan's mind. Outside, the wind howled and the sides of the tent rustled.

"I have the illusion of duty, but I'm driven by my goals and desires.

When I have gathered enough of my own rewards, I will stand tall, knowing I have not surrendered my time to anyone else."

Abdul Aziz stood tall to emphasize his confidence, and placed his hand in his jacket pocket in his best impersonation of a European king. As always in this weather, his pocket was full of sand.

"It may appear from an outsider's point of view," he continued, "that I follow this fool, and it may even appear that I believe in what he says, but soon—and it will not be long—I will strike the truth into his clouded and lazy mind. His time of reckoning will come. Malik will be weighed."

Abdul Aziz raised a clenched fist and cast aside the sand from his pocket. It reflected in the light as it fell to the floor and scattered over the matting.

Adnan had grown bored with the conversation. His crotch had started to tingle with his fantasy of the desirable Elissa. He would need Bijid shortly. He longed for the meeting to end.

"Yes, yes, I get your point," he said. "So tell me once again, Abdul Aziz, how you will fix the situation."

Abdul Aziz had tolerated all he could of the ego stroking he had given the foolish Adnan. He had lured the fool into the den, and the bait had been laid. It was time to take charge. He smiled, clapped his hands together and licked his lips.

"I'm glad you asked," he started.

CHAPTER 5

IS THIS THE WAY TO AMARILLO?

W"ould you like a drink, ma'am?"

The flight attendant glared at me, daring me to ignore him. I relented and had one. In the old days I would have had a dozen just to serve him right.

I turned back to the poisonous contract I was expected to inflict on the unsuspecting recipients. It wasn't the first time I'd done this, but I was feeling tarnished by the whole process. I put it away. I couldn't bear to think about it at the moment.

Newark to Singapore was the mother of all long hauls. It was taking forever, even in business class. There was too much time and I'd started thinking about things. One of the things was that the longer I was in the air, the greater chance I had of falling out of it. After all, it was only statistics.

And when I thought about the plane crashing, I started re-evaluating my life decisions.

Did I want to crawl my way through an isolated life, just to die lonely and sad? Or was it better to have someone, anyone, around who I could annoy? David was hardly perfect. No man was. In fact, men were, as the bumper sticker said, like toilets: they were either vacant, engaged, or full of crap. None of them were dashing, heroic, smart, handsome, fashionable, cool, sexy, with great hair, and excellent dental hygiene.

Maybe one.

Actually, I guess I could add in George Clooney and Brad Pitt. And it would be irresponsible of me and practically a crime to leave out Daniel Craig. Well, besides those, what had the Romans done for us? This was what sitting in a plane for twenty hours did to you. Sigh.

Was David the best option? No. But he would always be there when the others got bored and wandered off looking for some young, thin Kazakh wife, with olive skin and everything. Cheating bastards. Especially you, George. How could you leave me for one of those … those exotic tarts? Well, if that's the way it's going to be, you can take your—and it gives me no pleasure in saying this—Dolce Gusto coffee machine and leave. And never come back. I'll miss that coffee machine.

I wouldn't get that with David. For one, I would keep the coffee machine. No man was worth that. Except George, Brad, or Daniel. Or Ax. You see what sitting in a plane for twenty hours does. Sigh.

Two hours in Singapore for a quick stretch of the legs and a humungous long black, then straight to Dubai for the interchange to Doha. Why did flying take so long? I thought the world was meant to be getting smaller.

After twenty-two hours in the air, when I landed in Dubai I had no idea where or when I was. Was it today, tomorrow, or even yesterday? My brain was orbiting the moon. And so, while standing on the escalator coming up from duty-expensive trying to work out if I needed breakfast, dinner, a new iPod Nano, descaling, or if I was even human, while standing on the escalator not paying attention to the thoughts in my head, that's when everything went wrong. If I'd been paying attention and had ignored him, well …

"Ax?" my mouth said without the permission of my brain.

"What? Who?" Alex looked around for the person who had shouted his name. "Ellen Martin!" He stared back at me in disbelief as he passed me on the down escalator. He shouted, "I'll meet you in the Irish bar."

"Ah … okay." I had the immediate feeling that this was a bad idea. Why had I opened my mouth? If I'd said nothing, he would have gone past without noticing me, and I wouldn't be about to do something really stupid. I hated this place already.

I could run. I could hide in the business lounge. I could choose to be strong and simply walk away. These were real options. So why did my legs walk into the Irish Village? I'd heard they did great sausages … no, that wasn't any kind of excuse.

There was still time to escape. He had to go all the way down then come back up again. This meeting could only end badly. It wasn't likely we would end up on some desert island somewhere, locked away from the troubles of the world with him sunscreening my back.

I could go, right now. But wouldn't that be showing weakness?

I could go. It wasn't as if I *had* to stay. It was my choice.

I could go. Damn. He was here.

He had walked briskly into the bar and was scanning the crowd. He spotted me and made his way over.

"I can't believe it," he said. "What are you doing in Dubai of all places?"

"Well, it is a common interchange airport these days. I'm just flying through on company business. What are *you* doing here?"

"I'm tendering for a security contract on the Palm."

"You're not a spy anymore?"

"No, I'd had enough. It was time to move on before I got hurt. Seriously hurt. They do that to you. Keep pushing until you break. I had an out so I took it. Now I'm out here running a security company with some ex-SAS friends. The locals are hard to deal with, but they're loaded."

He smiled, but his eyes didn't sparkle like they once had. "What about you?"

"Oh, same ol' same ol'. You know. I'm a senior partner now. More work, more pay. Great new place to live. Something's coming up that might get me onto the board." I tried to be up, but my head was spinning. "That would make me the first woman on the board. Times are a changin'."

This was an apocalyptically bad idea. Looking at him, I could feel my insides crumble. Some say that men improve with age. I'd believed this was only said by aging men, but running my eyes over that ... that beautiful face, so full of passion, hurt and defiance, I was now a transitory believer. And I hated myself for doing it, for weakening in front of this man who had given so much only to be abandoned by me. I doubted whether I could last long before it became imperative to leave, to abandon him again.

"Like a drink?" asked Alex.

"I think I can have one." Any more than one, I thought, and there might be uninhibited consequences.

"Hey, let's have champagne. Everything's better with champagne."

"I ... okay ... what time is it?"

"No idea. But this is Dubai. It doesn't matter. I think it's late morning, if that makes you feel any better. And the other good thing about champagne: it's the all-day drink, acceptable from morning to midnight."

"Okay. Why not? I've got an hour to kill."

He smiled and dashed off to the bar.

I could go now, I thought. I was sure he wouldn't mind. But it was champagne. And I knew it would be a good one, too.

I could go. No, I'll stay for the champagne. Then go.

He came back with a couple of flutes in one hand and a mini bottle in the other. He waved them both. He filled the glasses and handed one to me. "A toast: to meeting friends in exotic locations."

We clinked our glasses together and both took a sip. It was good. Maybe I should have ninety-two.

"Shorter hair suits you," I said.

The compliment took him by surprise. "Thanks. Had to change to be more corporate-y. It's hard to sell a multi-million-dollar project if you look like a dropout. I had to change otherwise things would've stayed the same."

He paused and looked over my face. "The longer hair makes you look good, too. Like Beckham's wife. I like it tied back like that."

"It's only tied back out of necessity, for the long traveling. The rest of the time it's down. It distracts the men I do business with. When they're thinking of trying to make it with me, I'm getting them to sign their lives away. Just like an illusionist: you watch one hand while you should be watching the other, which is stealing your wallet."

We both took another sip, trying to think of something to say.

"Hey, you had a book written about the Colombian incident," said Alex.

"Yeah, by some sci-fi-fantasy wannabe. Wanted it full of aliens, Armageddon and robots."

"Not Evanovich then?"

"Hah. No such luck," I sneered. "Guy was useless. Hasn't got one solitary percentile of Janet's talent. Ow. I just got burned by a cigarette."

"So they really, actually, tried to get Janet?"

I nodded. "It's a great name. Evanovich. I wish it were mine. I'd just go around telling everyone my name. In a Russian accent. No, French. 'What's your name?' 'Evanovich.' 'What's your first name?' 'Evanovich.' 'No, your *first* name.' 'Ellen Evanovich.' Then I would stand like this with a look of disdain on my face, like Jessica Rabbit with a gun." I arranged myself into a stance Farrah Fawcett would have adopted in some seventies revenge thriller. "And I'd need a cigarette." I took a pretend puff. "Evanovich."

"Yes, well."

"Evanovich."

"If we could move on ..."

"Evan—"

"That's *enough*."

"Evanovich," I whispered in a low breathy voice.

We had a moment where we both stared at each other, in quiet contemplation. Then we laughed.

"I've missed you," Alex said.

"I'm sorry. I can see you're angry. I thought the scars would've healed."

I stroked the old scars on his face from when he saved me, dashing through the South American jungle. My mind flicked back to when we escaped from the combined military and police forces, when we kissed under the waterfall, when he was beaten by those horrific thugs because he was protecting me ...

"Scars make us stronger," I said. "They show we've survived."

"They've healed."

"Not on the inside."

"I'm all right. Everything ended up okay. Are you happy?"

"Yes," I lied. Sorta. Occasionally. Once a year. "Career's going well. That's still the most important thing for me. I'm getting lots of contacts for when I decide to leave to form my own company."

"It's good to have a plan. As long as you're happy doing what you're doing."

We had reached an awkward moment. There was a choice to be made. Did we discuss everything? Or nothing? Everything would be a monumental mistake. If we started down that road it would take days to cover it. There was a lifetime of issues to discuss, and I had a plane to catch.

This left nothing. So this is how it ends, I thought. With the opportunity to rekindle something amazing, or let it pass and suppress it forever. It was time to go.

"I've got a flight to catch," I said.

"Oh, okay. Well, it was fantastic to see you. I hope it all works out for you, with your job and everything."

"Thank you. I hope your contract comes through."

I picked up my briefcase and we both walked out.

"I have to go this way." I pointed toward the business lounges.

"Okay. Well. I have to go this way." He indicated the opposite direction.

We stood looking at each other. I was screaming internally with the millions of things I wanted to say. He appeared to feel the same.

What did we do now? Did we hug, shake hands, kiss? Or, my preferred option, rip all our clothes off and do it right here. In the end I felt I couldn't touch him without consequence so I offered my hand. He gave me a quizzical look, brushed it aside and gave me an engulfing hug. Again, I didn't know what do. I closed my eyes and let down the barriers around my heart for just a moment to remember what it had been like. But just for a moment. I remembered David and my promise, and pushed Alex away.

Well, it wasn't the worst day of my life.

I put my sunglasses on. I walked calmly down the main lounge drag. The world seemed to slow down around me. I could feel my jaw tightening. I pursed my lips together. I checked into the Emirates lounge and walked to the restroom. I grabbed one of the complementary towels, walked into a cubicle, locked the door. Sat down. Carefully folded the towel. Took off my glasses. Placed the towel over my face and howled into it.

I wanted to scream, but it was a post-Alex world and I had to get used to it. So I sat and sobbed until the mountains crumbled and the sky turned black, and I was left to linger on in darkness and in doubt, bound to grief until the world changed and the years of life were utterly spent.

CHAPTER 6

ALL ALONG THE
WATCHTOWER

A re you sure this will work?" asked Adnan Muanietha. He was reclining in the passenger seat of Abdul Aziz's Land Cruiser. His foot rested on the dashboard and he was idly playing with his prayer beads.*

"That's up to you. How convincing do you think you can be? Look, we know the man. He's a gullible, proud old fool who's blinded by his pride in his daughter. Take his pride, like a blade, and twist it into the doubt that lingers behind every man with a daughter."

"Is this his house?"

"It's the third one along the bay. I checked earlier. Stop texting. Who are you texting?"

Adnan sheepishly returned his phone to his pocket. "I was instructing a servant to tell Mohammad ..."

"No, *you* must do it."

"But it's a long way over there. And it's hot. Can I phone him?"

"No, and faxing's out too."

"Surely he'll know when she updates her Facebook relationship status."

---

* Not a euphemism.

"Stop trying to find the easy way out. He's a skilled politician. Sound worried and make it convincing. Anything less and he'll see through you."

Adnan eased his way out of the Toyota. He looked at the hundred yards to the house. "Are you sure I can't text him?"

Abdul Aziz shook his head. Adnan sighed and waddled his way to the great house of Elissa's father. He knocked furiously on the door. After a few moments a servant appeared and bowed when he saw the sheikh standing there.

"I need to speak urgently with Mohammad."

"It is very late, sir."

"It is of the most utmost important urgency."

"Most urgent things are important. Is there something wrong with your eyes? You seem to be raising your eyebrows a lot."

"Tell your master that Sheikh Adnan is here. Habib Mohammad, come quickly!" he shouted over the servant's shoulder.

"Sheikh Adnan, can I request a moment of peace while I fetch Sheikh Mohammad. Please wait in the men's room. I shall see if Sheikh Mohammad is able to see you."

"Quick, you must fetch him now. It is vital."

"Please, Sheikh Adnan, keep your voice down. Sheikh Mohammad may be asleep." The servant turned to go.

"Mohammad!" Adnan bellowed. "There is terrible news that will cause you great concern. There are bad people doing bad things with what you most treasure. Check your house."

"Please, sir, enter the men's room." The servant indicated the doorway to the conference room.

"Raul, who is causing that intolerable racket at such a ridiculous time of night? Who shouts my name, and what is so urgent that it cannot wait until a civilized hour?" Mohammad's voice boomed out from upstairs. There was a creaking from a set of double doors as he emerged at the top of the landing and made his way slowly down the stairs.

"Sheikh Mohammad, sir, I tried to divert him into the meeting room, but he will not do as requested," protested the servant.

"Don't worry, Raul, I will deal with this now." He dismissed the servant with a wave of his hand and glared at Adnan.

"I've had word that Elissa may have stolen out from under your guard," Adnan said. "She may be planning sacred vows and dishonoring your name with an outsider."

"She hasn't updated her Facebook status. I would know. I have to approve every post."

"She may not have had the time or inclination while she was getting married."

"Rubbish. Women can't wait to tell their friends about anything intimate about their interactions with men, and in the most disturbing detail."

Mohammad and Adnan entered the men's conference room and the door closed behind them.

Abdul Aziz was flicking through recent messages on his phone when Adnan opened the passenger door. After several moments of Adnan trying to lift himself into the car, Abdul Aziz lowered the vehicle to disabled-access level.

"Tell me all the details, Adnan," Abdul Aziz said as the large man closed the door.

"All went to plan. You can call me the puppet master. I was like, 'Oh, your house has been ransacked and the whole community will whisper behind your back.' And he was like, 'I don't believe you. I'm so great and you're so not great.' Then we had a pretty good coffee, and the servant came back and said Elissa was gone, which made him really cross. Then we had another coffee. Then I had to go to the toilet because coffee sometimes goes straight through me late at night."

"Ransacked? Does anyone say that anymore?"

"Then he said stuff, including 'You're a monster.' And I said,

'You're a politician so we're equal.' No, wait, before that I said that she was getting it on with this guy, except I did it in some smart way that I can't remember at the moment. Something about whales, sheep ... No. Some other beasts, and the two were joined as one, if you know what I mean. Then he got his back up. Then I made a comment about *their* backs, which didn't go down too well, but you can't please everyone."

Adnan continued, warming to his story. "Then he was, 'Watch what you're saying in my house about my family.' And I said what you said about only having concern for his, Mohammad's, standing in the community. He sort of liked that."

"Yes, yes, I get the point. So you were you able to convince him?"

"Yes." Adnan smiled an evil smirk.

"Our plan is now in motion. If you keep your focus and stick to the plan then we should win this. I'll drop you back at your house, but we need to be careful from now on. If people see us together and know that you're undermining Malik, they'll think the same of me. By tomorrow I'll make sure the parliament knows of Malik's endeavors. If it wasn't for this Iran issue I could guarantee he'd be reprimanded and dealt with according to traditional law, but with Iran getting out of control they may hesitate to get rid of him."

Abdul Aziz started to fume, just thinking about Malik. "They think he has the gifts of some ancient warrior and that he's so special he's irreplaceable. Oh so wonderful Malik. Save us, Malik. They're such blind fools, believing in his dumb stories. Oh Malik, please lead our armed forces. Such *fools*."

He smashed his fist into the steering wheel. "I *hate* him. They think the sun shines out his—" He looked over at Adnan, then breathed deeply to calm his nerves. "But I've got to show Malik signs of loyalty. So don't fret if you see me standing by him. Remember, it's all an illusion."

Mohammad paced furiously around the foyer. After a few minutes Raul appeared, looking grave. He bowed before his master and offered him a fresh cup of coffee.

"I don't want to know how he knew," Mohammad said, his voice barely above a whisper. His face was creased with the anguish of betrayal, concern, and consequence. "Elissa has gone. The dowry will be huge. What am I going to tell her mother? She'll be furious. Worse, she'll be silent."

He stared down at his feet as the improbability of it all sunk in. "There are so many questions that … *man* … needs to answer. Did she speak to him, and if so, what did she say? I hope she hasn't been stupid enough to do something she can't undo. Why did I have to be cursed with a daughter? She's nothing but an expense to the heart and wallet. Raul, tell me you knew nothing of this."

"Sheikh, it is complete news to me. Elissa must have been planning this for a long time. Or perhaps it was a complete spur-of-the-moment decision. It would've been hard to organize something like this without someone in the household knowing about it. It has come as the greatest of all shocks."

Raul paused. "*If* it is true, sir," he cautioned. "Let's establish some facts. At this point we know she's not in her room, but we only have the word of Adnan that she has run away. Let's see where she is first."

"Thanks, Raul, I would be lost without you. Did Adnan tell you where she was? I don't recall him saying." Without waiting for a reply he raced on. "Where was my mind? Raul, I have become useless in my old age."

Mohammad paced around the room. "He used the word 'outsider,' didn't he? That's what all the purebloods call those who've married outside the family. I wonder if he means Malik. This gets worse. The bastard son of that wayward prince. Ring everyone. Make sure all the family is awake."

"I think they already are, sir," replied Raul.

"By the grace of Allah, my daughter, my blood, sneaking out past my authority. She seemed happy enough. Was it all just a ruse?" He shook his head. "Do you have such troubles with your daughters, Raul?"

"No, sir, they were raised under the tyrannical rule of my wife's mother back in Goa."

Mohammad let out a brief smile. "Fathers, from hence trust not your daughters' minds, by what you see them act. Is there not charms by which the property of youth and maidenhood may be abused?"

"I have heard similar things." Raul smiled back.

Mohammad patted him on the back. Adnan wasn't the only one with a classical education.

"Get my brother on the phone," Mohammad said. "He can use his contacts in the police services to get some answers."

CHAPTER 7

BRING ME SOME WATER

Time was pressing. The sign above the entrance to the control room indicated they were on high alert. A guard was standing to attention inside, watching the general activity. Soldiers and officers sat behind desks, frantically typing, phoning, and negotiating with the outside world. Tea boys hustled around, keeping up an endless supply of coffee. A roving officer drained his cup, picked up a series of notes from the various stations, and handed them to a senior officer standing in the center of the room.

The officer was taller than the men around him. His black hair was slicked back, and much like his face was showing few signs of aging. Malik al-Thani, commander of the Qatari forces, still dressed in his ceremonial uniform, quickly read through the notes then returned his focus to the bank of flat screens. It displayed a map of the region, with the various countries shaded in relation to their alliance. Iran was currently a vivid red.

Abdul Aziz entered, and the guard alerted the room to his arrival. Abdul Aziz marched across to Commander Malik and stood to attention next to him. Malik turned and waved him at ease.

"Abdul Aziz," he said. "Thank you for joining me at such short notice. It's good to see you again. Do you bring news?"

"I've just had Adnan on the phone." Abdul Aziz removed his beret and placed it under his epaulette. "He's heard that Mohammad is furious about your involvement with Elissa."

"He'll live. How did Adnan find out?"

"I assume it was through the servants' network, faster than fiber-optic cable. It was just a courtesy call so you could prepare yourself. Adnan is emerging as a very solid and capable individual. He should go far, don't you think?"

"He's certainly solid." Malik laughed at his own joke. "I've only ever considered him a greedy, self-obsessed fool. Maybe I was wrong. Or maybe he is growing up." He shrugged. "Time makes fools of us all in retrospect."

"Adnan was saying he described you in such insulting and despicable terms. If I'd been there I would have found it hard to restrain myself against such foolish and thoughtless words."

Abdul Aziz looked over Malik's face to see if there was any reaction. "Are you absolutely sure your marriage is secure? Mohammad is an important man in this city. There are rumors that the emir favors him as the next prime minister. He will try to annul your marriage, or else inflict whatever punishment the law and his power will allow him to."

"Thank you for your words of support, Abdul Aziz, You can leave it with me. We have more important issues to deal with."

"Are you sure?"

"Let him do his worst. I can stand proudly next to my achievements, my heritage and actions. What's that noise?"

"Mohammad Kalifa, I would presume, with some of his pretend guards. Maybe you should go. We don't need this distraction now of all times."

"Let him come in ... as an invited guest. I must appear strong and unwavering in front of his concerns. Running would make it look like I believed I'd done something wrong. His pride is all that's at risk. Are you sure it's him? He doesn't sound very angry."

"Praise to Allah, I think not."

Malik gave him a concerned look.

Captain Saif al-Noor marched into the room and saluted Malik, standing rigidly to attention.

Malik gave him a smile. "At ease, Saif, and please tell me some good news."

Saif relaxed into his at-ease position and clasped his hands behind his back. "The prime minister sends you his best wishes, Commander, and kindly requests you to visit him at your earliest convenience, which I believe means now."

"Any idea what he wants?"

A junior officer handed Malik a clipboard. He glanced over it.

"I would guess from his actions that it's something about Iran," Saif said. "And eavesdropping on his phone conversation. And looking at the documents on his desk. And observing what he was watching on the TV. In fact, if it wasn't about Iran I'd be worried. Parliament's been burning with activity all night. The prime minister has called a special assembly of selected experts to discuss our options. They're all there now, with you being the notable absence. He has sent me to request your attendance when possible, if you know what I mean."

"Now?" Malik signed the document and handed the clipboard back to the waiting officer, who turned and marched away.

"Yes, Commander. Now. In fact, then." Saif stared straight ahead.

"Saif, I enjoy your Americanized way of talking. It's so friendly. If I didn't know you or the prime minister so well I would not treat this with the utmost urgency it requires."

"He has sent out quite a few people looking for you."

"He could call."

"He has been calling."

Malik patted his pockets. "My phone must be in the car. Just as well it was you, as I would have ignored the other messengers. One moment, Lieutenant, I need to"—he paused and looked at Abdul Aziz—"make a quick call. Then we will go."

Malik turned and left the room, closing the door behind him. The two soldiers stared at the door, then at each other.

"A private call is more important than meeting with the prime minister? What's that about?" Saif asked.

"Allah has bestowed a great but treacherous gift, which has courted much controversy."

"That's a bit cryptic. Say it in normal words."

"Malik is now married to an important, young, rich woman who has the body of a goddess."

"No way! The old dog. He kept that quiet."

"However, it was done in secret and her family's very angry. He'll need to do some heavy negotiating if he wants it to work. If he can, he'll have his feet under the table, as they say, but the father's furious."

"Fathers, from hence trust not your daughters' minds by what you see them act. Is there not charms by which the property of youth and maidenhood may be abused? And all that."

Saif smiled, but Abdul Aziz gave him a blank stare.

"Who is he hitched to?" Saif asked.

Abdul Aziz opened his mouth, but before he could speak Malik barged back into the room.

"Okay, Lieutenant, let's get going."

There was a commotion outside the control room. Abdul Aziz nodded to Malik and went to investigate.

"You seem to be popular tonight, Commander," Saif observed, "but none of your visitors appear to be happy."

Abdul Aziz strode back into the room. "Commander, the civilian Mohammad Kalifa is here to see you. He has assailed our building with a number of police and some of his personal guards. Are you sure you want to meet him? I also note they bear arms, which is against the control-room regulations."

Abdul Aziz stood aside, and Mohammad and his men entered the room.

"Gentlemen and civilians," Malik said. "What can I help you with? Please be brief as I have been summoned away."

"Don't pretend you don't know why I'm here," Mohammad said. "Don't insult me. Police, arrest him."

"With all due respect, Sheikh Mohammad, I think you'll find I have authority over the police at this time," said Malik. "And the presence of force has less influence than the respect you command with your wisdom and years. But please, tell me your concerns."

"My daughter ... how *dare* you take her like a thief in the night," said Mohammad. He pointed an accusatory finger at Malik. "Where is she? Anybody with eyes and half a brain could tell you there's no way a beautiful and happy young girl like her would run off with a man like you unless you tricked her, drugged her, or kidnapped her. In fact, that's probably what did happen, so I'm arresting you."

He turned to his men. "Arrest this man. If he struggles, use force."

The policemen shuffled uneasily. They were witness to two powerful men who were locked in a debate that was certainly in the gray area between modern law—as championed by the emir—and the traditions upheld by the powerful families.

"Calm down," Malik boomed.

Saif and Abdul Aziz stood behind him. They looked menacing, strong, and resolute.

Most of the security guards and police paled in the face of Malik's huge frame and powerful voice. He dominated the room with his presence, and had a personality to match. They hesitated.

"Don't instruct me to calm down." Mohammad's self-confidence rallied against Malik. He was old and haggard compared to Malik, but he compensated with an abundance of self-assuredness.

"You've thrown some serious accusations at me," Malik said. "Where do you want me to go to respond to these charges?"

"Prison."

"Prison? I am commander of the Qatar forces. My actions are not against the law."

"They are against our way, against our traditions. Just because you were raised hidden away … you live here now and must abide by our ways."

"I'd like to help you, I really would," Malik said, playing his trump card, "but I've been summoned by the prime minister under the direct instruction of the emir to attend parliament and provide expert advice on pressing and vital issues of state. Captain Saif al-Noor is here, waiting to take me to his eminence immediately. On pressing state business," he repeated.

"This is true, Sheikh Mohammad," Saif said. "The prime minister is in council. I thought you would already be there. You have also been sent for."

"What? Parliament has been called now? At this time of night? I have half a mind to march you down there right now and have this issue dealt with," Mohammad told Malik.

"I'm not sure it would be seen as appropriate under the circumstances," said Malik. "Do you not know what's going on out there at the moment?"

"All I need to know is what's going on in my household, except everyone else seems to know but me."

"Would it be better if Elissa spoke to you directly?" said Malik. "She's here, texting her friends, who appear to be in the same room."

"She's here? Bring her to me. I'll put an end to this deception and take her home immediately."

"Please let her speak first. If she admits she wanted this, then please allow her to live her own life. Lieutenant Abdul Aziz, please fetch Elissa."

Abdul Aziz saluted and left the room. There was silence as everyone looked uneasily around the room. The atmosphere was electric. A few moments later Abdul Aziz reappeared, with Elissa following closely behind.

"Elissa. Tell me this is all some great hoax," Mohammad cried.

"Father, habibi," Elissa said. "It's all so boss. You are my father. I'm your little girl. I'll always be indebted to everything you've done, but it's been a minute and it's time to go. There's nothing bent here. Malik is, like, so my man now, he's so totally shut up until we ROFL, just like Mom was with you. Malik is so cool, the real deal. He's like so OMG and totally rules. And I will follow him, my man." She giggled.

"Did anyone understand any of that?" Mohammad asked.

"Some of it," Malik said.

"All I heard was vowels and initials."

"I did," Saif said.

"So she's speaking American," Mohammad said.

"Not quite. She speaks reality TV," Saif said.

"What's the point of my spending all that money sending her to the British school when she ends up speaking like that? It's so disappointing." He looked sternly at Elissa. "You must stop this speech pattern right now, do you understand? You're an adult now."

She nodded, but reluctantly.

"I'd rather adopt a child than have one of my own," said Mohammad. "Come here, Malik. I'm forced to give my blessing to this marriage. With all my heart, I give you that thing which, if you didn't already have it, I'd try to keep from you—Elissa."

He looked defeated. "Now, down to business. Malik, how much do you want for the dowry?" His face dropped in expectation of the cost.

"Nothing."

"What? Really?"

"I'm very comfortable. The cards have fallen well for me financially. I should be paying you. You've paid for her education and living expenses for nearly two decades. Let me honor you for the excellent job you've done in raising such a wonderful woman with a gift of, say, five hundred thousand riyal."

"She went to the best schools, you know."

"How about six hundred and fifty thousand?"

"She went to the very best schools, and had the finest clothes handcrafted for her by the finest Italian designers."

"Okay, my last and final offer. Eight hundred and fifty. And not one riyal more."

"Call it a million and you have a deal."

"Done."

They shook hands.

"Saif, we must go," said Malik. "Let the prime minister know we're on our way."

"Oh, woe betide me and the loss of my most precious ..." Mohammad started, but his heart was no longer in it. "Oh, well, you can't live their lives for them."

He looked at Malik and shrugged in resignation. "I'll reassign her Facebook account over to you in the morning. Good luck. And make sure you keep an eye on her posts. Women say more on there than to your face. Now I'm going home to lock up my remaining daughter. Then possibly throw away the key. But if I could get another million ..." He paused, lost in thought. "Malik, you don't need a second wife?"

CHAPTER 8

WE ARE FAMILY

The phone rang. Alex lifted it out of his pocket. The caller was blocked. He leaned back in the plush leather seat. One of the perks of working in the region was the seeming inevitability of someone organizing a suite at the Burj for any kind of transaction.

"Hello?" he said.

"Ax, it's me."

"Jess, what do you want? Especially so soon."

"We got shot down, surface-to-air took out the rotor."

"What!" he cried.

"The helo was taken out as we neared the coast of Afghanistan."

"Are you all right, any injuries?"

"Yeah, I'm okay. But Casey got away. I don't know how, but he got out of the handcuffs while he was underwater and upside down. Then he killed one of the guards. But I managed to keep the Fitzkie safe."

"If he has any kind of brains he'll lie low for a long time."

"I'll explain this to you because you're a male and therefore not very smart, but he's a male and not very smart. My big concern is that he knows what I look like."

"I think I might've found out why you're still single. Maybe you should have kept your mask on like someone who knows better suggested."

"But he was hot-looking. I don't meet many men. And the ones I do meet I usually have to kill."

"What is it with you women? You all seem to fall for any guy that's good looking, and to miss the obvious trait that he's a complete dick. Put Casey on stage in front of a band and I bet you'd be falling to your knees."

"Not until after the second date."

Alex sighed and drummed his fingers on the table. "Perhaps you should keep low for a while. Go do some training in the Antarctic and get friendly with the penguins. Above all, Jess, keep your eyes open and stay safe."

He hung up and looked out the window of the Burj. "Casey, you wouldn't be stupid or spiteful enough to come back, would you?" he muttered.

"Everything all right?" Damien asked. He relaxed on the sofa and shifted his gaze from the impressive view out the window to the desk where Alex was working.

"It's nothing. Jess has got herself into trouble. Again."

"What's she blown up this time?" Damien smoothed down the creases in his uniform.

Alex laughed. "You got a sister, Damien?"

"Hah! Can't tell you now you've left."

"You told me before."

"You were one of us back then," Damien drawled.

"She got shot down near Afghanistan."

"Send some of your guys up there." Damien waved his hand vaguely towards the north. "You still got that crazy pilot, what's his name, Johnno?"

"I can't at the moment. Not with the Iran issue. You know what they're like. It needs to be quiet."

Damien's gaze drifted out the window. The horizon beckoned

him to jump. He stood up and wandered over to the glass wall. His finger traced the outline of the city on the glass and he arced it into the sky.

"I'd get her myself if I could be bothered," he said. "And if she had young, hot-looking friends."

"You're like the brother I'm glad I never had. Where's your next port of call?"

"I'm lookin' at a drug ring up on the Turkey–Iran border. We're getting close to source. Nice covert party, where I can wear civvies. We nearly had them a few months back off the east coast of Africa, but some maniac came in and blew the whole op. Wasn't you, was it, wishing for the old glory days?"

Alex looked up. Damien was still looking out the window. Dust clouds were collecting on the horizon and threatening to roll in over the city.

"You ever had an old flame suddenly come back into your life from the 'old days?'" Alex said.

"Only ever had one love in my heart," Damien said. "A love of the theatre." He turned, waved his hand dramatically through the air, and bowed. "This is where you applaud."

"You haven't done anything yet." Alex looked down and continued leafing through the document on the desk.

"How can you soar like an F-18 when you're surrounded by Ryanair flights?" Damien spouted. "I could do a monologue for you. I've been working on an edgy Shakesp—"

"God, no! Not interested unless you're a bad guy and you're telling me your grand plan. What's your guise, drama student?"

" 'Did my heart love till now? Forswear it, sight! For I ne'er saw true beauty till this night.' You met an old flame?" Damien ducked as a cushion sailed toward him. "Too slow, old man."

"Yeah, down in terminal one this morning."

"Is she hot? You know, in that old-woman way."

"She'd laugh at that," said Alex. "Actually, she wouldn't. She'd get angry and say something stupid. Anyway, she's not even forty yet."

"Some old chicks are all right, like Beyoncé or Britney Spears. You give her a quick one?"

"I'm sure I wasn't as dumb and annoying as you are when I was your age. No, I didn't give her a quick one. I got over her a long time ago."

"Sounds like it. What happened?" Damien wandered over to the sideboard and ran his finger along the marble, checking for dust.

"She left, but things happened and she never came back."

"Ah, 'Don't waste your love on somebody, who doesn't value it … For never was a story of more woe than this—'" Damien had his eyes closed when reciting and this time the cushion hit him straight in the face. "Everyone's a critic."

"It was unresolved with us. We never had a breakup moment."

"I see you still carry a flame," Damien said.

"I don't. She isn't a green light at the end of the jetty. I regret we never said goodbye, never had closure. After all the dumb things she said, she never said sorry."

"What for?"

"For not coming back."

"You realize how stupid that sounds?" Damien said. "Anyway, she sounds like a pain."

"She gets under your skin, a lot like Doha. Wherever she goes, she opens her mouth and disaster happens."

"How tragic. I'm sure you'll both end up happily ever after. You finished the paperwork yet? I have to mobilize soon."

"Yeah, here you go." Alex slid the paper inside a folder and put it back in the briefcase. He shut it and slid the case across the desk toward the younger man. "I'd better get back on the plane. I've got training later."

"How's the airport going over there?"

"Slowly. You know they have an emergency landing strip for the space shuttle?"

"Is that because the airport was designed in kilometers but built in miles?"

"I think you'll find that's a rumor."

"What about BA threatening to sue the airport when one of their 747s sucked recently laid tarmac into the engine and refused to fly into Doha for years?"

"Rumor." Alex said, getting up.

The two men headed toward the door.

"In the first Gulf war," said Damien, "on an evening training flight, one of the Qatari pilots reported in from the range that he had a missing bomb. It was suspected that the bomb fell off between the Marriot end of the runway and the Sheraton Hotel."

"Yes," said Alex, "just rumors."

"Why are there so many rumors?"

Alex opened the door and signaled for Damien to leave. "The media was tightly controlled for decades," he said, "so the only way news got around was via gossip channels. The habit's stayed, even though the media's loosened up heaps. Could also be boredom. Anyway, take the case back to your boss. Let me know if you hear anything on the wire about Jess."

CHAPTER 9

SHIP TO SHORE

Hussein al-Kalifa was pacing around the large table that dominated his main conference room. He had hoped that since the days of the coup, when he and the emir had escorted the previous emir, the man's father no less, at gunpoint from his office and exiled him to Paris, he would never have to worry about conflict again. The prime minister was a man of diplomacy. He excelled at it, and he had achieved much over the last decades with no more than set of large ears, a quick mind, and a friendly face. But this was war and people expected answers from him, which he was struggling to give. His primary ministers were looking at the various bits of information strewn over the tabletop.

"Have any of you read this advice?" The prime minister indicated the paperwork. "None of it makes sense. It's so vague it might as well have been put together by a consultant."

"Indeed," said the first minister. "The reports are wildly conflicting, even if I just look at my own records. I've got some saying one hundred thousand troops are readying off the Turkish coast. Some say they're on ships, some say it's an airborne army, and some say there's only a tiny reconnaissance force. How can we have such inaccurate records?" he asked the room in general.

"Our sources agree that *something* is going on," said the minister of the interior, "so we need to act as though we expect something to happen. They all confirm an Iranian force readying to move toward Turkey. First we had the Israeli military incident on the Iranian nuclear program, and now this."

"What do I do?" the prime minister said. "How can any decision be made from this information? Are we being attacked or not? I cannot believe it, *refuse* to believe it, until I see it with my own eyes."

There was a knock on the main doors.

"Come," said the prime minister. "Ah, Sergeant, please tell me something that will make sense of this."

The great wooden doors swung open. A soldier marched into the room and saluted the prime minister. He removed his beret and placed it under his arm. He stayed stiffly at attention as he gave his report. A Nepalese servant closed the doors behind him.

"The Iranian army is preparing to invade Turkey," the sergeant said. "I am fresh from air reconnaissance and can confirm this visually. General Ayden thought it important that I confirm this to you personally so there could be no doubt. I'm sorry to have brought bad news."

"You saw this clearly and can swear by it?"

The soldier nodded. "Sir."

"It's Ayden. You know him and what it means," said the minister of the interior.

The prime minister looked furious. "The Iranian commanders must be insane. They're behaving like an empire from two centuries ago. This is madness. Who invades today, other than power-mad buffoons? We know they're after the gasfield. Why storm Turkey?"

The minister of the interior hesitated, and then spoke.

"I'm no expert, but how about this for an idea. If their ultimate goal is to take the field, they need to protect themselves. The US air force is currently allowed to use the Turkish airbases. If Iran cut off access to those bases that would take care of their major threat, and by the time the US navy could get to the Gulf, it would all be over."

"Surely they're not that mad," the first minister said. "It's a foolhardy plan beyond comprehension."

"As I said, I'm no expert," the minster of the interior repeated. "I'm a man for times of peace, not war."

"And I'm a man for times of pizza. Who else is hungry?" the first minister asked.

There was another knock at the door. The first minister raised his eyes in the expectation of food. A grim-looking solider marched into the center of the room.

"Great, more news," said the first minister. "I don't think my blood pressure can survive any more updates." He collapsed onto an antique French Louis tapestry salon chair. It creaked under his weight.

"Sir, there may be some support from Kuwait," said the soldier.

"What?" the prime minister exclaimed. He slumped down in his seat at the head of the table.

"Yes, Kuwait, sir. Our men on the ground are saying they're going to join forces."

"Ay, I thought so," the minister of the interior said.

"Really?" the prime minister said, turning to face the minister.

"Yes, sir," said the minister of the interior. "It will be because of the deal with the Russians. You remember, Prime Minister. And that mess with the petrodollar-to-euro switch. It was only a matter of time, and opportunity, of course."

He turned to the soldier. "How many troops do you think they can amass?"

"The 25th, 15th and 35th Brigades have amassed at Al Jiwan Camp, sir."

"Moderate but deadly." The first minister nodded sagely.

"I think the first minister is a little optimistic," said the minister of the interior. "It would be over one hundred M1 Abrams. It's certainly getting toward a significant force, especially with the Iranians."

"Nevertheless," said the prime minister, "this development appears reckless and shortsighted. I hope it's a ploy to confuse us."

The soldier coughed. "General Ayden is currently stationed out there on tactical maneuvers with a handful of men, sir. He may have accidentally strayed into their waters and caught some coded information regarding possible targets. He's an experienced and trustworthy man and he wouldn't make these comments lightly. There's rarely subtlety in military tactics; I would not count on it being a trick. He's still there awaiting your instructions, sir."

"Where's their cultural ambassador? He can answer for their actions," said the prime minister. "This foolishness has gone on too long. What was his name? Mannard? Luc Mannard?"

"He's now in Dubai, probably hiding and drinking himself into a stupor," said the first minister.

"Get him on the phone now. Time is of the essence," said the prime minister.

"Are you sure?" said the first minister. "He may make no sense. But I'd be the first to admit he makes little sense at any time. I'll arrange the call for you, sir."

A servant entered the room and coughed. The ministers turned, dreading any further bad news. Their hearts lifted as Malik strode confidently into the room, followed by his trusted aides, Saif and Abdul Aziz.

"Malik, as commander of our combined forces, we must consult with you urgently about these foolhardy endeavors of the Iranians," said the prime minister. "Saif, did you find Mohammad?"

"Sir, yes, sir."

"And?"

"He is, that is, I have." Saif looked at Malik.

"He received some disturbing news about his daughter and won't be attending," Malik announced.

"Which one?" the prime minister asked.

"Elissa," Malik said.

"Which one is she?" asked the minister of the interior.

"She's the good-looking one. She takes after Mohammad rather than his wife," replied the first minister.

"What's his wife look like? I've never seen her. Well, I've seen her, but not what she looks like," said the minister of the interior.

"She stole away from her home and married secretly," Malik said.

"I ... what? Say that again. Elissa eloped?" The prime minister stared in disbelief. He turned to Malik. Malik nodded. "I ... I don't think I've ever heard of that before out here. Maybe if a young lady is overseas, but not locally." He turned to the minister of the interior. "Do we have any laws against that?"

Before the minister of the interior could speak, the first minister recited: "Fathers, from hence trust not your daughters' minds by what you see them act. Is there not charms by which the property of youth and maidenhood may be abused?"

They all stared at him in astonishment.

"What are you looking at? I had a decent education. And Western women seemed to love it if you recite stuff like that. Don't ask me why, it's just the enigma that we call the West."

"No, Prime Minister," the minister of the interior responded. "There's no law, as decreed by the emir since 1995. Maybe common sense and tradition recommend against it, but no law."

"Malik," said the prime minister, "do you know who the scoundrel was?"

"Me."

"Yes, you. Do you know who it was?"

"No, it was me."

"You what?"

"I married her."

"You?"

"Yes, me."

"You?"

"What's hard to understand about this?"

"Well, she's young and ... er ... young, and you are, well, not to put too fine a point on it, you are old," the prime minister said. "Perhaps not old, but certainly middle aged. Definitely not young. And we know your reputation. You chose to give up your bachelorhood?"

"There wasn't any ... trouble?" The first minister waggled his eyebrows.

"You know my past, you know me. I've always been rash when it comes to the ladies, and my decisions involving both love and war have often been ambitious. Maybe it was simply time for me to settle down. She's young and healthy. She should be able to cope. If not, Mohammad has already offered me his other daughter."

"You're serious?" the prime minister said.

"It is true," Malik replied. He coughed and prepared his talking-to-sheikhs voice.

"Here we go. He's putting on his talking-to-sheikhs voice," murmured the first minister.

"Oh god, do we really have time for this?" said the minister of the interior.

"No, we don't," said the prime minister. "Iran is heading for Turkey. Kuwait is amassing an invading force. All we need is for the Americans to butt in and stamp all over the region. We haven't faced a situation like this for centuries."

He turned to Malik. "You understand better than anyone how the defenses of our neighbors work, Malik. We've got good men out there, but no one's been prepared for this. We need your expertise for desperate situations. So can you possibly put aside your marriage celebrations and head up this dangerous expedition? I know it's a big request."

"I always rise to the occasion when faced with challenges," said Malik. "I will take charge of this defense against the Iranians. But I humbly ask you to make appropriate arrangements for my wife by giving her a place to live and escorts that suit her high rank."

"She can stay at her father's house," said the minister of the interior.

There was a sharp laugh from the first minister. "He won't allow it. Not until his emotions have settled."

"Neither will I," said Malik. "She's my wife and my responsibility now. She's a part of me, and that means being part of a soldier. I don't want to be separated from her at the moment. I wouldn't be focused and so would be of little use to you."

"Look, it isn't a concern of mine about your private arrangements," said the prime minister. "Believe me, the less I know the better. I attended the early birthdays of young Elissa, so please spare me the details. What I do care about is that your mind is focused on the task at hand. If you need her near, then so be it, but I can see it backfiring. This is terrible timing. Next time, don't get married in secret."

"You'll have to leave very soon, Malik," said the first minister. "Prime Minister, maybe you should have counsel with the emir and let him know how tonight's discussions have progressed. He'll be pleased that Malik's on the case. Maybe we can get his American friend to advise as well."

"I shall await your instructions," Malik said to the prime minister.

"We'll reconvene at nine in the morning. Malik, have one of your officers stay behind." The prime minister indicated Saif and Abdul Aziz. "I'll prepare your man with the documentation you need, and anything else that may arise now that the events of the night have settled down. A calmer mind may pick up some facts we've missed in the excitement of the evening."

"Saif is my best man and is by my side most of the time," Malik said. "He'll join us on the endeavor. Load him up with whatever else you think I might need. Abdul Aziz, you can retire for what remains of the night."

"All right, let's conclude our council for this overly long night," said the prime minister.

Malik turned to leave.

"Malik, keep an eye on her," the prime minister cautioned. "She's young and passionate. She lied to her father, the most important man in her life, until recently. She may lie to you too."

"I believe, deeply believe, that she would never deceive me," Malik replied. "Abdul Aziz, please arrange with your wife to get things sorted out for the morning. I only have an hour to spend with Elissa, and certain requirements to achieve."

"I said I didn't want to know," called the prime minister.

The first minister laughed. "No matter what he says about the physical aspect, I would certainly partake."

"I don't think your heart could bear it," said the prime minister. "Or the bed. These days you're truly built for comfort. Damn. I've just conflicted with the other meeting with the American about the plutonium deal. I'll have to delay it. Please remind me before we finish tonight, First Minister."

CHAPTER 10

THE WINNER TAKES IT ALL

The jumbo set down on the tarmac of the Doha International Airport.

We were ushered off the plane and herded through passport control. The queue diminished as each person was directed to a counter. The locals seemed to just wander through in the special white-clothes-only section, waving officials aside with a look of disdain that could only be used by someone who owned the place. At the other end of the scale was a herd—there must be a better collective noun, I thought—of Malay women, all tiny and terrified.

I presented my passport for its stamp. The man took it, looked at me and waited. I also waited. Eventually he coughed.

"Visa. You need visa to enter the country," he said.

"I have Mastercard." In my chronically jetlagged state, I began to look for my cardholder. "And Diners."

"No, not credit card. Visa. Permission to enter."

"Yes, yes. I am aware of what a visa is, but I'm an America. Visas? Where I'm going I don't need a visa." I smiled at him, hoping to earn some brownie points. He looked blankly at me. No McFly here, it would appear.

"Visa. You fill in visa." He pushed a card toward me.

I sighed and looked it over. The text was mostly in Arabic, with some poorly translated English underneath. I finally filled it out, mainly by matching up the symbols on my ticket to the symbols on the card. Fingers crossed. I was last through, which always made me feel efficient.

Most people collected their luggage and were quickly on their way home or to a hotel. I stood by the carousel trying to remember my name and if I'd brought any luggage. The one good thing about being last through passport control is yours is the only luggage left on the carousel. It was a small comfort.

I came out of the airport and was instantly hit by the humidity. My sunglasses immediately fogged up. The heat hit like a hammer. I started to perspire. No wonder they covered themselves up in this place. Months of this heat would be unbearable. There was no shade, certainly no trees to speak of, but at least I didn't have to walk to the city. For one thing, it was right there in front of me; and two, there were about a million green cabs. Maybe this time things would work out okay. I jumped into a cab and gave the driver my destination.

Palm trees lined the Corniche. The wind blew in through the window, and the air conditioner cooled my toes. It wasn't Dubai, but on the other hand it wasn't as stressful as Dubai. This was the life—warm, laid back, ocean views, and plenty of space.

We left the main road and headed inland. We went through a large collection of small stalls—*souks*, the driver informed me—and the sweet smell of herbs overwhelmed my senses. Men were sitting around in the midday heat, relaxing in the cool shade of the little stores. Women seemed to be walking freely. Most were covered in shawls—*abayas*, the driver informed me—and some had scarves, some didn't. No one seemed to be worked up about it. Interesting place, I thought.

"Welcome to the Ramada, ma'am. We hope you enjoy your stay here."

I looked around. The Ramada was about one million times better than my Colombian hotel. It would be impossible to burn this one down, I thought, and I was sure it could absorb a bomb blast. Security was everywhere. Everyone got searched as they came in. I could feel safe in a place like this. The huge marble foyer gave way to restaurants—with people *drinking*. Were they allowed to do that? I would have to get onto the people back at work—the infopak they gave me seemed to be out of whack with what I was seeing. I could see through the lobby to a pool with a submerged bar. The humidity was going to make the pool an ideal spot to be splashing about, sipping cocktails.

"Your company called. We inquired if you wanted a good room," said the concierge.

Oh, here we go, I thought.

"And they said to give you our best room."

"Best? My company said that? Really?"

"Yes, a Mr. Hinde," said the concierge.

"Hinde said *best*? Did he sound drunk?"

"We hope you enjoy the business suite. It's on the top floor. Your cases will be brought up later."

If he says I have a minibar I'll marry him, I thought. He smiled and offered me the swipe keys.

I was somewhere outside of America, and it was nice. I wanted to stroke the marble walls, put my face against them and feel the coolness radiating out. The porter opened the door to the suite and beckoned me in. It was huge. I wanted to cry.

"Ms. Ellen, your suite. There is some tourism information on the coffee table." The concierge bowed and left me. I didn't even need to tip the little Indian fellow.

The suite was as big as my condo, but it was all on one level and I had nowhere to park a car I didn't own. It had two main rooms— one main living area with panoramic views, and another with one of the largest beds I had ever seen.

I may never go back to a normal one again, I thought.

On the coffee table was a leaflet selling the dream of five things to do when you visit Doha. Five! Better clear my diary. I was only there for a month. What was number one? Go for a run along the Corniche. In this heat? They must be mad. Number two? Forget it.

I turned over the sheet representing all that could be called fun in Doha, and saw that it was blank. Maybe it was more about the people than the activities.

The huge windows beckoned. I looked out over the panoramic view of the city. It was dead flat all the way to the horizon. A dusty world—a sea of concrete and sand—stretched as far as I could see. I marveled at this manmade place. Once there was nothing but flat desert here. I guessed if I went back far enough it would have been the bottom of the ocean. But when the continents drifted and the oceans retreated, it became land. Then men stood on it, taking in the majesty and grandeur of an epic horizon, and thought: *What a godawful, desolate place.*

Women would have packed up and found somewhere nice, like Fiji. But the men thought differently and hid the car keys. So, starting with the most primitive of tools, they eked out an existence, always building and developing, always with the dream of building a better tomorrow for themselves and their families. Then the Westerners turned up with their great drills, the Turks turned up with their concrete, and together they built great phallic monuments to themselves and everything was ruined.

Oh well. It was good to know men didn't change wherever I went. But we could've been in Fiji, fellas!

I flicked on the TV, hoping to get a sense of the pop culture. I caught Al Jazeera, which was showing a locally filmed debate. A young woman dressed in a modern business suit and scarf was giving her all for her two minutes of recognition.

"Dreams," she was saying. "These people were once simple fishermen who had dreams. Then the miracle of hydrocarbons was inflicted on them, and they suddenly got their dreams all right. In fact, the dreams were too small. Greed set in and, just like everywhere else in the world, the families bickered. War, destruction, chaos, and all the other usual manmade fantasies turned up. Then the emir said enough and brought them together."

Like King Arthur, I thought.

"Dreams," she repeated. "The Qataris had proved they could do anything here. Floating libraries. New islands in the shape of initials. Snow in the desert on a fifty-degree-Celsius day. Buildings one hundred and sixty stories high. If they could dream it, they could build it."

I looked out the window to make sure she was talking about the same place, and that she wasn't in some fairyland being sold on the back of developers looking to make a quick buck. I turned my attention back to the screen. I was riveted.

"It showed what we could do as a race," the woman was saying. "Someone said here is a pot of gold, build this for me. And they did. No limits. We were shackled by our glorification of the dream of the mighty dollar, but all it did was keep us small. This region showed that we could soar like the gods themselves, and the only limit was our imagination. If only we were brave enough to dream it and believe it."

But the traffic looked pretty bad.

She was right. We lived in a time like the roaring twenties, where money fell from the skies. Part of my job was looking over contracts for new civil projects costing hundreds of billions of dollars. We talked of debt in the trillions, yet no one sweated. We craved more things yet gave them less value because we forgot we were all once like the poor fishermen the woman spoke about. We all looked around our world and wondered if we had to keep moving, or if we could plant some food and live in a nearby cave. We bought imaginary things like stocks and shares with imaginary money. And it all worked because we all believed, and we all danced the rain-money dance. The higher the stakes, the greater the pressure, and the more we pushed to the back of our minds that it was all make believe, and the harder we tried to forget that the dance could end.

And Hinde had told me the dance would end on September 14. Economic disaster was coming.

At least I owned my penthouse, the one that overlooked the bay. Perhaps I could lock myself away with fifty tons of canned pineapples.

On September 15, when I locked my door against the rioters, who would I be dreaming about? I would have David, but he was not the dream. I knew the dream, but a coffee machine couldn't give you everything. All right, I confessed to myself, Ax would be the dream. But here was where our worlds parted.

The woman on the TV sold the dream that in Qatar everything was possible because no one had said otherwise. In the West we all told ourselves this couldn't be done, that couldn't be done. The dream was not reality because it was not cost effective. And we had to deal with it every day because we were too shortsighted to think big. From the government to the individual, we relinquished our dreams in exchange for flat screen TVs and the addiction of reality TV. Those people lived the dreams for us. What an appalling trade. Yet it was an illusion.

So, in this city of dreams, did I believe David was my future? Something didn't have to be visible for it to be true. A cynical and skeptical world, with its rules of transparency and accountability, would say that if it was not apparent then it was not true. In my business the saying was: If it was going to happen it would have happened already.

I wondered if we could have gotten to the moon in 1969 if we thought then like we do today. Oh, David, what have you done to deserve me?

Tomorrow I would meet the prime minister. My, I thought, the places that the control of money took you. Tomorrow I would meet the prime minister and try to fleece this country out of a trillion dollars. But it was okay because it was pretend money, and they were buying something that was not real.

I wasn't sure I liked my job anymore. It was getting to the point where I couldn't look at my face in the mirror, which could be a real problem when applying mascara.

CHAPTER 11

READ 'EM AND WEEP

Luckily the prime minister bumped the morning meeting from nine to eleven. The jetlag was killing me. In a state of half zombification I tried to get myself into some kind of order. I only just made the breakfast buffet. I was overcome with an urgency to try everything on offer in the most bizarre combinations. Yes, I would like some Dutch cheese with my muesli and soy dumplings.

I had gotten bored with hotel life, but not for hotels like this. Cowley & Tate was cheap when it came to looking after their non-board staff. That made my stay even more interesting. They obviously felt the need to give me a good suite in a good hotel, which pushed this contract to the top of the career-defining list.

I was picked up in a brand new Bentley and escorted to the parliament located next to the palace. The palace was huge. It could have housed an aircraft. I wondered what it was like inside. Then I was taken through several security gates, where men looked under, over, and in the car. My door was opened and I was met by more security. I went through a metal detector, was scanned, and then searched.

I finally got through the barricades and was greeted by a man wearing one of those all-white dresses … those clothes things.

He gave me a slight bow. "Greetings, Ms. Ellen. I am Alctah Mahommid bin Kalifa al-Dahnish. I am the minister of the interior."

His name rolled off his tongue like a well-crafted sonnet. Unfortunately, in my clouded state it flowed through my mind like a cresting wave, and left with hesitation.

"I would like to welcome you to our humble parliament," the minister of the interior said. "I look forward to our dealings. You are about to meet the prime minister. We have some issues developing with Iran at the moment, so please don't feel offended if he seems a little distracted."

"What kind of issues? Nothing too serious, I hope."

"I would prefer it if we could leave that off the table for the moment. It may be nothing. But in the world of politics nothing can become something in twenty-four hours, so it's weighing on his mind. Please come this way."

He led me through one of the largest set of doors I had ever seen, which led into one of the largest rooms I had ever seen. The room spoke to me, as a child of the eighties. *More is more*, it said. And didn't it say it loudly. Intertwined complex marble patterns covered every surface. Rich and exotic tapestries hung from the walls, and there were great chairs reminiscent of a bygone era of English supremacy.

There were several men gathered around a large circular table. They all wore traditional clothing, starched and pressed to within an inch of their lives.

"I'm sorry to welcome you to such an ordinary building," Al-Dahnish said. "It must pale against the great architectural achievements that have been constructed in your homeland. But we're working on something new that will hopefully be more fitting to the importance of politics and serving the people. As minister of the interior, it's my responsibility to correct such deficiencies."

Al-Dahnish stopped in front of an elderly, regal-looking man, who stood tall, poised and graceful. "Ah, here we are. Miss Ellen, this is our very esteemed Prime Minister of the State of Qatar, Hussein bin Mohammad bin Jaider al-Kalifa."

The prime minister leaned towards me. His face, although aging, wasn't what I would call old, but it belonged to a man who didn't laugh too frequently. His dark eyes were friendly, intelligent and warm. But his face was one that had to deal with power and not let it take him.

Al-Kalifa offered his hand, and I shook it, not really knowing what else to do.

I had read in the infopak from work that Qataris wouldn't want to touch a visitor, but so much of the information I'd been given had been in stark contrast to what my own observations had shown me. Sometimes it seemed as though the information had been written about another country altogether. Saudi, maybe. Or Qatar, but from a more distant era. I'd definitely be having a word with work when I got back.

"We welcome you, Ms. Ellen, to our humble country," said the prime minister. "I hope you have found it hospitable, and the heat and humidity have not been too uncomfortable."

"Thank you for the invitation." What was I supposed to I call him? I was too jetlagged to remember his full name, and in the infopak all the names just looked like a jumble of vowels. The names sounded melodious when the Qataris said them, but when I'd practiced earlier I sounded like I had a speech impediment.

"Prime Minister, sir, here is my card," I said. Hopefully he had one too. I kept my ears tuned to find out what everyone else called him.

"Suresh," he called, "please give Ms. Ellen my card."

Al-Kalifa returned his focus to me. "I hope your family is well. Do you have children?"

"Actually, I'm not married yet, so children have not been my main focus."

"You should not wait too long. A young lady like yourself will need plenty of energy once you have two or three children."

Hah. I'd seen *Alien*. I knew about the dreaded secret of childbirth. Every other woman may have fallen for it, but not me.

This asking about families seemed important. "May I ask how your family is going?" I said.

"Very well, thank you. My eldest son is just entering parliament here, as a junior. He's been well schooled at Harvard, but now needs some practical experience in the cutthroat world of Middle Eastern politics, where there is twice the number of alliances as participants. My second son is just finishing his business degree, also from Harvard. He has been awarded the MBA as your great previous leader Mr. George. No doubt much training will be required before he takes over the family businesses."

Without taking a breath, and before I could give an appropriate response, the prime minister continued his litany. "My eldest daughter has to study locally, obviously, at the foundation. She's becoming quite friendly with Sheikh Mosa, so I hope she can learn some modern skills from her and bring them to our family for greater prosperity."

And there was yet another son. "My third son is quite young, in both heart and mind. He's struggling a bit with his studies, as he is easily distracted by fast cars. I've been joking that if he doesn't improve his grades I shall send him off to race in the Formula One. However, he may see that as a challenge rather than the threat it is. But he would hate to be away from his family for six months of the year, only to be surrounded by those noisy, smelly cars, and women who are too thin."

"Do you have a wife … or two?" I inquired.

"Yes."

There was a pause.

"They are fine," he continued.

There was another pause.

"Okay. Well, I hope fortune and happiness come your way," I said.

"Would you like a drink?" the prime minister asked.

"I would love a coffee," I replied. I wheeled my documents holder under the table, opened it and retrieved a handful of documents. There was no need to scare them just yet.

"How about a Turkish?" suggested Al-Kalifa.

"I guess so. I haven't had one before."

"They are world renowned," said the prime minister. "Suresh, Turkish please."

Suresh poured from a large golden urn with a curvy neck, like a swan, into a small china cup. He placed it in front of me. It looked very dark. The other guests were intently reading their papers. I took a sip. There was nowhere to spit so I had to swallow.

"Ms. Ellen, your eyes have gone red," Al-Kalifa observed.

"!" I said.

"Sorry?"

"Aren't you having one?" I managed to splutter out.

"Good grief, no. We have Dolce Gusto. Perfect cappuccino every time. If it's good enough for George Clooney it's good enough for us. Turkish coffee is an acquired taste, and one I have failed to acquire after many attempts. I wouldn't think any less of you if you choose not to finish it. Perhaps you would prefer an espresso."

"No. I'll take this as a challenge. Me versus the Ottomans and their interesting refreshments." I took another sip and did my best to swallow without causing too much of a scene. I let out a tiny wince.

"I'm not sure you're winning," said the prime minister.

We all laughed.

"I would like to open the meeting, and thank you all for coming. Please acknowledge our guest, Ms. Ellen, from the American company Cowley and Tate."

"Gentlemen," I said, "thank you for inviting me to your wonderful country, and for entrusting me with the transaction."

"Let Allah see wisdom prevail over this meeting," chimed in Al-Dahnish, the minister of the interior.

"Er. Yes." The reference had thrown me. "Gentlemen, as you are aware, we—being Cowley and Tate, and me—as the authorized signatory on behalf of the company—are in possession of two metric tonnes of plutonium *in potentia*. The rights for the plutonium exist in the London Exchange and remain there. The actual plutonium is still in the ground in various sites around the world."

"Have readings been completed at these sights?" Al-Kalifa asked.

"As best they can be. Everyone must understand, as we did when we bought the ownership rights, that the readings are not one hundred percent reliable. They may be correct or they may not be. Such is the risk. However, if you choose to onsell the rights at some point in the future before the mining has been performed, at what I would assume would be a reasonable profit, it wouldn't matter. You're simply buying the idea of owning the plutonium, as we did."

"Could you tell us why you're selling?" said the minister of the interior.

"Our CEO, Simon Hinde, had a late-night revelation brought on by a bad pizza. He wants to invest in local biomedical research. I won't point out how this revelation comes moments after the relaxation of the stem-cell research laws our previous government enforced. Plutonium has been good to us, and over the last fifteen years it has increased at a generous twenty to thirty percent per annum. Bioresearch could go critical over the next decade, with some fierce patent wars. We—we being Simon Hinde—want in at ground zero. The value of bioresearch patents could be worth tens of trillions of dollars. Hinde also wants one of those fancy boats similar to the one you have in the harbor."

"That would be the emir's private yacht," the minister of the interior said.

"Hinde sees himself as a bit of a king, although we call him a queen."

"We're not sure we know what you mean," the minister of the interior said.

"Yes," I said with a smile, "that may be for the best. Two hundred billion, gentlemen. Two hundred *billion* dollars. That translates to seven hundred and twenty-eight billion riyal."

"That's a lot of money," the prime minister said. "Of course we don't have funds of that magnitude lying around."

"Not even behind the sofa," chimed in another minister.

"Not now, First Minister. Ms. Ellen, allow me to introduce the first minister and deputy prime minister, Dr. Hassah al-Thani bin Kalifa al-Thani. A man with a sense of humor."

He said it like it was a disease.

"There are various financial protocols and procedures we need to follow," the prime minister said. "It's double our last year's GDP so the emir will want to be present. We will, of course, have to arrange the ceremonial handover. Ms. Ellen, this will escalate your company into the top ten companies by capitalization. The world will change for the company. Are you sure everyone's ready to deal with it? We know a lot about dealing with sudden wealth, and it's not easy."

"I'm sure our government will become our new best friend."

"We will make arrangements," he said. "Will you or someone else be present at the handover?"

"I assume Hinde will want to be the one," I said. "He likes the glory. He'll be here in a few days and I'm not sure if he'll want me to stay around or not."

I looked into their faces and saw honesty and integrity. My heart sank. I had to warn them.

"Read the contract carefully. I'm advising you as a lawyer to read the contract very carefully. I also advise you as someone who doesn't like Hinde, and who is in a very bad mood, to read the contract carefully. You have twenty-four hours to read and sign the initial-works contract. If you don't sign, the deal is off, or, knowing Hinde, he'll double the fee."

"Is that the contract there?" asked Al-Kalifa, indicating the handful of sheets in front of me.

"No. That's my airline e-ticket. This is your contract." I wheeled out the document carrier. I opened it up and lifted out, in three goes, the contract. It was eighteen inches of paperwork. The table swayed under its weight. "Remember, gentlemen, it is vitally important you read the contract. All of it."

I paused and took a mouthful of Turkish coffee. My eyes bulged. It felt unfair how quickly I'd forgotten its taste. I swallowed. I felt like waxing my tongue.

"Would you like a moment to recover?" asked the prime minister.

I shook my head. "Once you've signed this contract," I said when I'd regained my voice, "you have two weeks—ten working days—to transfer the funds, as per international-finance laws as amended in Singapore, July 2008. I'm contractually bound to say Simon Hinde had nothing to do with that either. He may have been in Singapore during July, but that was for totally different reasons."

"Why don't you like your boss," asked the prime minister.

"It would take a book to explain why. Ten working days, gentlemen. Get that in your minds. I reiterate—read the contract and understand it. If you have any questions you can find me in the bar in the pool at the Ramada, although I'm not sure what state of mind I'll be in considering my jetlag and the amount of alcho—er, cockt—er, Turkish coffees I'm going to consume."

"Well, we'd better get going," said the prime minister. He called out to Suresh, "Cancel our lives for the next twenty-four hours."

"I'll be back here at the same time tomorrow," I said. "If you want the plutonium, I mean really want it—and think hard about that— then have the contract signed. Good day, gentlemen."

With that I grabbed my briefcase and walked briskly out of the meeting room.

CHAPTER 12

DANCING IN THE DARK

It was several hours later and Abdul Aziz was concluding his most secretive of all meetings. This meeting didn't even have a venue, only a GPS coordinate. A group of elderly men huddled in the dark around a collection of Land Cruisers. Their respective eminent positions within the community meant they needed to keep their identities secret, so each had his *smagh* wrapped around his face.

Abdul Aziz knew who each one of them was.

He had organized a shipment of seven identical Cruisers from a corrupt friend who ran illegal vehicles over the Saudi border. Each vehicle had an identical number plate. It was all for show, as each elder was too self-centered to make himself look ordinary. Some had tried, but they all had their little telltale signs that they couldn't do without: a specific cufflink; an angle of their smagh; a nervous habit with their beads. The others were too self-absorbed to notice, but he knew every single one. There were seven families represented.

In an attempt to shroud themselves in some form of secrecy, it had been decided that they should each have a code name. Going through various collections of sevens, they had tried the names of the seven samurai, but the names were too foreign and complex. They tried the seven deadly sins in a show of derision toward the heathen Western religions, but no one wanted to be called *greedy*, although *wrath* had been popular.

Abdul Aziz's personal favorite was to name them after the seven dwarfs, appropriate because of their voracious appetite for gold and all that glitters. In the end he had given up and named them, as a tribute to his favorite movie, after the colors of the rainbow.

Yes, he thought, there were better representatives from the families, but those men were all active go-getters. They didn't sit around complaining about how unfair life was because the most extravagant of lifestyles hadn't been handed to them. They would see reason, could debate the importance of social responsibility and of making your own way in the world, but as far as Abdul Aziz was concerned you could keep them.

He wanted the bitter, put-upon ones; the small-minded, the petty, the heartbreakers, the ones distracted by shiny trinkets; the ones who could be manipulated, and relied upon to be full of vileness, self-importance, and stupidity.

And assembled in front of him he had them, the worst of the worst.

"Shouldn't we have some kind of secret sign?" Sheikh Green said.

"Why?" Sheikh Yellow replied. His voice dripped with annoyance.

"So we can identify each other if we meet."

"What's the point of that? We're meant to be secret. Secret from each other, as well as the rest of society. How secret do you think a society should be that has planning a bloodless coup on the emir? Do you think it should be something that only a few people know, or something that should be casually discussed at dinner parties?" Sheikh Orange said.

"There could be strength in numbers." Sheikh Green said.

"There's never strength in numbers," Sheikh Yellow said. "People hate change. There's strength in might." He clenched his fist and raised it in front of the others. "We need to crush all who stand in our way."

"Gentlemen," Abdul Aziz interjected, raising both his hands to calm the situation. "Can I humbly request that we commence this meeting."

"Who made you leader?" Sheikh Yellow snapped.

"No one made me leader. I am merely facilitating the development of ideas from your collective great minds."

"We should have a leader," Sheikh Orange said. "I should be the general manager. I've had many years of experience in waiting, and I feel it's my duty to rise to the occasion and be the GM."

The room erupted in a babble of voices.

"You can't have a general manager of a secret society."

"Isn't there some Canadian society that has a Grand Moose?"

"You can be our grand ass."

"Well, the Freemasons have a Grand Master."

"There's no way in the world you're going to be the Grand Master of any society I'm in, unless I'm one as well."

"You can't have two Grand Masters. It's not chess."

"It's obvious that I'm the only person who pays any kind of attention to what's going on," Sheikh Yellow said, "so I will humbly accept the title of manager."

"If he's a manager then so am I," Sheikh Blue said.

"Me too," chorused the rest of the sheikhs.

"Okay, you're *all* managers," Abdul Aziz said. "Now can we move on?"

The men gave brief glances around the circle then all nodded in agreement. Abdul Aziz was sure that next they would want to discuss business cards.

"Now, down to the important business at hand. What do we call ourselves?" Sheikh Yellow said.

"No names!" Abdul Aziz spluttered. "Gentlemen, learned sheikhs, lend me your ears."

"What's in this for you, Abdul Aziz?" Sheikh Yellow said. "Why are you helping us?"

"When you originally came to me looking for assistance there were two personal benefits I could immediately see. The first, and most important, was the money. First, last, and always is the money. My years of being a mercenary have taught me there's very little you can rely on, but the most certain of all things is a large number in your bank account. But of course you all know this. I give you Adnan to meet your ends, but at a cost. The second benefit is Malik al-Thani, the forgotten bastard child of the disgraced princess. He owes me much, but refuses to recognize or reward me."

"Malik has been known as a real Casanova," Sheikh Yellow said.

Sheikh Orange looked puzzled. "Mmm … a new Spanish house?"

"I said pay attention. There are rumors Malik slept with some of his own soldiers' wives."

"How does he get all the luck?" Sheikh Blue asked.

"I hate Malik, and yes, there is a rumor that he's slept with my wife," Abdul Aziz said.

"No need to give us the grim details. Just because you've been unable to control your wife doesn't mean everyone has the same problem," Sheikh Yellow said.

"Maybe even some of your own treasures have been seduced by his deep voice and fancy stories," Abdul Aziz added darkly.

"Hah! Has he even *seen* some of my treasures? No one would want to touch them with a ten-foot hookah," Sheikh Red said.

"I'm not sure it's true," Abdul Azul said, "but just the suspicion is enough for me. The gullible fool thinks highly of me, and that's a weakness I plan to abuse."

"How?" chorused the collection of old men, all except for Sheikh Orange, who was beginning to doze. The chorus jolted him back into the world of the conscious.

The men huddled around Abdul Aziz as he laid out his plan.

Silence settled over the group as Abdul Aziz explained his vision. The quiet continued after he had finished while each man let the ideas settle into place.

Eventually Sheikh Yellow spoke. "All I can see is your own agenda being satisfied. If this all goes wrong we're the ones who will lose the most."

"You're also the men who have the most to gain," Abdul Aziz said. "This is the reality of playing for high stakes. You play for a country with over a trillion barrels of natural gas. Play your cards right, and you and your families will be unimaginably wealthy forever."

"These are empty words that may please the foolish or greedy," Sheikh Yellow said, "but we've heard them many times before and the promises always fail to materialize. How will your plan help us?"

"It's all connected," Abdul Aziz said. "Stick to your guns, make sure the events play out. You will have your right to march on the emir and force him out. But you need someone as a figure of authority, who appears to the outside world that he could lead a country. Adnan Muanietha is the right man for this task."

"But Adnan is a fool barely able to breathe," Sheikh Yellow blurted. "He knows nothing."

"Yes, but he's your fool. He's old family. Traditional. He's one of you, and like you he has lost much under the emir, who fritters away your money on the undeserving. Make the plan work and you'll be able to force the emir out. The next most powerful person will be Adnan, who will step up to take power. Then you will have your puppet in power. You can make it like the old days and forget all these modern ideas by a modern emir."

"Okay. We shall proceed with caution," Sheikh Yellow said. "I, for one, am not completely sold on the plan. You are a very skilled diplomat if you can achieve all you describe, one far greater than any of us."

"Agreed," said Sheikh Blue.

"We already have a deputy prime minister," Sheikh Green said. "Dr. Hassah. What will happen to him? Unlike the emir, he's in rude health."

"I will take care of him," Sheikh Yellow replied.

"And how will you do that?" Sheikh Green asked.

Sheikh Yellow chuckled and glared back at Sheikh Green with eyes full of malice.

The others hesitantly nodded in agreement with the more vocal sheikhs. The last to give his assent was Sheikh Green, who paused for a long time before agreeing.

CHAPTER 13

I SAID NEVER AGAIN
(BUT HERE WE ARE)

I was soaking in the pool, floating on my back. The sun was glorious. The pool was the perfect temperature, and the margarita was nice and strong. I felt the waves of heat roll over me, and my head got a little fuzzy. I was the only one there. All I needed was about four days' sleep and I would be as good as new.

I heard someone splash down near me. I opened one eye to see who was invading my space. It was another tourist. She was wearing a yellow bikini—how seventies. She swam over to the steward waiting in the submerged bar and ordered something with a name laced with Western innuendo. I wondered if the barman knew what a slow comfortable screw against the wall was like, other than some relaxing DIY.

The woman chatted inanely with the barman as best she could, but the only English he seemed to understand was the names of drinks.

Having a conversation with the barman would be interesting, I thought. Every other line would be a hint at sex. I wondered if he understood that. I wondered if Western women threw themselves at him using these terms and he thought they wanted drinks. Could work out to be a funny sketch for *SNL*.

After a while the stilted dialog got to me. I swam over to order another drink.

"Hi, I'm Brandi," said the other woman named Brandi. "With an i."

Well, I say woman. More like just past her teens.

"Well hello, Brandi," I said. "I would hope you have two." I floated onto an underwater concrete seat.

And she laughed, annoyingly, like she'd never heard it before. I bet she made friends really quickly, especially male ones.

"I'm Ellen."

And that's where everything went wrong. If I hadn't spoken to her, if I'd just minded my own stupid business, if I'd paid attention to her stupid name—knowing someone called Brandi with an i could only lead to trouble—if I'd remembered why I was there, then so much trouble could have been avoided. You would think I'd have learned by now.

"Are you on holiday?" asked Brandi with an i.

"No, I'm with work. I'm here doing contract stuff for a couple of weeks. And to work on my tan. How about you?"

"I'm with the military."

"You don't look like a soldier."

"No, my boyfriend is based at the US base here. He's away at the moment doing something manly, so I'm here ignoring the fact he's away."

"You from Arkansas?" She had a strong Southern accent, and if I guessed right I was hoping she would be impressed.

"Yeah. Where are you from?"

"Louisiana."

"Really, you don't sound like it."

"I left a long time ago, and I work in an industry that likes a flat accent."

"Huh?"

"I'm a lawyer."

"I'm just a girlfriend."

"Well, it's a dirt job, but someone's got to do it."

"What?"

"Someone has got to be a girlfriend, so the rest of us don't have to be."

"Huh?"

"Don't worry."

There were plenty of moments to escape yet I failed to notice any of them. So we sat and drank into the evening, getting more BFF-ish. And after more cocktails, Brandi with an i didn't seem so bad. She was friendly and I didn't have to talk too much, or even listen too much, truth be told. I don't think she knew much about anything, but she liked shoes so we had some common ground there.

"Then I got these amazing knee-high silver boots with a six-inch dagger for a heel, but I don't know how anyone walks with them."

"That's easy," I said. " You take them off when you get out of bed."

"Do you wear yours to sleep?" Her face wrinkled up in a way that I was sure soldiers everywhere would like.

"Don't worry."

"Hey, you know what we should do? We should go to Bubbles."

"I've been here a day," I said. "To me that could either be a relaxation center or a private zoo."

"It could be totally both. It's, like, the nightclub at the Marriott."

"Nightclub? I'm nearly fort—er, I'm late—I'm mid-thirties."

"Okay, Ms. Mid-Thirties, you're thin and fit looking, and, trust me, there you'll be a babe-in-arms. And the DJ plays lots of really old songs from the nineties."

"I have to admit, you're not selling it to me that well. The nineties were known for grunge, which doesn't translate well to the dance floor."

"No, no, no, the other stuff. Like those cute guys."

"I'm not sure … could you be a little bit more specific?"

"You know," she said, "the ones who had the brother of the guy who went to jail."

I racked my brain for some time. The five hours of cocktail drinking didn't help. Eventually a name rose from the mire with its head bowed low with appropriate embarrassment.

"You don't mean New Kids on the Block. I hope you don't mean New Kids on the Block."

"Yeah, them," Brandi shrieked. "Oh, I loved them sooo much."

"I'm not sure I can speak to you anymore."

"Back streets here, all right!" she sang.

"Shhh, we're in public, and people have opinions."

"Oh come on, you know you'll love it. Come on, pleeeeease. It'll be fun."

"Against all my better judgment, I'll say ..." I paused. Brandi was fit to explode with antici ... pation. "Okay."

She cheered.

"I'm sure I'll regret it in the morning," I said.

"Hey, we could get dressed together, and have drinks and talk about stuff like boys."

"I don't think so." I didn't need to be reminded of what I once looked like. "Come back in an hour. I'm in the business suite."

She giggled like—let's be generous—a young excitable lady, collected her things into a leopard-skin bag half her size, saronged herself, downed what remained of her drink, and headed back to the lobby.

My god, she had used the word *boys*. Do you remember that, Ellen? I asked myself. Talking about boys, doing toenails, giggling excitedly about who was going to be at the club with my roomy, Candice. I definitely did remember. Maybe a night out wouldn't be so bad. One for the glory days.

I remembered the days when the night was for the young, and we were young. More often than not the night would end in disaster, with Candice missing a shoe, or crying in the toilet over someone who refused to notice her. It didn't make sense, but when you're young nothing does. All that mattered was that we wore as little as possible, behaved in a way that said "look at me" and drank enough to not care how embarrassing the whole effort was.

I went back up to the room. I hadn't expected to wear it on this trip, but I carried it with me everywhere. I'm not sure why. It was a black suede jersey-dress with tan panels, which was a wonderful figure-flattering cocktail piece. I paired it with oversize earrings and velvet platform sandals. It was the ultimate party look. Classy. Cheeky. Fun.

Yeah, it was designed for a woman in her twenties, but tonight all bets were off and all the rules were to be broken. I'd bought the dress as an act of defiance when I was in London a few years back, surviving another disaster. French Connection. Or more appropriately, their moniker FCUK. What a glorious message to the world. It was how I felt a lot of the time.

My dress size hadn't changed. Time hadn't been cruel to me; I had been cruel to it. It showed that I was winning. Just because I was now older than a teenager didn't mean I was old. And what you forget, Mr. Advertising Man, is that I've got cash. And lots of it. So yeah, you can go French Connect yourself.

There was a knock at the door. I opened it and Brandi stood in the corridor wearing a set of torn denim shorts, cowboy boots, and about a million necklaces. Was the nightclub a fancy-dress place?

"What are you wearing?"

"Stuff."

"You've got glitter on your face. Are you eleven?"

"I've put it everywhere," Brandi whispered behind her hand.

"I do not want to know. The fewer people who know, the less chance it has of catching on and becoming a trend. Come in before you're arrested."

"Hey, nice outfit. You dress like my mom."

"You don't have many friends, do you?"

"Great room."

"Suite."

"Oh, totally."

"I seem to have sobered up too much. Let's attack the minibar before we go. What would you like?"

"Have they got any Jacks?"

She kept getting classier. I told myself not to be too hard on her. Her tastebuds, like her boobs, probably hadn't developed yet.

"I can't convert you to vodka?" Champagne was going way too far. I was sure she probably couldn't even pronounce the word if she saw it written down.

"Do you think there'll be some hot boys there tonight?"

"I thought you were a girlfriend."

She giggled. "It's not as if I'm married."

I sighed. It seemed all women attracted to men in uniforms were of loose morals.

"Have you got a boyfriend? Or are you married?" Brandi asked.

"You don't have a boyfriend when you get to my age. That's a bit tween. I have a gentleman friend to whom I am engaged. To be married," I added just to clarify the situation.

"Oh wow. Is he, like, totally hot?"

"No. He's in his forties. Men in their forties are no longer hot."

"Isn't Brad Pitt forty-something?"

"Well, yes."

"He's not too bad for an old man."

I would need to adjust my headspace. I wasn't sure I could cope in a world where Brad Pitt was seen as an old man. I couldn't argue. He was no longer that dripping pool of sex that any girl/woman/living female with any kind of taste or pulse would melt for. No. But for god's sake, he was *Brad Pitt*. He was *better*.

In fact, there were a slew of them these days, men who were still all right in their forties. Okay, they were all movie stars with infinite health budgets and weren't afraid of moisturizer, but still, it showed what was possible. No one had to let themselves go. I still trained five times a week. And I still fitted into this dress. So fcuk you, Old Man Time.

I thought of Alex. He was forty-two and looked … No, Ellen, we're not discussing Alex. Are we? No, Ellen, we are not.

"So maybe tonight we can be totally single." Brandi was stuck on this theme. "Maybe we can hook up with some hot bods."

Why was I even listening to her? I decided it must be the vodka affecting my brain. I, for reasons best known to my deprived libido, decided that a last fling before settling down, and turning forty—but there was no need to discuss that tonight—was excusable.

"Okay. Let's not tell them to go away unless they're total losers." Oh god. I was even talking like Brandi now.

"Here's to hot guys." Brandi raised her glass.

CHAPTER 14

MUSTANG SALLY

We walked into the venue. The music was pumping, and the bass fired up my emotions and recollections. It reminded me of long ago. My god, I used to love to dance. I didn't care if there was no one else or everyone else. It was always me and the beat, lost together, mixed in a cocktail of adrenaline and often something illegal.

With David's proposal, and being down here in the club with Brandi, the present didn't seem so gloomy. It was time to take a fresh look at my life. I was definitely going to do more dancing when I got home. I wondered if David danced. Probably not. Not well, anyway.

Perhaps I could get him into an MDMA habit. Then we could go out raving. Oh, yeah. Put your hands up for Detroit. And I didn't care what anyone thought. Dancing was for everyone. It wasn't only the domain of the young; it belonged to every one of every age. I looked around. I was young compared to most of the other people in here.

Brandi seemed to know lots of people, and within moments we were surrounded by admirers. It had to be the blond hair. Of course. And the cowboy boots. Now someone had gotten her a cowboy hat. I hoped there was no pole nearby; otherwise it was going to look very cheap very quickly. I hoped the night wouldn't end with her shaking her dixie around to desperate men throwing money.

A couple of sharp-looking guys were angling to buy us drinks. They were tall, dark and lean. Good-looking guys with heaps of cash. They were pulling out five-hundred-riyal notes, which was equivalent to about a hundred and forty dollars.

Brandi ordered something large and sticky. She had draped herself over one of the guys.

The other guy looked at me. He made some twisting-by-the-pool motion, which I took to mean *Would you like to dance?* I nodded and we headed for the flashing floor.

He moved well, and he was a smooth looker. It made me feel great. We spun around to eighties classics that were popular before Brandi was even alive until the sweat poured off us. We went back to Brandi, who now had both arms wrapped around her man. She was kissing him passionately and rubbing her body against his. This was going to end badly for someone.

The other guy ordered some drinks. I went for an old favorite from my clubbing days—a Bud. Oh, how it took me back.

"What's your name?" I shouted.

"Mo," shouted Mo.

"You look very healthy. What do you do?"

"I'm a member of the emir's personal search-and-rescue squad."

"Now that sounds dangerous and exciting."

I took a sip from the bottle. I wondered if he'd ever seen a woman drinking straight from a bottle. Most of the ladies in here were drinking cocktails or sparkling white, hence the name of the place.

I looked around. There were quite a few Filipina ladies, wearing not a whole lot, decorating the walls, waiting for … someone, I guessed.

"Hookers," shouted Mo.

"I hope you don't think I'm one," I shouted.

He smiled. It was a nice smile. He seemed like a nice person, unlike his friend, who was basically having sex with Brandi next to us. It certainly could be considered foreplay.

What the hell. I draped my arm over my guy's shoulder. I was the best deal he was going to get tonight, and maybe the last best deal of anonymous excitement I was going to get for the rest of my life.

The lights strobed, my mind blurred and the music kicked. I hadn't felt this happy in a long time. We danced more and drank more. We danced closer and closer as the evening went on. As the night wound towards midnight, I didn't know how Mo was feeling, but I was getting pretty worked up. He held me close and grabbed my ass. I didn't stop him. I gave him a deep, long kiss, and we hung there in time, surrounded by our desires.

"Do you have a place nearby?" I shouted.

"Yes," Mo shouted back.

"Shall we go there? We could ... talk."

The guys said they had a place at the barracks. It was quiet there, and we could all ... talk. It looked like Brandi couldn't wait to have a close and in-depth discussion with her man. I was thinking of him as the Brandi-man, but his real name—well, the one he wanted us to use—was Pax. I wondered what it was short for.

On the way out Brandi staggered around a fair bit and Pax assisted with a hand planted firmly on her backside. I guess it sort of worked.

A young guy, a local, was making a bit of a scene at the entrance to the club. He was beginning to shout. The bouncers didn't seem to know what to do with him. He was acting pretty smashed.

Brandi staggered in her boots and bumped into him gently. He went ballistic. He shouted at the bouncers, pointing at Brandi. No one looked very happy. Pax stepped forward and put his palms up to try and calm the situation. The young local started to push him about, but Pax just stood there, letting the aggression bounce off him. If he was a soldier, like Mo, then the young guy was going to be in a lot of trouble.

Pax must have said something bad because the young guy's face changed. He went red and took a wild swing at Pax. Pax spun him round and flung him to the ground. He kneeled on his back and placed him in an armlock.

The bouncers then got involved. They pulled Pax up, put him in some bizarre lock and in seconds had him kneeling on the floor. Mo tried to intervene but he was pushed aside.

I thought it best to try and inject some kind of peace message into the conversation. I placed my hand on the shoulder of the young guy on the floor to try and help him up. He started shouting and pointing at me. Amongst his jumbled and slurred speech he managed to form the word *whore*. His hand came around and left a ringing slap on my face.

How *dare* this little inebriated halfwit call me a whore. I thought about slapping him back ... then realized I'd already returned the compliment. Uh-oh.

The whole place went crazy. People were shouting and running around. More bouncers turned up. The police arrived.

"Oh, holy crap," said Brandi. "Cops. The kid must've been an important-someone's son. No wonder he's causing a scene. Ellen, listen to me, this is really important. If they ask what your relationship to your man is, say he's your cousin."

"Why?"

"Because they'll throw you in jail if they catch you out with someone you're not related to in some way. It's meant to stop prostitution. So, he's your distant cousin, got it?"

"Don't tell me you know exactly what to do because you do this so often. When you say jail, how long are we talking?"

"Ten to fifteen years."

I turned to Mo. "Well, cousin Mo, it's a pleasure to meet you again after all these years."

We were all escorted by the police to a van outside and taken off to the police station.

"Does this happen often?" I asked Brandi.

"Yeah, it's just another way for the local guys to scam some more money."

"How?"

"They might want bribes or something. They don't get paid much, and they don't get much respect because the powerful families think they're above the law."

"And you think this young guy was from a powerful family?"

"Yeah, just some punk with a skin full of courage. He probably wasn't old enough to go in the place. No wonder the bouncers were having a hard time. It's hard to deal with people like him. You either get in trouble with the family or your boss, depending on what you do. It's crap sometimes."

"You said bribes or something. I assume the something is sex."

She winked at me. "It's cheaper than paying a fine. Your arrest will also go on your record here. 'Something' gets the whole thing swept under the carpet. But don't worry. I know Mo and Pax's boss. We were discussing him at Bubbles. If I can get in touch with him he'll sort it out. Hey, Pax, the captain's all right, isn't he?"

Pax nodded. "Although he won't be happy to bail us out again."

"Again?" I said.

"Have you got a cell?" Brandi asked me.

"I think I may have left it in the room. Just for once it would be nice to go to a country where I didn't get arrested."

"You get arrested a lot?"

"More than I should."

"You go, girl!" Brandi wanted to do a high-five. I just stared at her until she dropped her hand.

"You guys got a phone?" I asked.

They shook their heads. Pax indicated that the police had taken theirs. Within a few minutes we were at the police station. We were hustled up some old stone steps into a decrepit old room with ancient seventies furniture. Not even the cool retro stuff. Just old crap.

The guys were bundled off into another room. Brandi and I were put in a rusty old cage. She seemed remarkably at ease with the situation. Mind you, so was I. I'd been in enough of these cells. And let me make this clear: it was never my fault. Well, nearly always never my fault. I hoped Brandi wouldn't start dancing. Women dancing in cages was never a good look.

She was leaning against the bars, smiling at the guard. She was twirling something in her mouth. She winked at the guard. He smiled back in a leery way and strolled over to her. She winked at me. She whispered something into his ear. He looked around and nodded. He unlocked the cage door, gave me a disapproving stare, and led Brandi away. She signaled *ten* to me as she disappeared.

Ten minutes later she came back.

"I'm going to Pax's place," she whispered quickly. "We sorta made bail. I'll call his captain from there and send him down. He's an American so he'll look after you. He's a good guy; he'll get you out. You never know, tonight could still be your night. He's kinda cute since you're into those old guys like Brad and George."

Inside, I shook my head. Ten years ago women would have lined up to kill Brandi after a comment like that. Now I guessed Brad wasn't cool because he wasn't a vampire. Pity they didn't know about *Interview with the Vampire*. Old Louis would've them wetting their panties in anticipation. It was a crap film, but we didn't see it for the art.

CHAPTER 15

JAILHOUSE ROCK

After half an hour of sitting alone in the cell, I heard a commotion. Raised Arabic voices went on for some time. Eventually an unmistakably American voice said, "Mo, get your sorry ass out here. You and your cousin are in a whole heap of trouble, do you understand me? I can't believe you got caught again. By the way, you have the largest extended family of anyone I've ever met."

I placed my head in my hands.

"Let's see who this latest cousin is," the man said.

This was about to be the worst day of my life.

"Yes, Captain, this is Ellen …"

"Martin," said Alex Heart. "Oh my, what a small world we live in. Mo, you're free to go. You're no longer in trouble."

Mo looked like he could sense something was wrong, so he took the opportunity to evacuate the premises at speed.

"Oh, let her out," Alex shouted to the desk. "Although I have three-quarters of a mind to let her stay in there," he muttered. One of the local police appeared from the front office and unlocked the cell door. I stepped out into freedom.

"What about the guy who hit me?" I said to Alex. I placed my hands on my hips.

"Forget him."

"But he hit me. I don't like being hit."

"For Christ's sake, Ellen, what are you doing?"

"I was out having a good time."

"Out for trouble, more like. What are you doing hooking up with my men?"

"I'm not hooking up with them. By the way, I don't like the way you said that, and I didn't know they were *your* men." I folded my arms and glared at him.

"That makes it all right?"

"I thought you were in Dubai."

"No, I'm here, but on occasion I visit Dubai. This can be a dangerous country, especially for people dressed like you."

"What's that supposed to mean?"

"Dressed like a hooker."

"This is French Connection, thank you very much. It's a class outfit for a classy person."

"Yeah, maybe if you were ten years younger. You need to get some self-restraint. I can't be in every country you're in when you get arrested."

"I didn't need you in London."

"You got arrested in London?"

"It wasn't my fault," I wailed. "It was ... unfortunate."

He grabbed my arm and took me around to the front office. There was a local policeman standing behind the desk with a considerable amount of paperwork on it.

"Everything is unfortunate with you. Every time I see you, it's because something unfortunate has happened. Then it usually happens to me too."

"Is the lady your wife?" the police officer asked.

"Hah! Life would not be worth living. No, she's my"—he rolled his eyes—"cousin."

"Yours, too?"

He sighed. "Yes. A very distant and annoying one."

"Speaking of family, how is Jessie?" the officer asked Alex. "Is she coming back to visit us again soon?"

"She's infinitely better and more grown up than this lady here," Alex said. "And no, I don't think she'll be back for a while."

"Tell her we still have her picture." The officer indicated a blown-up photocopy from a newspaper clipping stuck to the wall.

I squinted at the image. I could see the resemblance. She was running, and behind her something big had blown sky high.

"I see she got the looks," I said to Alex. "Probably got the manners as well." I turned my back on the men.

"Captain, you can't put this lady down as your cousin if Mo's claiming her as one, too."

"Oh, Christ, this is stupid. What is she then?"

"Wife?"

"Not in a million years," we both said at the same time.

"Fiancée?" the officer asked.

"This is making me feel very sick." Alex wiped his hand across his forehead. "Geez, okay, for better or for worse, yes, she's my fiancée."

He looked back at the other officer, who was sitting behind the desk. "I'm beginning to dread how many favors I owe you. Can we go?"

The officer nodded.

"You got any cash?" Alex asked me.

"Yeah."

"I suggest you donate generously to their Eid fund." He pointed to a large jar in the center of the desk.

"What's an Eid?"

"It's like Christmas."

I took out some notes and stuffed them into the jar on the counter.

"More generous than that," Alex said.

I took out the rest of the money in my purse and poured it over the desk. Alex quickly scooped it up and placed it in the jar. The policeman glared at me. I sneered back at him. Alex quickly dragged me out the door.

"Geez, Ellen, have you learned nothing about dealing with locals? You need to be careful. That stunt back there could be seen as disrespectful. And guess where you'd end up if the police thought you were being disrespectful."

"But I'm not the one at fault. I was having a great time, and some idiot hit me."

"You are at fault. Get in the car, fiancée."

"But he hit me. First."

We slammed our car doors in unison. Alex fired the engine into life and he roared off into the traffic. He screeched through a tight corner, mounted a curb and shot straight into a huge roundabout without stopping for the oncoming traffic. I quickly reached around for the seat belt. Of course it kept sticking as I tugged the belt over my shoulder. Eventually I managed to ease it around myself and buckled up.

"It doesn't matter. You're a foreigner here. If you hadn't been there the incident wouldn't have happened. So, because you were in the country, it was your fault."

"You cannot be serious."

Another cruiser was desperately trying to get past us. It swerved from side to side, trying to find a way around. It flashes its high beam and blasted the horn. Alex sat resolutely in the middle of the road. He coasted up to a set of traffic lights.

"It's the same on the road," he said. "If they run a red light and smash into you, it's your fault."

"That's stupid."

The other cruiser took the opportunity to career onto the sidewalk, through the chairs, and out the front of the shops. The driver waited for the lights to turn green, revving the engine to high heaven.

I looked over at the car. All the windows were pitch black, which matched the paintwork. I couldn't see anything through the glass.

"It's not stupid," said Alex. "From their point of view, you're here in their country taking their money and not giving them much back in return. And in a way it's true. They have a point. It is their country. If you do business here you have to understand how it works."

"Well, I'm not doing business here. I was just out having a good time. They're not paying me anything to be here."

The lights turned green and the cruiser next to us took off, wheels squealing and chairs scattering. It crunched back onto the road and roared off up the street. Less than fifty yards later it pulled over. The driver got out and strolled leisurely into the coffee shop he had stopped in front of.

"Still career obsessed?" Alex said.

"I am not obsessed. I have a plan, a vision I'm pursuing. I am what I do, I've told you that before. It would help if you listened."

"You said that ten years ago. I was listening, then and now."

"Then you should understand," I shouted. "You are so typical."

"Just get out," he shouted back.

"Don't be so inconsiderate as to abandon me in a place where I don't know where I am."

"Just get out. We're at your hotel. The Ramada." He indicated the big shiny building.

"Oh. Well, there's no need to shout."

He banged his head against the steering wheel. His cell rang. I got out, glared at him and slammed the door.

"Wait," Alex shouted. He climbed out of the 4WD and stormed in my direction.

"What now?"

"That was the police. I have to confirm, from your room, that you are actually there. Otherwise you have to go back. Christ, I am so over this."

We stood in the lift in silence. The doors opened. I looked

sideways at him with disdain and strode out of the lift. I swiped the card and burst into my room.

Alex followed. "Where's the phone?" he said.

"In the bedroom."

He gave me a look. I knew what he was thinking. He picked up the phone and dialed. He said a few words in Arabic.

He looked up at me. "How long are you here for?"

"Only two weeks, if you can stand it that long. Or as soon as my boss gets here. Then I'll be out of your stupid, precious country."

"Don't have a go at me. You're the one who's in trouble. Do you think you can stay out of trouble for two weeks?"

He said a few more words into the phone, hung up and turned to me. "These are the rules. Don't do anything wrong or stupid. Or both. I know that'll be difficult for you, but just try to be normal and not you."

I could feel the anger burning off me. Alex looked just as furious.

"Right," I said. "If that's the way it's going to be, I've got one thing to say to you."

"Tell me, I can hardly wait to hear your words of wisdom."

Right. That was it. I glared at him. He was going to regret tonight and those stupid comments.

I leaped forward. I wrapped my arms around him and pushed my mouth onto his. His eyes sprang wide open and he staggered back onto the bed. On top of him, I pushed my tongue into his mouth. He still seemed stunned. I ripped open his shirt and dragged my nails down his top. Oh god, his body was still amazing. Still lots of scars. Sorry about that, Alex.

He closed his eyes and kissed me back. He grabbed me tightly. My dress had ridden up and I tore it over my head. He rolled me over and ripped off his shirt. The cuff got caught on his watch, and he worked at it intently until he ran out of patience and just tore it off.

I clutched at his chest, feeling those great hulking muscles, then pulled him close. His back muscles flexed under my touch. His breath caressed my neck and sent shivers down my spine. My head was spinning out of control. I wrapped my legs around his waist and pulled him to me. God, how I wanted him inside of me, more than I thought was possible.

I bit into his neck and rubbed my face against his early-morning stubble. I ground my crotch into his and kissed him deeply. I rolled him back over so I was on top again.

I slowly licked down his bare chest until I reached his faithful old cargo pants with too many pockets. He still wore them, and he still looked good in them. His body had a light sheen of sweat and it made him smell delectable. I slid my hands over his chest and stomach, reached for his belt and began to undo it. I looked up at his body. I knew all the scars so well. And they were all my fault.

I rested my head on his stomach. It drove me wild seeing him there. Every fiber of my body wanted him so bad, but it was wrong and I knew it.

"No, I can't do this," I said.

"What? Why?"

"I just can't. It's too difficult."

"Oh, for Christ's sake, Ellen. Don't tell me that while you're lying there in Victoria's Secret."

"It's wrong."

"How can this be wrong between us with our history, when you were about to go home with one of my juniors?"

"It just is."

"That is so typical of you."

"How is it typical? You think I wanted this?"

"Who knows how you think. You are just a mess. Your whole life is about you. You don't care about anything or anyone else."

"How dare you say that? I've given up everything for other people."

"Really? For ten years ..." He looked so angry. "For ten years, Ellen, nothing."

"Well, it wasn't long enough. My life is perfect without you in it."

"Fine. Get what you wish for."

"I never—and I mean this—want to see you again. Not in a million years."

"Well, that's fine by me." He glared at me, grabbed his shirt and left.

The door closed and Alex left my life, forever this time. I collapsed back onto the bed, pulled the pillow over my head and burst into tears. He hadn't even looked back.

CHAPTER 16

GREAT BALLS OF FIRE

As always, the night had ended in disaster. At least I hadn't lost my shoes. They'd cost six hundred dollars, so I would have been inconsolable. I would've had to buy another three pairs to recover. What a night.

I managed to string together a couple of hours' sleep before I had to face the world, and I felt in no mood to suffer any fools, or men, which were the same thing in my book. I felt emotionally dead. I never wanted to meet any man who could hurt me so much. And that's why David was really the right option. I was never going to be so involved with him that he could hurt me.

I decided to call him and let him know that everything was all right, and tell him how excited I was about the future. But before I could make the call, reception buzzed and derailed my agenda.

My ride was on time and whisked me away to the meeting. A lot of me wished the council had decided not to sign that immoral contract. I struggled to see what was in it for them, but they had been the highest bidders so there had to be something there. The machinations of international politics were beyond my understanding or caring this morning.

The heat seemed worse today. I was already fatigued, and it

crushed the remaining energy out of me. I wilted under the sun like a Ruby Giant in a blast furnace.

They ushered me through the various layers of security and within minutes I was once again being led into the parliament offices. The same men were present from the previous day. It would have been humorous—at least in my eyes—if they had been there all night.

The gentlemen rose. It was good to see manners weren't dead everywhere. Al-Kalifa, the prime minister, came to greet me. He smiled. I felt in no mood to respond. He extended his hand, which I shook.

"Is everything all right, Ms. Ellen? You seem distracted," he said.

"I'm sorry. It was a bad night."

"Anything you would like to share? Has the hospitality not been acceptable? Your room has not been adequate?"

"Oh, Lord no. I cannot fault your generosity and hospitality. It's nothing. The less you know the better. Shall we begin?"

He nodded and indicated the expectant faces waiting around the table.

I waited until he was in his customary position at the head of the table. "Gentlemen, Prime Minister, we have concluded our twenty-four-hour period. Have you chosen to sign the contract?"

"We will sign," said Al-Kalifa.

"You have read it all?" I looked directly into the eyes of the prime minister, searching for any sign of doubt. But his face radiated generosity, and his eyes were friendly. At this point I would have believed anything he said.

"Yes, we have read it all," he said.

Deep down I felt that this job, this life, had hit a point of no return for me. I either had to face my conscience or run from it forever.

"I must remind you, gentlemen, that prior to signing this document you *must* understand all the implications of the contract. I will happily highlight the most important sections to confirm you haven't missed what I would consider vital clauses."

"We have read it and understand," the prime minister said. "You act like a good person who wants to see a fair outcome. For many decades we have been fleeced by overseas companies that have no further interest than making as much money as possible, no matter the consequences. We don't like them anymore. We like dealing with people like you."

"Okay, we shall continue." I felt dirty. "Are you a recognized and qualified representative who has been given the authority to sign this binding agreement?"

"I am," responded the prime minister.

"In that case you need to sign on the cover of each volume, with two witnesses, of which I will be one. Gentlemen, sit yourselves down, this is going to take some time."

I sat down and Al-Kalifa opened the cover of the first volume. Printed, signed and dated the document. His name took up half the page. I added my details, and we ploughed on in silence through the encyclopedic documentation. It took forty-five minutes, but we got there. Wringing our hands, we all put down our pens and sighed.

"I'll need a Turkish after that," I said.

The others laughed.

"Suresh, serve Ms.—" began the prime minister.

"No," I said quickly, "I was only joking."

The others laughed again.

"Okay, gentlemen, that's it," I said. "We're all signed. The meeting is over. You have fourteen days to come up with the funds; otherwise the penalty clause listed in appendix A for volume seven will be invoked. Do I need to remind you what the penalty is?" The collected men shook their heads. "In that case, gentlemen, I wish you all the best."

We all stood up and put away our various bits of information. The members of parliament shuffled out until only the prime minister and myself were left.

"You seem a little happier now," Al-Kalifa said.

"Yes. I'm sorry for my attitude earlier." I felt vulnerable after the turmoil of last night, and this man was throwing me a lifeline whether he knew it or not.

"With the formalities over, you can talk to me more informally," the prime minister said.

"It's nothing," I said. "Really."

"In my family I have been greatly outnumbered by daughters, wives, and sisters. I know when it is something."

I sighed. The man was a master at making a person feel at ease. In his great warm, brown eyes I couldn't have found a better father figure.

"I ran into someone last night," I said. "I was never expecting to see him again, and it made things complicated."

"I hope you had a chance to work things out."

"In a way."

"Good. It's unhealthy to leave bad feelings between friends. This is one thing I've learned from aging, and the many difficult decisions I've had to make in politics. Being friendly and sympathetic can get a remarkable amount of information out of the unsuspecting, and turn the most stalwart enemy into your ally. Sometimes an ear is the best weapon we have."

"I ... to be honest, it didn't end well, and I'm afraid it will stay that way forever. And in the cold light of day I feel very bad about it."

"Perhaps you'll see that person again one day, and fix things."

"I don't think that can or will happen. And the fault lies with me."

"Maybe you need a night out to relax and forget. The emir holds an annual ball for animal welfare, called the Fur Ball by the expatriates. A friend of mine has pulled out at the last moment, so there's a spare chair available if you'd like join the merrymaking."

The idea of getting glammed up lifted my spirits. "I've seen the ladies walking around in *abayas*," I said. "Do I need to wear one of those?"

"No, but I would ask you to remember our culture and dress with some sensitivity. If you show too much skin the first minister will have a heart attack. Especially with a lady as pretty as you."

That got a smile out of me. I weighed up my options. It was the best I was going to get.

"Fine, it would be an honor. I'm off to buy a gown, and I shall go to the ball."

The taxi pulled up at the front of the Intercontinental Hotel, which was located a few miles out of town and, as such, was surrounded by sand. The valets bustled around the vehicle. One opened the door and bowed to me. He even smiled. My nerves were a bit shaky, even after the minibottle of champagne from the hotel minibar. I was going to dread that bill.

I'd never been to a formal ball. I was in a foreign country, which frowned upon drinking, so I assumed there would be nothing to drink. I didn't know anyone here. Didn't know anyone sitting at the table. The only people I did vaguely know would be busy talking to their friends and other important people. But at least I had some killer shoes and a fabulous gown.

The evening could go either way. I could be a terrible nervous wreck, or I could meet someone charming who would talk and dance with me. Two options.

Or I could leave. No one would miss me. No one knew I was here. I could leave.

"Ms. Ellen, I'm so glad you could make it," said Al-Kalifa. The prime minister was standing in the foyer, greeting the more important guests.

"Mr. Prime Minister, I'm surprised to see you. I thought you'd be inside dealing with … important issues and people."

"And you can call me Hussein. Unfortunately, relations being what they are out here, this is the most important thing I have to do most of the time. Calming the more fiery individuals is vital to the smooth running of our country. I think it's the heat and humidity. It gets to everyone eventually and can turn the most reliable man into an emotional wreck. We need these functions to remind ourselves that we are not all work obsessed, and business goes smoothly if we respect one another."

"How often do you have these balls?"

"Easily two or three a month. Stay with me while I pretend to like the people coming through."

The prime minister chatted to me as the people came in, enlightening me of the various alliances. He was amiable, personable, and thoroughly entertaining. He complimented all who came past, and gave many of them to me. Maybe the night wouldn't be too bad.

"It looks like we're in another era," I said. "It's all so formal and elegant."

"They won't be so elegant by the end of the night." He winked at me. "And this is the captain of the emir's personal special forces, Captain Alex Heart. He's an American like you."

"Prime Minister—" Alex began.

"Oh my god," I said. "How small is this planet? Excuse me, Prime Minister, I may have to leave, urgently."

"Be nice in front of the royals," said Alex.

"Do you know each other?" asked the prime minister.

"Yes, Mr. Prime Minister," I said. "This was the person I was talking about this morning."

"Well, good fortune has smiled on you. This is your chance. Excuse me while I smooth the plumage of the first minister." Al-Kalifa made a very small bow, so small it looked like he was farting. He smiled, turned and left.

I turned to Alex. "You're in a uniform."

"I'm in the army. They called me Captain last night in front of you."

"You're right, they did, but I guess it never registered with me."

We stood in silence, looking at each other.

"It looks like you've had your last wish revoked."

I smiled. "I'm glad. I'm sorry. It was a very bad night. My life is changing and I'm not coping well with the changes. Sometimes I lie awake at night with the total understanding of the inevitability of death, and I wonder if this is how I want to live my life."

"Sounds like a mid-life crisis. Welcome to the human race. Shall we go in? It's cooler inside. Walk with me." He extended his elbow and I linked arms with him.

"I've never told anyone what I just told you," I said. "I've been keeping it inside and taking out my frustration on everyone, and you were the last one in the line."

"I have to deal with hotheads all the time out here. The stories I could tell of grown men crying over the most ridiculously small and unemotional reasons. I blame the heat and humidity."

"Hussein just said the same thing."

Alex grinned. "On first-name terms with the prime minister. You are doing well. Most of his ministers, who have known him for decades, wouldn't dare call him by his first name. What you are here is more important than who you are. Juice?"

A waiter offered a tray full of various juices.

As Alex picked up the glass, he took the opportunity to check out my new outfit. "Nice dress," he said, after his eyes had finished their roaming.

I smiled. "It's a gown, thank you very much." I curtseyed. "It's a Dolce and Gabbana princess gown. My first one."

"Are you expecting to lose a shoe?"

"Not at six hundred dollars a pair."

"There are many princes here who would happily check to see if it fits to win your hand in marriage, especially with you looking like that."

"I'm more of a shining-knight gal, rather than a precious princess."

"Really? I thought all girls wanted to be princesses at some stage. I met a princess once who lived in a castle. She said it was drafty."

"The men all look so regal in their, er, dresses."

"*Thobes.*"

"In their *thobes*. Funny word."

"Or *thawb*, but that word can be used to refer to women's clothing as well. It's the standard Arabic word for a garment."

"Well, they look very nice in their dresses."

We both laughed.

"They should, they cost thousands of dollars," Alex said.

"Really?"

"Yeah. Take a close look when you can. Most of them are designer labels. I know the prime minister prefers Armani."

"Armani makes *thobes*? I don't believe it."

"Huge market. Lots of wealthy Arabs who need to show off their money somehow. They can't wear gold, so sharp clothes are the next best thing."

"This place has made me change my thoughts on so many things. Your life can become so small when you're only thinking about your job. Out here, where the sky is the limit, things that might seem impossible in your small world suddenly seem possible. All you need to do is change."

"That's easier said than done. Most are afraid of change. Even on simple things like clothes or hairstyle. It usually has to be something major to make people change. Speaking of hair, your hair is still tied up. I thought you only did that for traveling."

"I had a change of heart. I like it like this for now."

"So do I."

I wondered if he knew, but I wouldn't put it past him. It didn't matter if he didn't remember, but I would know and it could be my secret.

The band oozed in the background and I tapped my toes. "Do you know how to dance?"

"Of course. I had to teach Jess when she got interested in boys. The waltz, foxtrot, everything. You'd be amazed how far the agency training went. Did you know the Viennese waltz was the first dance where the participants danced close to each other. Very scandalous at the time."

"You know, after everything that's happened, we've never had a simple dance, other than the horizontal kind. Would you lead me around the floor?" I curtseyed and presented my hand. "Please say yes," I hissed through my teeth, "or I'll end up looking really stupid in front of the royals."

"Even if it means we have to touch?"

I nodded.

He took my hand and smiled. "My pleasure." He led me to the dance floor.

We passed the prime minister, who seemed to be smiling at us.

"Are you going to let me lead," Alex said, "or will that be a struggle as well?"

I smiled at him and presented my arms. "Lead away. Unless you're terrible. Then I shall stab you with the heel of my shoe as punishment."

The music played and he twirled me gracefully around the floor. We started quite far apart, but I subtly moved closer as we waltzed. His hand had been quite high, but it had slid down into the small of my back as I moved in.

Crazy thoughts invaded my mind. In a world of princes, princesses, and the impossible being built, why couldn't my fantasy become a reality here? It was a crazy thought, but it gave me a warm inner glow.

"My, Mr. Kowalski, I do believe we are Viennese-ing. You know, I've noticed something with you, besides the smell, of course. Normally if I'm holding some guy's hand, I'll hold it from above, but not with you. You're the only one I let lead."

"I'm privileged."

"That's the general idea."

"That attitude must make you popular."

"Hah. I'm considered a right bitch at work. I guess they consider me one everywhere. The winter feeds my heart while summer blows and burns my disappearing youth. All because of you."

"It's not my fault," said Alex.

"No, but you came into my life and changed everything. You made me focus on what I was feeling rather than what I could achieve."

"Generally, people would say that's a good thing."

"People have preconceived ideas about what's good and what's bad. Some of us, such as myself, don't want to be like everyone else. Some of us don't want to live in the suburbs, shackled to a kitchen, with a sticker on the car bumper that says 'Mom's Taxi.' In a world full of Pacific Islands, soaring Alps and majestic vistas, some of us want more."

"You know love and achievement are not mutually exclusive."

"They are for most people."

"I thought you didn't want to be most people," he said.

Damn. He had a point. We stared into each other's eyes and the music played on. I yearned to be closer to him, to wrap my arms around him and never let him go.

"What are we going to do?"

"Commit suicide. Like in *Romeo and Juliet*." I smiled at him.

"I meant with you. But it wasn't suicide, it was stupidity."

"That's not very romantic."

"Killing yourself is hardly romantic. It's tragedy. I read that somewhere. Ready for a twirl?"

"What? Oh yes."

"Wish me luck." Alex gracefully twirled me under his arm then pulled me close. "Mission accomplished."

"Not bad. For you. But did you notice my exquisite footwork?"

"No, I was staring at you. Anyway, the dress—"

"Gown."

"The gown hides them. In fact, it's pretty good at keeping most things away from you."

"You need to push in harder." I smiled at him.

"You need to let some things in."

"You know my life. We've been over this before. Let the past be the past."

"That's your problem. The past is *important*. It defines us. If you continually throw it away you have nothing to base your future on. And if you throw away the past you throw us, what we had, away."

Alex wasn't smiling now. He loosened his grip and let go. We stood there, looking at each other. There was no expression on his face. No anger. No sadness. Nothing.

He turned and left me standing on the dance floor. I reached out for him.

"No, I ..."

It was too late. He was walking away. He wasn't listening.

"... didn't mean it like that," I said quietly as he went to join his table.

CHAPTER 17

JUST THE TWO OF US

"You don't look happy," Malik said.

"I don't want to talk about it." Alex sat down with a face full of thunder.

The large round table took pride of place at the head of the hall. The various ministers turned to welcome the only non-Arab present, then carried on texting either their employees or the other men sitting at the same table.

"Women?" said Malik.

"What do we do to deserve to be treated like this?"

"Ah, the magic and mystery of the fairer sex." Malik poured himself a large glass of orange juice from the jug at the center of the table.

"Fairer? Hah! Why couldn't … how can she … why does she …" Alex gave up and rested his head on the table.

"All fair questions, I give you. But you're not being an idiot, are you? I find that when the man is angry it's usually because he's been an idiot, even if he doesn't know it. You should rethink things if you're being an idiot."

Alex gave Malik a sideways glance. He sat up straight. "Let's talk about something else. Elissa. Let's talk about her. Hopefully, she won't give you as much grief as she would if she were a Western woman."

Alex leaned across to the first minister. "She has a fantastic voice," he said, indicating the woman standing in front of the band, sweetly singing a contemporary love song.

"Thank you, Captain. I shall pass on your compliments."

"How's the marriage going?" Alex asked Malik.

The first minister clapped his hands. "Yes, Malik, tell us how you scored her."

The minister of the interior frowned. "First Minister, decorum if you please."

"You know the stories," said Malik. "My storytelling was the secret. All my life I've been fighting one kind of battle or another for my family or country, and I've learned you need to act fast and decisively when you want something."

He's using the voice," the minister of the interior muttered. He wriggled to make himself more comfortable on the chair, expecting a long sitting-and-listening-to-Malik session.

Malik looked at each of the men at the table. "Some of you have been there to see my mantra in action. Life wasn't easy for either my mother or me. The only institute that would accept me was the army. I had to start as young as they would take me, and in the only position they would hide me: the bottom. It's taken me decades of loyalty and hard, dangerous work for our emir and the state to earn my place before you. The emir's eventual recognition of my skills over the years has allowed me to ingratiate myself into the world I should have been born into."

The minister of the interior checked his texts, hoping the story was over. He was about to rise when Malik continued.

"One of the first men to show me any kindness was Mohammad, and we built a great friendship over the years. He used to invite me to his house, continually asking me about my life and the battles I've fought. I told him about my hair-raising adventures in the air, and on the sea and land, and the near catastrophes and disasters I've experienced."

"Which ones?" the first minister asked. "Most of the ones I've heard you tell I wouldn't recount to my wife, or anyone else's for that matter."

"I told him how I was captured and tortured, how I fought for my freedom, and how I wandered through Afghan caves and Saudi deserts. And I would show them all the scars. When I retold these stories, Elissa listened attentively and always wanted to hear more. Her eyes would fill with tears as she ran her fingers over the scars. When my stories were over, she'd sigh and tell me how strangely wonderful they were, but that she wished she hadn't heard the sadness that had been within them. She also wished there was a man like me for her. She thanked me and told me that if a friend of mine had a story like mine to tell, she'd fall in love with him. I took the hint. I loved her for her beauty, humor, caring and passion."

Malik finished his story and stared off at some distant memory that brought a tear to his eye. There was a moment of silence as the assembled men allowed the old and battered hero his tender, reflective moment. He who had given so much for his home and family had finally found acceptance, peace and love.

"Well, that was the dullest story I've ever heard you tell, Malik. You need to beef it up more." The first minister licked his lips. "Maybe put a late-night rendezvous, stolen kisses, moonlight reflecting off silken, untouched skin …"

The minister's eyes glazed over. They all looked at him suspiciously.

The first minister snapped to. "Eh, what would I know? Did you tell her about the time you were in Kuwait, when the diagonal drilling was going on and the US army invaded and you were caught in the middle? I like that one. They should make a movie out of it."

"Yes," said Malik, "she knows all of them."

"What about the time in Monaco, when you—"

Malik hastily interrupted. "Except that one."

"Well," said the first minister, "you were a lot younger in those days. Maybe there are some aspects of your past that should be kept quiet. I don't think I'll ever forget the look on those three ladies' faces. I told you at the time you should've taken pictures on your Polaroid. We could've made a fortune."

"I've tried to ease Mohammad's pain by paying a reasonable dowry."

"To him?" The first minister nodded in appreciation. "He would like that, shows great respect and understanding. Good decision. How much, if I could ask?"

"Just a million," Malik replied.

"I want your job," the first minister shrieked.

"At least he can buy that luxury Mercedes he's had his eye on," Al-Dahnish said. "I'll bet he's on the way to the showroom now."

"You can imagine him eagerly looking in through the window as they unlock the doors. It's so romantic. S-Class AMG," the first minister whispered.

All the men sighed.

"You don't think he would go for the Maybach?" Alex suggested.

There was a long reflective pause as each was caught within their private fantasy.

"The curves," the first minister said.

"The power," the minister of the interior said.

The first minister smiled. "Is it wrong to call it sexy?"

"Hmm … yes. That would be worshiping a false idol," the minister of the interior reminded the assembled cast.

"You're right," agreed Malik. "In that case I shall call it well engineered. Those curves. The power. The material. It's like business class in emirates."

"Well, if you want to slum it," Al-Dahnish said. "I'll schedule a visit to pass on my best wishes to his family and tell him he'll need to make the best of it. I'll remind him that there are worse men than Malik in this world."

"Yes, and my daughters all seem to be married to them," the first minister said. The others laughed. "Lazy, stupid boys with nothing more to offer than the importance of their family name, draining the generosity of the emir like leaches."

"Well, they are locals," Malik pointed out, "and the emir thinks they should share in the fortune that's arisen from their land. It's a fair idea. But it would be nice if they actually tried to contribute something back to the country a little more frequently than they currently do."

"You were very brave going against tradition," Alex said.

"Why is it that young girls see this as responsible behavior?" the minister of the interior said to the table at large. "I admit there's drama and what have you, but someone needs to pay for food."

"The minister of the interior, full of romance," the first minister said with a caustic glare at Al-Dahnish. "Perhaps he's forgotten what it was like to be young."

"I remember very well, thank you," Al-Dahnish said, "and if I didn't follow the correct protocol there would be no yearly allowance. There would be no gift of land from the emir. There would be the service bills. There would be no loan-relief bonus. It all makes practical sense. All parties should recognize this when engaging in a contractual arrangement."

"When you put it like that, how could a girl refuse?" the first minister said. "I bet you were beating them off with many pages of delicately crafted accounts. I bet they swooned over your general ledger."

The minister of the interior spread his hands out on the clean white tablecloth. "All I'm saying is that there are practicalities. Especially here. Even though tradition isn't law, it's still tradition."

"Tradition is not what it used to be." The first minister put on his grumpy face.

Malik waved his hand. "Mohammad will come around. No man is perfect, but I offer more than many. Sometimes a young lady needs the steadying hand of a more mature man. I think eventually he'll like the idea of having royal connections, no matter how tenuous. You never know your luck; if twenty-eight Al-Thanis suddenly die, I could be the next emir."

The men laughed, then instantly started plotting potential mass assassinations.

"Quiet, the boss is coming," Alex said.

All the men stood as the prime minister approached the table.

"Sit, sit, please sit," said Al-Kalifa. "We don't need to be at the mercy of ceremony tonight. Anyway, the prime minister already looks exhausted from standing and it's only nine o'clock."

A waiter stood by the table.

"Would anyone like a Turkish?" the prime minister said.

There was a chorus of urgent no's from around the table.

"Juices will be fine," the prime minister told the waiter. "Captain Alex, you may drink if you wish. It won't offend us, although the first minister may get jealous."

"Thank you for the offer, Prime Minister, but it's been a difficult couple of days and my head's already muddled enough."

"As you wish." Al-Kalifa waved the waiter away. "Commander, tell me, what are we going to do about Iran?"

"They have been very aggressive since the Israeli incident," said the minister of the interior.

"You can't blame them," said Al-Kalifa. "It was unfortunate. Then when the Americans got involved, it all got very difficult. But this whole gas-field controversy's getting out of hand. We made the agreement and we were generous. Why are they so intent on using force to dispute it?"

"I think a lot of it has to do with the plutonium deal," Malik said. "If that avenue is cut off for them, their energy options will be severely reduced. They will be between a rock and a hard place."

"Is it inevitable that they want to attack?" the prime minister asked.

"It looks like it. They're building a strategy that would look very odd if they didn't."

"So what do we do?" said the first minister. "They vastly outnumber us."

"Have you all seen the weather projections?" Malik asked the table. The men gave various interpretations of maybe. "What if we took out their communications? We could send in a couple of men and disable the hot spots just before the storm hits."

"That's what I was thinking," said Alex. "Something small and covert."

"I like where this is heading," said the prime minister.

"If we could get the emir to stall things for a week, we could go in and take the communications," Malik said. "It would leave them paralyzed."

Malik and Alex looked at each other and nodded in professional agreement.

"Do you have the men?" asked the prime minister.

"I will do it personally, with the assistance of Captain Heart."

"Me?" Alex was surprised. "Wouldn't you prefer one of your younger men?"

"No. Two old war dogs with decades of experience and cool heads are what's required."

"I'm not that old, but it would be my honor to assist."

CHAPTER 18

I'M TOO SEXY

I found my place at a table. It was close to the table where the prime minister and Alex sat, but thankfully my seat faced the other way, onto the dance floor.

"Hi, I'm Britney." She was a youngish blond who had a sunbed addiction by the looks of it. Mind you, she could be very young but have badly aged skin from the sun. Anyway, she was blond, tanned, young and thin. Sigh. This evening was going to be hard work. I wondered how soon I could leave without being rude. Three minutes?

"Hi, I'm Ellen." I went to shake her hand and realized that was more of a work thing. She didn't look corporate.

A waiter came by with two bottles of wine, one red, one white.

"They have wine here." I said. It was more of a question.

"Yes," said Britney "but it's a very new thing at functions like this. The Qataris are becoming quite broadminded in some aspects, although some of the old families don't like all the changes."

"But isn't everyone profiting from it now?"

"Yes, and that's the problem. In the old days, under the old emir, it was only the big families that got any of the riches. With the new emir, the wealth has been spread far wider. He's made real investments in the country's infrastructure and its future. But, given the chance, the old families would overthrow him and go back to the old ways. Stuff like that happens all the time in this region."

"How do you know all this?"

"I'm seeing Captain Saif, one of Commander Malik al-Thani's friends. Malik is a prince, you know." She indicated the grand table a short distance from us. "Malik is the one sitting next to the Westerner." My heart sank with the reference to Alex. "Saif has to keep quiet about me because I'm not the traditional choice for a lover. But he's been Americanized so he's a modern thinker, and fantastically good looking. And rich. He's thinking we might elope and avoid all the parental interference."

"Where is Saif?"

"He's busy tonight. He has to do family things. They want to make a big fuss out of his promotion, and I'm not invited." She took a sip from a glass of water and looked a little dejected.

"With two people from very different backgrounds, it isn't always that easy. Even after the happy ending. Sometimes the fairytale isn't so great."

"I think it is. I would do anything for him. Follow him anywhere."

"And this is where we differ," I said.

"You got any men in your life?"

"Don't ask."

"Oh, go on. There's not a whole lot to talk about here, other than how terrible the traffic is."

Alex looked to be locked in deep conversation with the men on the other table. I just couldn't seem to get a step right at the moment. Everything seemed to be going wrong. I doubted he would be spending much time with me again.

"All right," I said, "let's have some drinks. Then dance. Then talk. With more drinks in between each stage. It's a long story."

The night wore on and we chatted. Britney was an interesting person, unlike Brandi, who just wanted to get into trouble all the time. We did that two-girls-dancing thing, but there are not a whole lot of moves you can bust in a gown. We generally twirled, which is what we all did in the eighties, so it was no stretch. Then we got dizzy and crashed into those standing nearby, who in turn got irritated.

"Is that your friend over there?" asked the prime minister.

Alex's heart sank. He knew that when senior people in power asked questions like that, it never bode well. There was always going to be some awkward and difficult task to follow.

"Using the term 'friend' might be a bit generous. I am unfortunate enough to know her," Alex replied.

"You may need to escort her home, as I'm not certain she could find her way there."

"She'll be fine. A taxi will get her there."

"No, you should do it. She needs reassurance from you. She and I have been speaking and I know she's having a difficult time. You haven't been an idiot, have you?"

"Oh, not you, too. I'm being ganged up on. All right. I'm only going to do it because you're the prime minister and you'll probably have me flogged if I ignore a direct instruction from you."

"I'm glad you've learned how our system works so quickly." The prime minister smiled and patted Alex on his arm. "Now, go and rescue her. Be her knight in shining armor."

Alex glared at the prime minister. He stood up and gave the man the smallest allowable bow. He looked over to Malik and gave him a suspicious look. "I'll see you tomorrow, Malik, troublemaker."

Malik smiled and waved.

"Alex! Oh Alex, you came back." I attempted to throw my arms around him.

He extracted himself from my clutches and looked heavenward. He eased me away and I fell back into my chair.

"Alex, this is Britney. She's married to one of your men over there. Oh, where'd she go? Helloooo?"

"She's not under the table. Ellen, we have to go. The prime minister's getting a little worried about you."

"Oh, what's he kno—the prime minister, you say. That's bad. I guess that means—no, wait. 'I'm Too Sexy.' I *love* this song. Dance with me!"

"No."

"Oh, come on. Then I'll go. But I have to be sexy first. Please."

Alex sighed.

"Oh, new drinks," I said.

The waiter had appeared with a tray of assorted glasses of wine. I grabbed one and tried to take a sip, but Alex steered it away from my mouth, leaving my neck craning as it went past.

"Oh, all right," he said.

"Oh, goody." I clapped my hands together. "Dancing was my life when I was eighteen to twenty-two inclusive. Every weekend, when I should've been studying, me and Candice would go out and jump and shout and swirl and party till the early hours."

I moved onto the dance floor, twirling about on my toes. I gave Alex some sultry looks over my shoulder. I raised my arms and did a shimmy around him.

He just stood there.

"Dance, boy."

"How do you dance to this when not completely drunk?"

"That's the secret." I winked at him. I went to drape my arms around his shoulders.

He did a quick sidestep, grabbed me around my waist, and hauled me off the floor. "I remember you being lighter."

"Are you calling me fat?"

"Yes."

"Well, you could be weaker, considering you're old now."

"You've aged the same amount as me. That makes you old, too."

"Put me down, *now*. Are you calling me fat *and* old? I'm not even forty, unlike some."

"But you're old for a girl."

"If I had any vague idea where my feet were I would kick you."

He grabbed my hand and pulled me out of the ballroom, through the foyer and into the parking lot.

"Why are you always dragging me places? What's the hurry?" Sexy time appeared to be over.

"It's time to go. You're making a scene and I've been given instructions."

"He was a terrible DJ anyhow, playing all that eighties cheese. Where the hell is Amarillo anyway? Is this the way to … Oh great, now I'm singing it. Sing something so I can forget it."

"YMCA," Alex sang.

"No, that's worse. Is your car far? I'm not sure these shoes are actually made for walking." I giggled after a random thought. "I know a joke about that. God, it's hot. I'm still hungry. I need KFC. KFC! KFC! Your car's not in Amarillo, is it?"

"It's good to see some things don't change."

"Is this the way to Amarillo," I sang quietly. "Hey, where's your Cruiser?"

"This is my go-to-balls car."

"Ooo, Mercedes SL-class, AMG edition. Expensive, black and sssexy. I like my cars like I like my men."

"Get in." The car lights flashed and the doors unlocked.

I sank into the rich leather seat. "Hey, this is a convertible. Where's the button?"

"Just leave it."

"No way. It's a fantastic night. Is it this one? No. How about this? No. What's this one do?"

"Stop fiddling with things."

"Is this an automatic? Is that the stickshift? Don't look at me like that. All the other guys like it when I do that."

Alex extracted my hand from his crotch and started the car.

I accidentally knocked a small knob and there was a whirring from the roof. "Ah ha!" It stopped whirring. "Oh." I fiddled with it again and the whirring started up. I held the knob in place as the roof arced over the top of us. I gave Alice—er, Alex—a broad grin.

"Where's the stereo? Turn it up, baby. Oh wait, will it all be Arabic music out here? Oh well. Who needs a radio when you can sing." I took a deep breath.

"No singing!"

I blew a raspberry at him. I folded my arms and stared ahead. Alex drove the sleek beast out of the parking lot. The rumble of the engine came up through the seats as he slowly accelerated.

"Oh wait, where are we going?"

Alex had entered a huge roundabout. "To your hotel."

"No, no, no. It's that way, I remember the big sign."

"It's not that way. I know where it is."

"Don't be a typical male. If you don't know, ask directions."

"I don't need to ask questions. I know the way."

"To Amarillo. No, no, no. It's definitely back there."

"I'll show you."

He continued slowly around the roundabout. "See how the headlights illuminate the dead end? Yet if we continue around, we see the lights of the city, which houses your hotel."

"All right, if you have to be mister Right All the Time. Wait, no, go back around, please."

"Why?"

"I thought I saw something."

"There's nothing there. Just sand."

"No, please go around."

Alex sighed and we went around again. The lights swung over the dark and obviously empty sand.

"Oh, I thought I saw the ocean. I'd love to walk along the beach. Wouldn't you love that too? It would be so romantic."

Alex glared at me, continued around the roundabout and we roared off toward the city. There was a flashing blue light behind us. Alex cursed and pulled the car over to the side. A motorcycle policeman pulled up alongside us.

"Hello, Captain. Is everything all right?"

"Ha! No."

"I noticed you went around the roundabout a few times. Have you been drinking? I can smell alcohol."

"That would be little Miss Sunshine here, who was giving me bad directions. She's consumed enough to kill a small camel."

"Is she related to you?"

"God, no. The prime minister suggested I escort her home from the ball. Stop singing!" Alex shouted at me. He rolled his eyes at the policeman.

"He's my fiancé," I shouted. "Wooo. It's official and everything. He told the police yester—yesterday, all my troubles seemed so far away. Don't you wish your boyfriend was hot like you, freaky. Woo."

"Stop singing!"

"Can I hum? Am I going the right way for a smacked bottom? Shh, donkey! I'm Princess Fioooona."

Alex rested his forehead on the steering wheel.

"I would walk five hundred miles and all I want to do is make love to you," I swayed my arms in the air. "Yeah!"

"I'll let you go," said the policeman.

"I'd ask you to arrest her, but it would be me who'd have to bail her out. I can't win."

CHAPTER 19

IN-A-GADDA-DA-VIDA

Alex pulled in the hotel parking lot. "Can you make it to your room on your own?"

"Of course. I can ask for help if I get lost. I know how to do that because I'm a woman." I pointed my thumb toward my bust. "With boobies and everything. Woohoo for the boobies."

"You're not going to get lost," Alex said.

"See, even you agree."

"No, we're in the parking lot. It's the big building right there, twenty yards away. With the big sign out front."

"Where?"

"Oh, good grief."

He got out of the car and came around to my side. He opened the door and stood back, waiting for me to get out.

"This may be a little bit difficult," I said. "The car is very low, the dress is very foomfy, and for some reason my balance doesn't seem to be too good at the moment. I'm blaming my shoes. Wait, I'll give it a go."

I struggled to get my feet out of the door. After several moments of grunting and groaning I got a foot out. I cheered. I swiveled in the seat and got the second foot out.

"I'm exhausted. Okay, phase two." I reached up and grabbed the windscreen. I tried to heave myself up but fell back into the car.

"This is ridiculous." Alex reached in, grabbed my hand, and pulled me out.

"See, I told you I could do it." I poked out my tongue at him. I wandered off toward the hotel.

"You're going to the fast-food shop. The hotel's the other way."

"I knew that. I was … hungry. Is it KFC?"

"No."

"Well, I am no longer hungry."

"Come here." He grabbed my hand and steered me toward to the hotel. "Do you think you can walk straight for a few yards?"

I shook him free. "Just watch me." I took a couple of steps forward and stopped. I signaled for him to come over to me.

"No," I whispered.

The shoes seemed to be getting the better of me. Alex looked heavenward. He doesn't need to do that, I thought. An angel was standing right in front of him.

He took my hand and we walked to the hotel. We managed to get through the foyer security without attracting too much attention, probably something to do with the military uniform. He steered me into the lift and we ascended. The lift binged and I staggered out. We had made it to my door.

"That'll do, pig, that'll do." I patted Alex on the head. He had some expression on his face that I couldn't make any sense of.

"Where's my clutch? Oh, that's right, I didn't get one. One thousand dollars for one of those teeny things. It wouldn't even *hold* a thousand dollars. But that's what boyfriends are for. Oh look, a little puppy." I bent over and patted the little dog. "Who's a cute little doggy?"

"That's a stone Buddha statue."

I straightened up and hitched up my top. "I knew that." I gave him a look of indignation. "What was I looking for? Oh, yes. My swipe." I slid my hand into my top. My brow furrowed with concentration as I searched within the bodice. "Ah ha," I declared as I triumphantly drew out the card.

I swayed a bit and took an unsteady step forward. I squinted my eyes to focus on the door. It took a couple of goes, but I eventually got the card in the slot. "A thousand dollars," I muttered to myself.

I collapsed through the door into the main suite. "Hello, home, I'm honey," I declared to the room. I teetered over to the sofa and collapsed in a bouffant heap.

"Alex, honey, can you do me a favor, and get me one of those freezing cold waters from the minibar?"

"Are you prepared to pay the forty dollars for it?"

"Yes. I'm rich. Miss Moneybags, that's me. Got to be some benefit in having no one to spend your money on."

Alex went over to the minibar as I continued to do battle with my footwear.

"Oh my feet. What's the point in wearing fancy shoes if you can't see them under all this flouncy stuff. I have an urgent inclination to take them off." I dived under the folds of exotic materials. "This is stupid. How much material do they need to make these dresses, gowns, whatever?"

I continued to search but the material kept falling through my fingers. "Where are my feet? I can't find them. I give up."

Alex handed me the water bottle. I ripped off the top. We both watched it arc across the room and skittle under the sideboard.

"Ax, can you be a gentleman and help me take my shoes off? It's like Cinderella, but in reverse. This way you can un-fiancée me. It could be symbolic or something." I took a long sip from the bottle.

He searched through the material until he found my feet. He couldn't see the shoes so he had to remove them by feel. There was a look of concentration on his face as he tried to unstrap them.

I took another big sip from the small bottle. "If they were a bra I bet you could remove them blindfolded in less than three seconds."

Alex smiled as he extracted the two shoes from under the mountain of material.

"I now pronounce you single. You may French kiss anyone you like. Oo la la. I forgot how silvery they were. I think I love these shoes. Shoes, marry me. I am now single. I did have a fiancé, but he just dumped me four seconds ago."

"You're going to suffer tomorrow." Alex sat down next to me.

"I could be suffering now. I could be hiding it extremely well. Being dumped by your fiancé can be traumatic. Oh, Ax, I'm so sorry about last night. Please forgive me. I'll make it up to you. I'll think of something. I'm good at thinking. Not much else, but I can think with the best of them."

"Don't be too hard on yourself."

"You look so neat in those clothes. I've never seen you in anything other than your cargos"—I placed my finger on his knee—"and your T-shirt. Maybe a sweater." I placed my hand on his shirt. "Definitely not a cravat. And, of course …"

I paused and looked away, then stood up rather uneasily. "Come here. I want to show you something. In here." I indicated the bedroom. Alex looked uncertain. "Don't worry. I won't hurt you. Well, no more than I already have. Sorry."

I took another sip from the bottle and dragged Alex in with me. I opened a dresser drawer and put my hands inside. "Check this out. I found the most extraordinary shops when I was shopping for my dress—gown. Special shops for women."

I pulled out a loose collection of small garments. "Matching underwear. It's taken me years to get that happening. Feel how soft they are."

I held them against my face. They were so soft and delicate. "I'm hoping they'll make me feel desirable again."

"You don't need them."

"Oh, Alex." I sat down on the edge of the bed. He sat down next to me. "I'm so sorry. I'm so sorry for so many things. If I wrote a list

I would run out of letters, even if I used all those weird European ones."

"Look, it's been hard for us. People don't normally go through what we do. It should never have happened. It was a gift and a curse."

I placed my hand on his knee. "Do you find me attractive?" I looked down, not really wanting to read his face.

He gently lifted my face and gave me a delicate kiss on the cheek. "Always."

"Oh, Alex." I went to kiss him back, but my head wasn't too good. I misjudged the distance and slid off the bed onto the floor. "I guess it's time for me to go to sleep."

I crawled back up to a standing position. "Could you do me a favor, Alex? Last one for the night. Could you just start my unzip zip-thing? I can't reach it."

I turned my back to him, hoping that he would help. Otherwise it was going to be an uncomfortable night's sleep. I felt his hand on my shoulder and the zip began to descend. I turned around to face him.

"Thanks. I've had a thought. I told you I was a thinking person. Well, this is how I want to make things up to you." I reached behind and unzipped the rest of the gown. It fell to the ground, and I was left standing in the latest Anne Summer bodice and suspenders. Yeah, I knew what he liked. I hoped.

"I need to finish what I ruined last night. As soon as I saw you in that uniform, which is so amazingly ironed, I melted. Have I told you I'm no good at ironing?" I stroked my hands down his sides.

"Yes. And I have seen your domestic adventures in action."

I smiled. "I'll be careful with your clothes."

"Sometimes less is more. Like when it comes to your talking. Any suggestions on how to shut you up?"

I stepped forward and kissed him on his lips. I slowly undid the buttons on his shirt until it fell to the floor. I kicked it under a chair.

He wrapped his arms around me and held me tightly. We just stood kissing and holding each other. I pulled out the scrunchie and let my hair fall over my shoulders. He ran his fingers through the strands. I sat on the bed and pulled him over. I undid his belt and let his trousers fall.

Well, hello old friend, I thought. I missed you so much I invented a name for you. And I named something else I have with the same name.

He pushed me back onto the bed and hovered above me. His hands slid down my body, teasing, caressing, until he reached my legs. Luckily we didn't have a thermometer or it would have exploded. He easily unhitched the suspenders and rolled down the fishnets. Oh, the hands of experience. He placed my leg over his shoulder and kissed the inside of my thigh, and gently kissed his way up.

Total OMG. What a mighty fine man he was. He really did bring the teenager out in me.

He bit into the pantie strap and teased them down. I kicked them off over my head. I giggled. Tada, I thought. He buried his head in between my legs. I closed my eyes with the absolute pleasure he was sending through my body.

I ran my fingers through his hair. "Ax, please don't leave me. Stay for a while, stay forever."

He stopped and sat up.

"Oh nonononono. Don't tease me."

"I can't do this." He turned away.

I sat up. "You so can. At least one part of you can. No performance issues there. Look at you. You're solid as a rock. If you don't screw me right now I'm taking it with me whether you're attached or not."

"We need to talk."

"Oh Christ, Alex. I really need this, and you want to talk? Talk about role reversal."

"I need to know what happened."

"What happened when? Last night? Oh, before." I threw myself back onto the bed and held my head in my hands. "What happened is what happened," I said.

"You left me."

"I stayed with you for a week. It's more than I've ever given anyone. And it cost me dearly in everything—my work, my heart, my future. And don't get me started about my mother." I threw my hands in the air in a mock strangling.

"You didn't stay for a week."

"I did so."

"You may have been present for a week, but after the hotel you had gone."

"Okay, I know what you mean, and I'm so, so sorry, but it's what I do. I have to leave. How could I have gone back home and done what I needed to do with you wrapped around me? I would have loved to, more than anything. I was crazy about you, but it never would have worked. I can't see you being a househusband, or me giving up my career to be with you. It could never have worked. And you, of all people, should know that."

"But you never gave it a chance. When you want something badly enough you have to give it a go, but you just walked away and never came back."

"It broke me in two, shutting you out, but if I hadn't done that it would've destroyed me. We both have the rest of our lives to live out. We had no common ground, except for one week together. And I haven't forgotten either. I carry it around the time, and it hurts. I knew real love if only fleetingly, and everything since has been awful and hollow. What am I meant to do with that?"

"It's simple. You hold onto it and don't ever let it go."

"I go with other men but I cry when it's over because it's not you. You're the one I think of when I hold them. You and that fantastic body, and the heady moments in those hot jungle nights. You're still tearing me in two now. I'm crying, and every part of me wants to jump on top of you."

"Stop trying to grab me. When I said 'hold onto it' I didn't mean that. I'll have to hold you down."

"Promise?"

I placed my finger playfully into my mouth, but he wasn't buying. In fact, the whole shopping center had closed. I slumped back against the bedstead and sighed.

"There'll never be another you, and there never was. There never should have been. Maybe we had our moment, and maybe we stole it from the world and took it for our own. But it's over. Just let it go. I've got to let it go."

He was still standing hard in front of me. I glared and calculated a last lunge. I could be a lady who lunges. But Alex could see my plan and he backed away.

"I have to admit you were the only one who could screw me into submission. Oh lord, how you used to make my legs shake. Bottle that, and I'd buy a swimming pool's worth. That's something I really miss." I let out a long sigh. "But I have the memory, and it's more than a lot of other people have. Anyway, the rules have changed. I'm meant to be a married person now."

"You're married? But we were about to …"

"Engaged, to be married. Oh Christ. This isn't good, is it? Do you think it shows that my heart isn't in it?"

"Yeah."

"One day ago I was going to be married to David, and I was okay with that. And then you turn up and ruin everything, again. My life lurches from one kind of ruined to another, and I don't even get great sex out of it. How about oral sex? If you do me, I'll do you. That's not real sex, is it? That won't count. Does this make me sound desperate? It's a good deal. I do sound desperate, don't I?"

"A little." He nodded, then let out a half-laugh.

There were so many things I wanted to say, to scream, so I did. "What do I do? I love you, Alex, with all of my heart, with every fiber of my body. I always have, but I can't live like this. I have the feeling, rightly or wrongly, that to be with you means it has to be me who compromises. But my life is everything I am. If I give it up, what am I? What do I become? I didn't even know what I wanted to be until I put the clothes on. It defined me, gave me meaning. What do I do without that? What would I be worth to you? As we are right now there's no way."

Alex opened his mouth to speak, but I waved his turn away.

"And I keep thinking, why should it be me who has to compromise? Why do I have to give up everything after all that I've worked towards, after all I've sacrificed. I've had dozens of imagined arguments with you about how unfair you've been. And I imagine you say this, then that, and I know that underneath it all lurks my conscience saying it's not about any of that. It's about guilt and making excuses."

"I would've followed you anywhere if you'd just called for me. You are what is important to me, not what we do, either of us."

"You can't say that," I cried. "You don't know." I took a deep breath. "I know I couldn't tolerate it if I took you out of your natural environment and you ended up hating it, and worse, hating me. Because of my selfishness, because I'm afraid of change and losing who I am, I've blamed you for it all because I was always afraid of losing you, and the easiest way to avoid that is by not having you. I've fought long and hard in my head to not want you."

"But how can you do that? To us. To me. I have dreams where we meet by accident somewhere, and it's wonderful. But then I wake and it's heartbreaking. It's been hell for ten years, wondering, waiting, looking ..."

"Don't give me ten years. For me it's felt like a century, and it's worn me down to this horrible, bitter person I can't even recognize anymore when I look in the mirror."

I sagged forward and felt that I let something go. Then I straightened and traced my fingers over his arms to his hands, feeling the curve of his muscles.

"I've seen you in action. That day, that most amazing day, when you were every teenage girl's dream come to life. But the problem is we are not, and were not, teenagers. The fairytale has ended. And there's no way I can see you in the suburbs putting up shelves and mowing the lawn. Even if you did, I wouldn't hold you, you wild and untamable beast, to a caged future like that. You belong in that environment."

"But it doesn't matter," Alex said. "The thing about being together is that we find a way to meet somewhere in the middle. Everyone has to do it."

"Maybe we aren't everybody. I have thought, really thought, that my life isn't worth anything without you in it, and there have been times where I've had dark thoughts about long walks off short bridges. And it is all my fault."

I started to cry. I turned away to salvage some dignity.

He came to me and engulfed me like a large winter coat. "Okay, there's no need to be melodramatic."

I needed his embrace like a Pacific Islander living on a Russian steppe. I retreated into his comforting arms and tried to pull myself together. We sat for a long time wrapped around each other.

When I awoke he was gone. Gone for a while, or gone forever?

CHAPTER 20

I GOT THE POWER

The winds were beginning to pick up, and a loud, low-pitched rumble was beginning to emanate from the *barchans*. The roar was accompanied by the usual avalanche of sand off the top of the arcing dunes. The singing usually lasted for fifteen minutes. Abdul Aziz had that long to conduct the meeting with the heads of the elder families.

Each elder had his *smagh* wrapped around his face, concealing who he was, with his eyes barely visible. Abdul Aziz didn't bother to hide his identity. He knew the concealment gave the others a false sense of security. They also needed to believe that he was a man who had the confidence and conviction to follow through on whatever desperate measures needed to be carried out. They could see it in his eyes.

"Gentlemen, we have until the dunes stop singing to conclude our meeting."

"Why?" Sheikh Yellow demanded.

"Our voices are only completely obscured audibly for that duration. After that any noise will carry for kilometers. It's an old military trick carried over from the days when Marco Polo attacked the region."

"So we're using the djinns to protect us? I'm glad I'm not a superstitious man."

"I heard that Mars has *barchans* and *djinns*, too. Not sure why they would be there. Not many people to tempt," said Sheikh Green.

Abdul Aziz wondered who should be calling whom a *djinn*. The men certainly had no great benevolence in mind. He decided to reinforce this. "I declare the Majlis al-Jinn started."

Hearing the old term for a council meeting made Sheikh Red nostalgic. "Majlis al-Jinn. That brings back memories. I haven't been to Oman for years," said Sheikh Green.

"It hasn't been the same since the sultanate collapsed," Sheikh Orange said.

A heated debate broke out among the old men.

"Have you seen the Graves in Al-Ayn? They are astounding."

"Not as good as the caves."

"I might drop in on my next visit to Mecca."

"Mecca, you old fool, is the other way."

"Where am I thinking of then?"

"Who knows?"

"No, wait, it was in that movie with the young guy. The one with the old guy."

There was silence.

"And it had the Germans in the planes, and a zeppelin."

"Oh, you mean the one with the guy from the space movie."

"Why are movie tickets so expensive?"

"I'm sure all of us can afford them. Some of us have our own cinema chain."

"That's not the point."

"It's not the tickets. It's all the other stuff you get. It seems stupid to pay twenty riyal for a bottle of water."

"We live in a desert. Water is a commodity."

"But a twenty-liter container only costs fifteen riyal at the shop. And that includes the little Indian fellow to carry it."

"Times must be hard for you."

Abdul Aziz was reminded that these elders were, in fact, elderly, with an attention span as such. "Gentlemen, may I refocus our attention on the matters at hand. Time is at a premium."

"Much like cinema tickets," muttered Sheikh Yellow.

"The news is good," Abdul Aziz continued, ignoring the interruption. "Dr. Hassah was involved in a car crash last night on his way home from a ball. He's in a serious condition. It's uncertain if he will be able to resume his duties. This is our chance. Well done, gentlemen."

The sheikhs burst out with a series of exclamations of surprise, except for Sheikh Yellow, who was looking pleased with himself, and Sheikh Green, who was giving Sheikh Yellow a dark look.

"I've known Dr. Hassah for decades, and although I've never seen eye to eye with him on anything, I would never harm him," Sheikh Green said.

"Someone needed to rise to the occasion. Someone needed to have the courage and conviction. Otherwise we're just a collection of old men standing around in the desert," Sheikh Yellow said.

"I wonder how it happened," Sheikh Green said suspiciously.

"You know him; he probably wasn't looking where he was going. Reading his texts, or some such nonsense."

Abdul Aziz quickly clapped his hands to focus everyone on him. "I'm arranging with Malik to present Adnan to the prime minister as the best candidate for the position of deputy prime minister. It will look good as a balance of politics. The prime minister is an ally of the emir. The deputy must be from one of the old families, this the emir knows. He's not a fool and he's also not a threat. He knows this is how it should be."

"But that doesn't get rid of anyone. It just installs an idiot into a position of power that any of us would kill for."

"He's our pawn. We can't win without someone like him in place."

"What if he recovers?" asked Sheikh Green. His eyes darted between Abdul Aziz and Sheikh Yellow, and he shifted uneasily in the sand and wind.

Abdul Aziz glanced at Sheikh Yellow, who gave a barely perceptible nod.

"He might get sick," Sheikh Yellow said.

"And how will that happen?"

"Perhaps something he eats. You can never be too careful out here with out-of-date food."

There was a very long pause as the two men looked at one another.

"If the contract fails and we lose the fields, then you have your chance on removing the emir," Abdul Aziz said. "The prime minister will go as he's with the emir, leaving the deputy prime minister, and whoever is currently in that position, as the most powerful man in the country."

"So how do we make sure the contract fails?" Sheikh Red asked. "We have the money. We always have the money."

"What if it isn't collected by the American?" Abdul Aziz said. "The prime minister is meant to be organizing it. He's been specifically chosen by the emir to complete this task successfully. If he does then the rewards will be great. If not, then we'll make sure the penalty is just as great."

"You're not saying we should kill her. I would be completely against that," Sheikh Green said.

Abdul Aziz shrugged. "She's an American. It's an option."

"You know what they're like, "said Sheikh Red. "The rest of the over-zealous US army fools would charge in and ruin things."

"Maybe it's best to delay her."

"Delay? As in …" Sheikh Green left the question hanging.

Abdul Aziz noted that once again Sheikh Green sounded hesitant over the plan, and had been the most difficult to bring to the table.

He seemed a bit sharper than the others. He'd have to keep an eye on him.

"I'll arrange it," said Abdul Aziz. "I know some freelancers who can assist. The more extreme ones would do it for a sack full of salt and some airtime on television."

"It sounds very risky," Sheikh Green said. "Is there no other way?"

Abdul Aziz shook his head. "We need our hands, *your* hands, to be clean. If something goes wrong you can deny any knowledge, then secretly give them a field as a reward."

Sheikh Green was incensed. "Give them a field? One of our fields? Are you mad?"

"Which question would you like me to answer? You have thousands of fields. Just give them something small that's from the area of debate," he said dismissively. "Are we agreed, gentlemen?"

One by one each elder nodded. Abdul Aziz stared at them intently until they all had bought into the idea. He watched them get into their Land Cruisers and disappear over the dunes. He got into his own one and took off as fast as the vehicle would go so he could catch up.

Sheikh Green was beginning to sound like someone who was losing his nerve. If one person crumbled the whole plan would collapse. Then there would be no chance of dealing with Malik. It was time to find some more information on Sheikh Green.

Abdul Aziz parked his Land Cruiser around the corner from Sheikh Green. It was dark and secluded with an uninterrupted view of the mansion. Time ambled past, and Abdul Aziz felt the need for relief. He opened the door and stepped out behind a wall. He fumbled with the buttons on his trousers, cursing the lack of a simple modern zipper.

After two buttons, a figure stepped silently out of the shadows behind him, raised his fist and swung toward the back of Abdul

Aziz's head. Abdul Aziz spun around and parried the attack. The dark figure tried a series of attack combinations but Abdul Aziz deflected them all. The figure lunged with his hands outstretched toward Abdul Aziz's throat. Abdul Aziz intercepted and the two were fixed in space, struggling against each other.

"So you're the one who's been following me all day. You finally got your chance to strike." Abdul Aziz looked over his opponent's ragged clothes and stared into his eyes. Recognition dawned. "I know you, Casey."

The man slapped his hand over Abdul Aziz's mouth. "I don't use that name anymore. Because of you I am Kasim. It's a name I never wanted to hear again, but now, because of you, I'm forced to use it."

"Because of me, Kasim? Your freedom is owed to me. How do you think they got you out? Do you think the Americans can come strolling in here without anyone knowing? How backward do you think we are?"

"Because of you, *you* owe *me*. I had my exit planned, the people arranged, and paperwork in order. I was going to walk out a free man, keeping the wealth I'd amassed. Then the Americans came, took what was most valuable to me, and now I have nothing. You owe me, *friend*."

"I owe you nothing. The trouble you brought on by yourself. You make your own life, friend. I let you in, and I let you out. I don't need to do anything more for you."

"While you walk and talk you're in my debt. You will always owe me until your dying day."

"You hang onto the past too much."

"The past? You've left me with no past. I have nothing. I can't use any of my old accounts. I have millions, which I will have to abandon. I can't even use a credit card. I had to steal one to get here."

The two men stood, locked in an intense, unflinching stare.

"Maybe there's something you can do for me that will benefit both of us," said Abdul Aziz. "How's your Turkish?"

CHAPTER 21

GET ME OUTTA HERE

M s. Ellen, how are you doing?"
I glared at him.

The Indian, or Asian-Middle Easterner, or whatever names they call the people who actually did any work around here, refused to wilt under my stare. He grinned like the male simpleton he was.

"Here's your ticket to Istanbul. We have organized a special visa so you can leave. It was a bit difficult as you didn't have a husband to authorize your short-notice trip."

I gave him a double stare. No stupid, godforsaken, imbecilic, brainless, dimwitted, obtuse man was going to tell me what to do. Whatever it was, I wasn't listening. But I would watch if there was some chance of them being injured in an amusing way.

"I hope you have a pleasant trip." He grinned, all teeth and smiles.

It was first thing in the morning and I had booked a ticket to the closest best place that didn't remind me of Alex. I was going to have a holiday for eleven and a half days. After that I would come back to Qatar and do whatever with the contract and then go home. If there were any kind of fairness in this world my plane would crash on the way home.

I had turned off my phone, and only under imminent threat of nuclear disaster or zombie oblivion would I turn it back on.

In five hours I wanted to be on some beach with my head in a book, being ignored by the men of the world. I would have to make a decision regarding David, but I already knew what it was. It wasn't fair on him. I couldn't love him. There was nothing he could do or be to make me love him. He had shown more emotion toward me than I ever could toward him, and for that he deserved someone who would respect him and show him the same kind of feeling and consideration. I was destined to become some sorry old woman surrounded by cats. Pity I was a dog person.

On the flight to Istanbul a businessman dressed in a smart Savile Row suit who was returning to Turkey spoke at me. He smelled strongly of cigarettes and coffee. He got very excited talking about all the amazing places I should see. I then made the mistake of saying that I had studied ancient history briefly in college. He hyperventilated over the ruins, effervesced over the milk pools, and effused over more. He kept repeating that there was so much more than Istanbul to see. He recommended that I get out into the heart of the country and see the amazing sights.

His breath nearly killed me. Thank you, Mr. Travel Agent. If I get amazingly bored I'll look. But for the moment I would be happy locked away in my Marriott executive suite with free access to the executive bar, which I intended to abuse.

The sun bore down and I sweltered in the heat. I had grabbed a few books from some vampire series all the girls at work were going on about. The idea seemed to be that you didn't have sex although you really wanted to. Weren't everyone's teenage years like that? That sure was how I remembered it.

Oh, for a decent man who shone like the sun, and would come and rescue you from the evil mother-witch and defeat the deadly

daddy-osaurus in mortal combat, and then whisk you away to a land
of flowers and candy, then lay you down on a bed of roses, caress
your skin and gently kiss your face then screw you senseless as your
head crashed into the headboard. Ah, good days.

Where had all the good men gone? And where were all the gods,
or a streetwise Hercules to fight the rising odds?

By the second day I was bored, but I was still determined to give this
chilling out a go.

Should have bought Anne Rice, I thought, putting down the book.
I mean, what author worth their salt ripped off a Shakespearean
plot?

And what was it with these tourists with their swimsuits wedged
up their backsides? Why exactly were they tanning their cheeks?
I could understand if they wandered around all day in mankinis
or G-strings, but as soon as they got up they put on clothing that
covered up what they dared to bare. People were weird.

By day three I had taken to ringing errors in the hotel-supplied Bible.
Revelations made much better reading than the vampire books.
Much more death and suffering, and fewer annoying teenagers.

I found it hard to concentrate on one thing at a time. I wasn't
sleeping properly either, even on the magnificent Marriott bed. So
many thoughts were auditioning in my head for acknowledgment,
as though I was some attention-deprived preteen.

I tried to formulate what to say to David. I also kept alternating
my views on him. Should I stick with him, or let him go? Deep down
I knew the answer, but I was afraid to admit it. I knew I needed to
be honest with him, and the truth was, he deserved someone better
than me. I felt like I wanted to run, just go from one place to another,
a constantly changing vista. I craved a horizon that never ended,
with nothing ahead but infinite possibilities, always drawing me in,
with no time to look back at a broken past.

That was the real problem: the past. It possibly deserved a capital. The Past. Better. With a capital it had so much more implied meaning and reverence.

Alex was right, of course. How could I build a future when I refused to acknowledge or fix the past? I mean the Past. The answer, of course, was to keep running into a new future, and maybe at some point I would be able to look back at a more recent past and not be too ashamed.

I lasted a few days beside the pool. There's only so much lying around you can do. I hired a car. My US license was good for a week, so I thought I would see the great wonders Mr. Travel Agent had tried to sell me on in the plane.

I looked at the place names. They all harked back to my ancient history 101 classes. This was my chance to revisit those dreams I'd had when devouring the textbooks. Oh, the fantasies—er, dreams—I used to have about a great strapping, bronzed Spartan warrior rescuing me from the Trojans, bringing me back to Sparta and then, under the sun, by the waters of the Cretan Sea, I would reward him and we'd ... yes, well. Even if the places themselves were totally lame, reciting the names to the excitement junkies back at work would sound fantastic. Maybe I would keep an eye out for any Spartans hanging around.

I would start by driving down by the Aegean Sea to Ephesus. It already sounded exotic and exciting, and it was just day one.

I wandered around the great city ruins of Ephesus, ancient as all modern mankind. Ancient history was my thing. I originally took the subject in college because I thought you'd meet a better class of man. I didn't, but I learned lots of interesting stuff.

I sat in the main amphitheater, constructed by a comparatively young Roman Empire, and looked down the main thoroughfare, which ended abruptly a few hundred yards away. It was hard to believe this landlocked city was once a port. My mind imagined what it would have been like all those millennia ago, with waves lapping at the promenade, the hustle and bustle of street traders excited by the arrival of a great galleon, its sails flapping in the breeze.

If my history lessons served me well, Ephesus was one of the twelve cities of the Ionian League during the Ancient Greek era, which had had a population of more than a quarter of a million in the first century BC, which also made it one of the largest cities in the Mediterranean world, which was all the world that mattered at the time.

Yeah, there were other people, but they hadn't invented history or flags. It was over three thousand years old and had been mentioned in the Book of Revelations I had read back at the hotel.

Can't get cooler than that, I thought. There would've been great big strapping men, Greek then Roman warriors—dare I say it, gladiators—flouncing around in their togas. Maybe not flouncing. They were both pretty aggressive and warlike races.

Heroes glinting in the sun. Maybe that was my problem. Maybe I was holding out for a hero, a teenage dream drawn from overwrought eighties bombastic songs. But didn't every woman?

Trouble was, we didn't always hold out. Sometimes we settled for a David.

It would have to be someone pretty heroic to put up with me. Who was my hero?

The ruins were built by heroes. Today, they were even being saved by them. There had always been heroes. I just needed to change the way I looked for them, and not send them away when they came knocking.

I kicked a small rock and it skittled off down the ancient steps made of sterner stuff than me. The tourists looked up at me, their faces full of confused concern.

Don't worry, folks, I'm not a Visigoth. Although I'd like the music.

After drinking about five bottles of water I got back in the car, turned on the aircon to maximum overload, and headed down to Kuşadasi.

It was about a four-hour drive, which involved me continually retuning the stereo trying to find something I could understand. Occasionally I got lucky, but the station would fade out after a while, leaving me with the white noise that made me want to fall asleep. But the coast kept being amazing and made up for everything else.

Kuşadasi turned out to be a lot bigger than I thought it would be, so I decided to stay overnight. It had an island with a castle on it. We didn't have those back home. Alas, there were no knights in the castle for me.

When I was at the hotel bar someone told me that about three hours' drive east was the ancient city of Hierapolis. After seeing that I could head up to Cappadocia and check out the caves. From there it was a quick trip over to the milk pools then a leisurely drive back to Istanbul, where I could rest for a day or two before heading back to Doha. What a plan.

So I joined the caravan of tourists and headed over to the site the next morning. I joined up with a tour guide, who led us around the place. It felt good to be just a person in the crowd.

"Founded in the second century BC, Hierapolis is a UNESCO World Heritage site whose name translates as Sacred City. It is surrounded by a beautiful and majestic landscape," the tour guide rambled.

Someone knocked me from behind, forcing me out to the edge of the group.

"The amphitheater has been rebuilt twice, in 17 AD and 60 AD, both times after an earthquake. In 352 AD it underwent a thorough restoration and was adapted for water shows. Note the baths. Please feel free to have a swim if you are suitably prepared. Towels are available for reasonable hire. For those wanting a little more history please follow me to the historic remains of the city, including the tombs of the Necropolis and the remains at the Temple of Apollo."

And when the sun was this hot you really wanted the reason to be because some self-righteous god, who hated people, wanted to make mere mortal life hell. If you built a temple you could go shout at him and complain, then duck off to the souvenir shop and get the temple in a small snow dome so you could take it home and vent your anger in the comfort of your own air-conditioned house.

Most of the crowd took off for the baths and a respite from the heat, leaving a handful of us behind. While surrounded by tourists shouting at the god of choice in the temple, I felt someone staring. In fact, from the amphitheater to the temple I felt like I'd been followed. But among the tourists it was near on impossible to be certain. I put it down to a lack of caffeine. Anyway, it freaked me a bit so I took it as a sign to move on to somewhere more secluded.

The road took me east and I drifted absent-mindedly behind the wheel to the Goreme National Park. The hours of solitude it took to get there helped me calm down. The road was quiet and isolated, and the empty horizon made me feel at ease. Eventually the tourist traffic started to build up to a moderately steady stream, which allowed me to drive to Cappadocia nearly on automatic. It was better than having to work out the signs.

The horizon gradually changed, evolving into the bizarrely shaped mounds of volcanic rock that had been deposited by now extinct volcanoes.

I, and several dozen other people, arrived at the volcanic rock formations at Cappadocia. Obviously this was a popular tourist attraction in the region, and a handful of large tourist coaches were parked near the entrance to the caves next to the huge pay-lots-of-money-here-to-enter booth. There was also a hot-air balloon ride offering flights or floats over the area to view the rock formations from an alternative angle. It surprised me that there wasn't a Ferris wheel and a casino.

Around four thousand years ago people decided they needed protection from the inhospitable elements and, using spoons, started carving cave dwellings into the volcanic rock. Yes, spoons. It was the Silverware Age. It came just before the Bronze Age, which was better because visitors kept stealing the silverware, making the people eat things using mud and sticks.

So with spoons and various kinds of experimental sporks they built a unique network of caves and tunnels that stretched down a dozen floors. It was a remarkable effort in excavation that plunged nearly one hundred yards into the ground. The cave complex was truly inspirational and captivating. But considering the number of tourists around, I was surprised to find it quiet and empty. I could hear other people nearby, but it was hard to make them out in the faint glow of the ancient lanterns.

And there I felt it again. Someone nearby. But whenever I turned to look there was no one there. Perhaps I was just getting jittery being so far away from familiar Western corporate coffee and fast-food icons.

I got back in the car and felt shivers run through my body. I felt the urgent need to be far away from here. I pulled out onto the main drag and headed east in search of a large, friendly and Western hotel.

CHAPTER 22

HOTEL CALIFORNIA

The wind was picking up and I could feel it beginning to buffer the rental around on the crumbling tarmac. The undulating road surrendered to a flatter terrain punctuated by mountains on the horizon. As the sky darkened I could make out a light in the distance. As I approached, the light revealed itself to be a solitary streetlamp in front of a rundown building.

I consulted my tourist book. Apparently it was a bed and breakfast for the more adventure-inspired backpacker. Great. I assumed it was going to be full of smelly, pimply, backpacking youth, full of hormones, knocking each other over when they turned around, thereby giving themselves an opportunity to speak to each other then get laid.

There was an old Citroën sedan, possibly abandoned, out front. It was one bumper sticker away from being a complete derelict. Still, it was French, and that had to count for something. Or maybe not. The dust and rust meant it certainly lacked the ooh-la-la factor.

I drove the rental up next to it and got out. The horizon still looked dark and forbidding. I gazed out toward the incoming clouds, and the wind blew back my hair. The stinging sand blew into my face. I put on my sunglasses for some protection. Behind me, on the road, there was no sign of life. Just an empty, dead horizon. I felt a sense of ease here.

I walked over to the entrance of the building. It had a huge old wooden door that could defend the house against any invading crusaders. Probably.

I tried to open the door, but it didn't move. I heaved against it and it creaked open. The wind was trying to close it back up, but I managed to squeeze in before the elements won. The door slammed behind me.

There was a young man behind a counter located in the center of an anteroom. He was writing something on a big stack of paper. He glanced up when he heard the door. He looked a bit weird, but he seemed quiet and the sort to mind his own business so that was all right by me.

His face had sharp features, which made him striking but not attractive. His hair, black as a raven, was slicked back, and face and body were gaunt. He was in some black slacks and a stained white singlet. His skin was pale, which seemed unusual out here in the middle of desert country. He could have been pushing the short side of twenty. He looked like a punk.

"Hi, I'm Ellen," I said.

He stared at me, unblinking and unsmiling, swinging gently from side to side, uninterested in the introduction. The wooden floorboards creaked in the heat. All else in the room was quiet. I heard the tortured squeaking of the rusty sign as it swung in the breeze out front.

"Do you speak English? Have you got a name?"

There was a considerable pause. "Damien," he drawled.

"Where is everyone? My tourist book says this is a popular and exciting place, capturing the transient charms of global excellence. But then it was written by a Thomas Cook representative."

"The wind comes in and blows all the people away, leavin' this place like a ghost town."

He sounded like a punk too. "Do you think they'll come back?"

"Nevermore."

"Oh-kay. Do you know if there's anywhere else to stay?"

He looked out the windows, lost in some far vision only visible to him.

"Storm's comin', Ellen," he said. "Ain't nowhere you can go. Nowhere to hide"—he smirked—"from the shadows." He finished it off with an unsettled, intent look that went right through me.

"Nowhere else at all?"

"Nevermore."

"Look, if you're going to keep saying that I may have to slap you. Are you going to say it again?"

"Never—no."

"Good. I'm glad you understand. Is that your old car out front?"

"No." He stared back at me.

"How long do I have to stay to avoid the storm?"

"Never—" he caught himself.

I raised a cautionary finger at him.

The wind picked up significantly enough to suck the door open. Papers scattered around the room and somersaulted in the air. Damien made his way to the door through the paper tornado and forced it shut against the strengthening gale. He slid a large bolt across from the wall and rammed it into the door.

He cast his gaze over the mess on the floor and glared at me in an unsettling way. "Better be prepared to stay for a while."

"All right. Give me a room."

"You can have 1408."

"I can easily see that you neither have fourteen floors nor eight rooms. What's up with that?"

"Probably someone's idea of a joke."

"Just give me the key." I snatched it out of his hand and glared at him. "It's okay, I don't need any assistance with my luggage."

Damien looked back at me vacantly, his eyes awash with indifference. I sighed and headed upstairs to the only other floor in the building.

The stairs were old, wooden, rickety and narrow. A solitary lightbulb hung from the ceiling. It was on but did little to puncture the brightness of the day. Things may be a bit different in a few hours, I thought, where it would do little to puncture the darkness of the night, and the storm. It was an old, cheap incandescent bulb. The ones that had been taken off the market but were dirt cheap and lasted about ten minutes—unless you turned them on, then about five. Cheap globe. Cheap place. Hopefully the building would be able to stand up in the storm.

The top two stairs were weird, too. There should have been one normal one, but there were two half-sized ones instead. Surely that was an accident waiting to happen. And, of course, since I wasn't expecting crap stairs I stumbled over them and fell against the base of the door of room 1408.

The room was minimal to say the least. Even a backpacker may have thought it too basic. It had a bed, a tiny table and a light suspended from the ceiling. No aircon. No minibar. Things were looking grim. It was a warehouse for hormones and depression.

I flicked the light switch and nothing happened. I sighed then got angry. I turned and stormed downstairs. And of course I wasn't thinking about the stairs and tripped up—down—on the stupid half-step and crashed into the wall.

"Do you need to turn power on or something?" I snapped at Damien.

He slowly looked up at me from whatever he was writing. "I'll see to it." His vacant stare lingered on until I got bored.

I went out to my car and grabbed the tourist book. I went back in and shook it at him for the only reason that I could think of, which was that it seemed like the right thing to do.

"And what's up with the stairs?" I shouted.

"Count 'em."

"Eh?"

"You'll see."

I turned to clamber up the uneven steps when some guy, who I could only describe as hunky, came out of the kitchen. A great big strapping guy with arms like tree trunks and a jaw you could grate cheese on. He had a T-shirt that may have once fit him but was now a couple of sizes too small, and in a good way. He had a baseball cap set casually back, half covering his short dark hair, and a set of shorts that ended past his knees. He was drying his hands on an old dusty dishtowel.

"Hi, I'm Ash. Who are you?"

"I'm Ellen. I was passing when the storm started to whip up."

"Yeah. Should be a beauty. You staying here long?"

I glanced over to Damien. He was still writing and shuffling. "Yeah. I guess so. I don't know much about surviving a sandstorm."

"As long as you stay inside while it's blowin' you should be right. But it sure looks big, this one. I'll let you know if you need to take any precautions." He threw the towel over his shoulder and winked.

I didn't like the way he said blowin', but he looked good so I'd allow him to get away with it for now.

"Hey, hon."

Ash had turned to some young thin thing coming into reception through the door, exposing a small and tired bathroom beyond. Her legs were so skinny you could have driven a horse through them. This was made apparent by the incredibly short shorts she was sucked into. She also had on a tight red tank top that had some faded slogan on the front. She wasn't wearing a whole lot else.

The girl threw her arms wide and gave Ash an amorous hug. The word *cling* came to mind. As did *desperate*.

"Ash! I missed you so much." She planted a dozen or so kisses on his face, which he seemed to relish.

He grabbed her skinny ass and squeezed. She lifted her legs and wrapped them around his aptly named love handles—if he'd had any.

I thought the world was getting fatter. Where did all these skinny people keep coming from?

"Did you miss me?" Ash managed to squeeze out while squeezing other things. Lucky his fly was done up.

"So much it made me sad." She put on a little sad face and pouted behind her long dark hair.

"Ooh there, my little kitten. I'm here now and we're together."

"My manstar, you've saved me."

Excuse me while I vomit all over my shoes. There was a moment when they were locked in an embrace that seemed to go on way too long and be way too passionate for such a public place. Eventually, and it was a long eventually, they broke to come up for air or another pack of condoms or something. Ash caught me out the corner of his eye.

"Cheryl, this is Ellen. She's staying here while the storm blows."

Cheryl giggled and hid her mouth behind her dainty hand.

For crying out loud. "Have you been away?" I inquired.

"No. I was just in the can," she replied. "But every moment apart makes me sad." She grabbed and squeezed his crotch, and her face changed into something a little darker. "I hope you haven't been a bad boy while I've been away."

Double-vomit time. With class like that I was sure there was nothing she wouldn't do for Ken doll.

"Well, I'll be in my room," I said.

Cheryl was kissing Ash again, and I thought I saw her glance at me as I walked past. Maybe she was a little insecure and lacking self-esteem. Or just plain insane.

This time I counted the stairs. Fourteen. What was so significant about that? I still managed to trip on the last one. I swore.

I went into my room and clicked on the light, which now worked. I lay on the bed and started to read through some of the info about recommended tourist spots. I made a mental note to write to the authors and take this place off the list.

There was a knock at the door. I had fallen asleep with the book on my head.

"Ellen, the dust cloud is gonna hit real soon," Ash shouted through the door. "It's a lot bigger than we originally thought. Best come downstairs into the kitchen. It's a safer place."

I opened the door and there he was, flexing in his T-shirt, fit to burst. He still had the dishtowel over his shoulder. I tried to shake the grogginess from my head, but my mind was in a pink haze. I nodded. One place I wanted to be out here was in a safe place.

It occurred to me later that he hadn't said "safe" place. He had called it "safer."

CHAPTER 23

REALLY GET ME
OUTTA HERE

The wind blew fiercely around the house and sent an eerie howl through the rooms. We sat in the heat and the dust, sweating, with the crackly old radio fazing between white noise and some lo-fi traditional Arabic music. It eventually died and a silence settled over the group. There was a loud bang from outside, which made me jump. A breeze made the lightbulb swing slightly. Darkness crawled uneasily around the room.

Damien, who had been rocking back and forth, slumped forward, dropping his eyes into shadow, and stared at the tabletop.

And the tap dripped into the broken sink.

"What happened to the dog that was scrounging around outside?" Cheryl asked.

"You have a dog?" I asked Damien.

Ash answered. "There was a stray runnin' 'round yesterday. Haven't seen it today. I always feel safe when there's a dog 'round. Somethin' that can sense fear and danger."

Damien spoke. "They tell me things. They say they might walk again."

"The dog? Who ya' talkin' about?" Cheryl asked.

"The spirits of the dead."

Ash sniggered. "Do you see dead people?"

Cheryl whacked him on the shoulder. She tried to hide the fact that she was laughing too.

I really didn't like these people. I'd been watching her, and I believed she wasn't in love. There was no denying she was all over him, but she didn't listen to him. She didn't look at him that much, and she didn't lift when she was next to him. Obviously there was the physical stuff, but I wondered what else she was getting out of him.

"My mother!" Damien exclaimed, jolting my thoughts back to him. "My mother appeared to me last night; standin' there in front of me. Floatin' like some hideous creature dragged from the pit of regret, sometimes her head on one side, then on the other, like she was tryin' to work out somethin'. She looked so sad, like no one else I had seen. So full of sorrow, yet her breasts were pressed out, pointin' through in the cold. So filled and so becomin', in that pure white nightdress. Pure dress, dark heart."

And the tap dripped into the broken sink.

"Full of the wounds of those stabs and slashes from that butcher's knife. She didn't stop. I begged with her to, but she never listened. So I warned her. I warned her so many times. Why didn't she listen? And when she stopped she was lookin' this way and that like she was tryin' to work somethin' out with that thing in her hand."

He paused. "Smilin' at me," he snarled. "Laughin'. Looking this way and that, like she was hangin' from the ceilin', eyes buggin' outta their sockets, with her hands gnarled and twisted 'round that thing."

He brought his hands up above the table and stared into them. They were shaking.

"And I looked down, and there was the blood ... all over the knife ... all over the nightdress ... all over my hands. And she just stood there lookin' at me. Why didn't she listen? Like a mother's sanctity, she approached where I was lyin', and she bowed, not once, but three times. And gaspin' as she tried to speak, her eyes spewed forth blood and grief until her fury was spent."

Damien looked up. "Then she croaked, 'Child, fate ruined me for you as my father ruined me, made me what I am, one who defiles the young and pure of heart. The lord did not—would not—save me when I cried out for him. You wish to see me spent in places scattered among the circles of hell? Well, child, weep for me and leave your soul crying; as you are a child lost forever in the darkness. The almighty will not come for either of us.' She took what was given by the Lord, then ran to hide from her own judgment. 'You will never see me again,' she promised me with those empty eyes. And so, screamin', she melted into the air."

We were all staring at Damien.

"I know this weren't no dream," he said. "Dreams are a kiss of forgiveness from the darkness, and don't torment you. I ain't one for superstitions, but I saw this and I've been tested by this. There she lies, fornicatin' with the nightmare of her own character, which may, if the Lord can be bothered to look the other way, gestate into a disgustin' and disfigured horror that will rain down a pretty disaster and breathe the foulness into you. So we sit here as the storm rages around us. Pity us for ya mother's fault. Feel the loss and all that may follow."

And the tap dripped into the broken sink.

"My eyes cannot cry, no matter hard I try, but my heart finds it too easy to bleed, and it's left me cursed for the rest of m' life, until the last farewell. The days grow darker an' darker, an' comfort is only found within tortured lullabies, which reflect upon a time when it weren't too dire and her voice did not fill me with dread, and my life was not filled with the screams. I try to find redemption in the last ride that flies to heaven, but the screams they pull me away. I long to get aboard. This is the chase and I gotta run forever. I wait with the past in my hands."

Damien stroked his fingers over his palm. "And the blood won't wash off. Stained into the hand like I'm holdin' a beatin' heart, her heart. Remindin' me of what happened. And the blood ain't washin' away. It never goes away."

He turned his dark, sullen eyes on Ash. "Yeah, I see dead people."

"That's it. I'm going to bed."

I stood up and left for the upstairs rooms. I was more prepared to take my chances with one of nature's more destructive forces than spend any more time in the kitchen with that lot and the stupid dripping tap.

I stormed up the stairs, with Damien's stupid monologue replaying in my mind. What kind of weirdo was he? And what kind of weirdoes were Ash and his psycho girlfriend for choosing to stay out here? Obviously Damien had murdered his mother and buried her. Or maybe he hadn't buried her, but had just set up her skeleton in his room in a rocking chair so she could stare out the window.

I tripped over the top step again and let loose a long chain of expletives. I got up and opened up the door to my room, stepped in and slammed it shut. It bounced back, whacking me in the head. The surprise of it made me stumble backwards. The only piece of furniture in the room then conspired against me, tripping me over and landing me on my back.

I breathed in deeply. Outside, seen through the savage sandstorm, the lone streetlamp exploded. I finished swearing. If I'd been lucky enough to be French, I could've kept going.

I lay on the floor, staring up at the hanging light swinging back and forth like a pendulum. All was quiet again, except for the roaring of the wind. I clambered up and threw myself on the bed. I shoved my head under the pillow and burst into tears.

"I want my mommy," I whimpered.

After about an hour and a half the wind eased off. It was still strong, but the house no longer felt like it was in imminent danger of falling over like a deck of cards. I wondered if I could make a dash for it. But my nerves had calmed down and rationality had raised its head, at least for the moment. I decided to just lie there, still and quiet.

There was a knock on my door.

"Who knocks without?" I shouted.

"Without what?"

"Without the door."

I got up and swung open the door. Damien stood there with a blank look on his face, his eyes distorted by the old light swinging in the hallway.

"Don't worry," I said. "Don't try to understand."

"I'm bored. You wanna go dancin'?" he drawled.

He was dressed in black from head to toe, with a pair of dark wraparound Versace sunglasses holding back his hair. A bit odd, since it was night. His shirt only had a couple of buttons secured, exposing some of his slender frame.

"What? *Dancing?* Out here?"

"Gotta' do somethin'. Too much time on your hands out here. The heat and humidity can bring dark and unsettling thoughts to a man."

"But we're in the middle of nowhere. It can't believe there's a club around here. We are still in Turkey, aren't we?"

"Not a club, but there's a party not too far away."

"A party? Out here? In a sandstorm? The heat does make you all crazy."

"The storm has pretty much passed. The next wave won't get here until tomorrow. You got any other concerns?"

"What am I going to wear?"

"Is that the pinnacle of the problems you got?"

"Hey, it's a biggie. You never know who you'll meet."

Damien laughed.

"Why are you laughing?"

"You'll find out. Come as you are, unless you got a ballgown."

"I don't even have decent shoes. I *never* go out without the right shoes."

He lowered his glasses over his eyes. "Shoes? Where we're going we don't need shoes." Seeing my puzzled expression, he added, "No one looks down."

We bumped along the track with the headlights scything through the fog-like dust. I wondered what was up with Damien. I knew nothing about him. Here he was pretending to be an axe murderer, but I knew *The Winter's Tale* when I heard it. He said the heat made a man go crazy. What if *he* had gone crazy? What if ... he started reciting more? Oh, the humanity. Or would it be tragedy?"

"You got a GPS?" Damien asked.

"Ha."

"What?"

"You just reminded me of something. Ten years ago I wouldn't have known what that was. Now we've got them on our phones. But no, I've got no GPS."

"You got one of them new smartphones?"

"Not yet. The company is slow on moving on things like that. They make a big deal of providing you with a cell and laptop, and it's the cheapest, oldest crap they can get their hands on. It's a corporate thing. Unless it's the board, of course. Then they want the latest or greatest as misled by our paranoid IT team, who are more interested in buying old, cheap crap that won't work without their continual expert guidance, thereby ensuring their own jobs. Not that I'm cynical."

"We ain't too far away," Damien said. "See?" He pointed out the windscreen at a distant light.

"Are we ... will we be safe?"

"Oh yeah. You'll be safer here than if you slept a night on the Bronx subway."

"You done much of that?"

"Best not to talk about it," he replied. "Most folks won't pay us any attention. What they're after we won't be supplying."

He certainly was an enigmatic and intriguing weirdo.

"What's the light?" I asked.

"It's the house."

And that was it. I couldn't draw any more information out of him.

As we approached, the lights haloed around the house. It was a huge two-story mansion, like the ones I'd seen back in Doha. There are no words to describe how weird it was to see a place like this in the middle of absolutely nowhere. Lights were searing through the sky like some old World War Two war film: lights looking out for signs of danger from above.

The music seemed subdued, but as we approached the volume increased dramatically. By the time we were at the front door it was thumping. Heavy, hard house music. Out here that had to be rarer than water.

I felt a sense of relief seep through me. Damien hadn't axe-murdered me, yet, and there was good music to be grooved to.

Damien knocked on the door. It opened to an astonishing sight: a very large man with a full beard who was wearing a full formal gown. There was a brief interchange of some Arabic words and we were in. But what were we in to?

CHAPTER 24

TO THE CLUB

The place looked like an authentic nightclub. Music was thumping, lights were flashing, and the smoke-machine was smoking. They even had a bar. Then the patrons became apparent. There didn't seem to be any other women in here. Lots of ballgowns, though. Lots of fat men wearing ballgowns.

Holy mother of magnitude, it was a full-blown transvestite party.

We wandered around the room and made our way to the bar. We passed the DJ, who gave us a subtle nod.

"Hang on for a minute, I just gotta do something," Damien said. He had that eternal blank look on his face.

He quickly looked around and headed off toward some dark corner to do something secret. Maybe work out where to bury me. The music pounded and, although enjoyable, I felt vulnerable in this unknown place. I stood there for a few minutes, feeling more and more conspicuous.

Eventually Damien returned. He was putting something in his wallet, which he slipped into his back pocket.

"Done?" I asked.

"Yeah."

"What was it?"

"Ash asked me to come and get somethin' for him up here."

"What?"

"Drugs. Looks like heroin."

"How do you know?"

"I'm an arts student."

"Really?"

"What would you like to drink? Ash arranged a small tab."

"Would they have a Bud?"

"They got everythin' here, sister. Solid and liquid. If you want a pill they can purty much guarantee it'll be the best you can get."

"Let's start with a Bud. I'm not sure if I want to run around a place like this telling every guy here I love him. The worst part would be being ignored."

The bartender got a couple of bottles out of the fridge. He made a big deal about opening them in front of us.

"What was that all about," I asked Damien. "Him doing the big arm wave thing?"

"He wanted to show you he didn't tamper with the drink."

"Does that happen much out here?" I was suddenly concerned.

"It'd be a very brave person to try. If they were caught it'd be instant death. Probably out back, then their body'd be dumped in the desert. This is a place of trust. Lots of influential people here. They don't wanna worry about stuff like that, they want a simple good time where they can be themselves. And wear great clothes."

We watched the men parade and dance around, and rather distressingly, kiss each other passionately. I wondered how illegal this place was. I knew how it worked. The only way the venue would be allowed was if there were some very important people here. Prohibition, eat your heart out.

Everyone floated around the floor gracefully, regal and flamboyant. Certainly more so than I had been at the ball. I bet they didn't wear heels. The gown was only half the challenge. The hardest part was balancing on your toes all night while your calves cramped. Then spinning around. The drinks helped numb the pain, but then you lost your balance.

We all deserved accolades for such dexterity. Certainly free drinks.

"How on this floating ball of rock did you ever find out about this?"

"It pays to be observant, Ellen."

"Jeez, you sound exactly like my friend ... a guy I knew who said he was a musician."

Damien looked impassively at me.

I smiled. "So, what do you do, Damien? Really."

"I paint."

"The guy I knew who said he was a musician turned out not to be one."

Damien slowly turned his head and gave me a stare that went right through me.

"What do you paint? Houses? Walls? Still-life flowers? Family portraits? Kittens?"

"Sometimes kittens. More abstract. Mainly black."

"Are the kittens alive?"

"Of course. There's enough death and despair in the world without adding to it."

I took a swig from the bottle and looked around the room. The DJ was cranking out some fine Detroit tunes, and the place was really beginning to pick up. "Do you do anything else?"

"I write stories."

"What kind?"

"Scary ones."

"You any good?"

"Yeah."

"I could've used you ten years ago."

That remark finally got some kind of expression out of him,

although only fleeting. He looked at me through narrowed eyes, then instantly got distracted by a huge man with a massive beard and an amazing purple gown.

Already he had brushed off my comment. I wondered if I was really that uninteresting to Damien. What kind of person would he be interested in, I wondered. If he had a girlfriend, which he obviously didn't because he was out here alone and was bafflingly weird, was she some neo-goth-slut-emo-punk? Or simply dead?

Damien turned back to me. "What do you do?" he asked.

The question surprised me. The only other question he had asked me was whether I wanted to come out here.

"I'm a lawyer. Corporate. It's amazingly dull. Especially when compared to house music."

"What's a lawyer doin' out here? Shouldn't you be in some big fancy city somewhere?"

I sighed. I wondered if I should bore him with the story. But it would only depress me. In the end I simply shrugged at him, hoping he could project some kind of response into it.

The blank look was back on his face. I wondered what went on in there. Was he really as tortured as he made out to be, or was he just some drama student bumming around, waiting for his trust fund back home to kick in? I liked the idea of him being the tortured artist, especially as he hadn't axe-murdered me yet.

I asked for another drink. The barman came over and did his special little presentation dance. It was really hot in the house, which was having a direct impact on my thirst. I realized I hadn't eaten in a while, and now the drinks, heat, and excitement were rushing to my head.

I decided to do something about it before something bad happened. "You dance, Damien?"

"Yeah. You can find solace in the music."

"I look forward to seeing solace in motion."

I found a place in the centre of the floor and gave him a quizzical expression to see if he was okay with dancing in the middle. He seemed cool with it. In fact, he loosened up heaps. He was an amazing groover. He was young so he knew all the latest moves. I danced as freely as I always did.

He laughed.

"What are you laughing at?"

"You dance like my aunt."

I narrowed my eyes and put my hands on my hips. "I'll have you know I've faced down the Colombian military, overcome London gangsters, done something unspeakable in Paris, and been imprisoned in the Middle East. My wise counsel to you would be to watch your step, bucko. And another thing—at least I come from an era when we did actually know how to dance, unlike you guys, who only seem to be able to jump up and down on the spot. I even know how to waltz. Do you?"

"What'd you say? I couldn't hear you."

"Forget it." I wasn't going to mime it all in the hardest game of charades ever. Three sentences, eighty-one words. First word: idiot. Next eighty: idiot.

I tried a different tack. "Do you see anyone you fancy?"

He looked around at the all-male ensemble. He returned his appraising gaze back to me and twisted it into a what-the-hell-are-you-talking-about one. "There ain't no women here."

"I didn't know if that was your inclination."

He didn't respond for a while. "You never meet anyone interesting in clubs."

"I think clubs are a fit-for-purpose, decision-making platform. You can tell a lot about someone by the way they dance and how they try to communicate with you while being hampered by excess volume."

"True. I refuse to sleep with a girl who can't dance."

"That's a bit harsh, but it's not the first time I've heard it. And finding a man who can dance is the same. We forgive a lot of vices if they're good in the sack, er, on the floor. Dancing. Not having sex on the floor, unless that's some kind of exotic cocktail. We should ask the barman to make one and see what he comes up with."

I smiled, but Damien looked back at me blankly. I didn't know if he didn't understand or couldn't hear. Alex would understand. I sighed, and then chided myself for thinking about him.

"Let's get a drink," Damien suggested.

We went back over to the bar and placed ourselves on a couple of stools.

"How long have you been looking after the hostel?" I asked.

"It's not mine."

"Sorry. I thought, I assumed, it was your place."

"No, the others."

"You mean Ash and Cheryl."

"Yeah, them weirdos."

"But you were out front."

"Ash asked me to look out while he was doin' somethin' out back."

"So you're the backpacker?"

"Somethin' like that."

Oh. Maybe the place wasn't as dangerous as I'd originally thought. My imagination had built a horror-movie drama of epic proportions around these people, and they were all just normal. And it was only made apparent to me while dancing with one of them, in an all-male, very gay party nearby. Life can teach you wisdom in the strangest ways.

I felt the stress leave my body. I had the feeling that everything was going to be all right. A few more drinks and a few more dances and I would be as right as rain.

"We should go now before it gets dangerous," Damien said.

"What? How's it going to get dangerous?"

"They take all their clothes off and then the action starts. They'll expect you to do the same. Anyway, I think we're being watched. You never know who's around at these things."

I didn't feel that relaxed anymore. I nodded. We got up and made our way out into the stifling night air.

"Do you think Ash and Cheryl just wanted us out the way so they could have crazy sex in the kitchen?" I asked.

"Don't say that. We eat off that table." He shook his head and shivered. "Great. I got that image in my mind now."

"Are we all right to drive after all the drinks?"

"Hah. Who's gonna check it out here?"

In the darkness to the side of the house, sat a dark dual cab. In the dark dual cab sat a dark man. In the dark man there was a dark heart. He watched impassively as the two Westerners drove away. He picked up his cell and dialed.

"They come," he said, and disconnected. Ten minutes later he received a text. He started his engine. It cranked into life, and he gently eased the vehicle away from the party. It rumbled down the empty road, sounding like a hungry lion.

CHAPTER 25

UNDERNEATH
THE RADAR

W e are flying the right way up, aren't we? Everywhere I look I see sand," Alex said.

"Roger, Iceman, over."

"Saif?"

"Yes, over."

"Did you just call me Iceman?"

"Er, no. Over."

"Sounded like it to me."

"Saif's been in America too long," Malik interjected. "He thinks he's in the movies."

"If he was in the movies it would only be as a bad guy," said Alex. "Foreigners can only be bad guys in Hollywood blockbusters, unless it's a chick flick. Then he can be the exotic romantic interest."

"What's a chick flick?" Malik asked.

"Man, you need to get out more, especially since you're married now. They're movies designed to make women realize the man they're with is a loser. Your Saturday nights will be booked up for years. You'll be forced to watch *Pretty Woman* at least four times a year. And don't get me started on *Thelma and Louise*."

Alex compared the electronic readouts to his paperwork. "Okay, we should be passing over a river in the next thirty seconds. Malik, let me know when you see it. Hey, does this take you back to ninety-four?"

"What was in ninety-four?" Saif asked. "Over."

"Gulf War."

"This is a lot worse. But I'm a better pilot now."

"Saif, drop back about five hundred meters."

"Copy. Over."

"Stop saying 'over.' It's annoying and unnecessary. There are only two planes."

"Understood. Over."

Alex sighed. "Malik, would you shoot Saif?"

"Not if he's behind us."

"Good point."

"Alex, we just went over the river," Malik said.

"Drop to three hundred. Target should be five hundred meters and seven degrees. The intel's been good so far. Who did it?"

"General Ayden. He's a very skilled logistics man. He would be happiest spending every day with his compass and maps, sneaking around enemy boarders."

"He also has the smallest writing I've ever seen. Lucky I bought my reading glasses. Okay, Saif, if we miss the target you take it out. And if necessary, use the Force."

Saif laughed. "Need it in this weather. How about if I use the Excessive Force? Over."

"Target acquired. Weapons hot. I'll drop the plane and you shoot," Malik said.

"Okay, got it. Engaged and … target neutralized. Thank you, ladies, gentlemen and ball boys. Let's go home. Easy flight for you, Saif, you didn't do anything. What is this? Work experience?"

Saif brought his jet up next to Malik. He wiggled his wings in a victory dance.

"Now shoot him, Malik," Alex commanded.

Saif pulled back on the throttle, kicked the nose of the jet skyward, and somersaulted over the other jet, flying in close behind Malik and Alex.

"Impressive stuff, hotshot," Alex said as he watched Saif's aeronautical maneuvers. "I bet the chicks dig it."

"They have to dig something," Malik said. "I've seen him dance. And you know how obsessive they are about that."

"That's another thing you'll have to learn, old man," Saif said. "Dancing is different these days. Over."

"Call it in, Captain Saif, and don't stray too far away," Malik said. "I would hate for you to get lost in the storm."

The wind roared across the plains. The ferocious sand made it impossible to see more than a few yards. The two soldiers made their way slowly along the track. It had taken them fifteen minutes to travel the two miles from the security gate to the command center. They had parked as close as they could to the control-room door, but it was still going to be difficult to get there. They wrapped their *smaghs* around their faces and tried to run to the doors. The wind buffeted them and they staggered against the elements.

Once inside they brushed themselves down. Sand fell over the floor. The entrance was buzzing with staff bustling around. They walked forward and saluted to the most senior officer.

"Issam, Jasham, how is the visibility outside?" General Ayden asked.

"Sir, it's terrible. No more than a few meters at best. You can't tell the sky from the desert, let alone anything in it that may be camouflaged," Issam said.

"I think the wind speaks. Allah has shown his preference. He favors the pure of heart," Jasham said.

"Yes … possibly. Or it was an appalling decision by the Iranian army. Passion over logic," Issam countered.

"This storm is ferocious. It's taken out most of our communications.

There's no chance that Kuwait and Iran are in a better position," said General Ayden. "We're all isolated."

"I think this may give us an opportunity to press the advantage." Issam's excitement grew. "The bases at Salmās have no cover for aircraft. Their fighters will be full of sand and dust, reducing the force to tank battalions at best. It's such a simple and often repeated mistake—trying to get too close to the enemy without proper coverage."

"Analyze the weather charts and see when we can organize the squadrons' strikes."

"Yes, General," replied Issam. He saluted and turned to leave.

Major Isifan entered the room with a smile on his face. A soldier alerted the room to his presence and the juniors stood to attention.

"I have great news, General," the major said. "Our friends, Saudi, have backed us and Iran is backing down. It's over. The sandstorm's been so fierce that they're locked down in Salmās. The storm is far more intense there as well. Our small country has been smiled on."

"Really? Is this true?" said General Ayden.

"We've had a surveillance plane arrive back with the news."

"A plane? Up in this? They must be madmen, or foolishly brave. Who authorized this?"

"I believe it comes from the top. Captain Saif al-Noor was the pilot and he'll be with us in a minute. He'll be able to explain."

Abdul Aziz strode into the room. A soldier alerted the room to his presence and the juniors shuffled to attention. A woman was in mid-tirade against Abdul Aziz. He appeared to be unhappy about it. Elissa followed a respectful distance behind.

"… and you were late," Najla said to Abdul Aziz, not worrying about following at a respectful distance behind. "Why are you always late? And who are you talking to on your phone?" She gave him a push on the arm.

"It's work. Some of us have to work so others who don't work can feed their big fat mouths."

"Watch who you're calling fat."

"There is nothing fat about you, dear, except for your mouth and brain."

"Abdul Aziz," General Ayden said. "Greetings to you and your good wife. It is a pleasure to see you, Najla. And this attractive young lady is …"

"Elissa. She is the new wife of Malik, and my ward," Abdul Aziz replied.

"Commander Malik got married? Why are we the last to be told anything?"

Saif strode into the room. A soldier alerted the room to his presence and the juniors slowly rose to attention.

"Captain Saif," said General Ayden. "It's a great pleasure and relief to see you."

"Thank you, General, sir. But I'm more concerned about Malik. We were separated in the storm."

"This is terrible news. Do we need to mark him as missing in action?"

"I hope not, General. However, even though he's one of our top guns, saving the country is risky business. But the mission is not impossible. Far and away he's got all the right moves."

Najla poked Abdul Aziz. "Why aren't you up there saving the country?"

"I was tasked with doing something far more important." He gave her a look of disdain.

She placed her hands on her hips and glared at him. "What's more important than that?"

"Looking after his wife."

"I thought I was meant to be doing that. Malik instructed me, because he knows where real responsibility lies."

"You can barely look after yourself. I assume he chose you so Elissa had someone to talk to. Little did he realize she wouldn't have the opportunity to talk with you around."

"At least I have something interesting to say that isn't about my mother."

"You leave her out of it. You didn't know her. Your tongue is as unthinking and violent as a wasp."

"Then you had better watch out for my sting."

"That means nothing as I can easily pick it out."

"Not if I sting you in your wallet or backside, as you can find neither with both hands."

"Move, woman. You're like a troubled fountain: muddled, ill-looking, thick, and bereft of beauty."

"You have worn goodness from me. If life were a cake, all I would be eating is dough. And there's no feast."

"You babble."

"And you burp and fart like an ill-mannered camel."

"Does this happen very often?" Elissa whispered to Saif.

"What, them arguing? They're at it like cats and dogs," he replied.

"No. This missing-in-action bit."

Saif laughed, and then stopped abruptly when he saw her expression. "No," he lied. "Very rarely. And not with Malik." He became aware of the growing horror on her face. "I'll shut up now."

She gave him a suspicious look, and then tweeted an emoticon (☹) to her followers.

"It's not even missing in action," he said. "More *delayed* in action."

"Is Malik far away? More importantly, is he safe? I was hoping he would be here before we arrived."

"We were all hoping that, but no, he's not here yet," Saif said. "We think he's safe, but when communications are lost we can never be one hundred percent certain until we see him. In this manner you don't need to feel alone as he gives HQ as much grief as you."

"Is he a good pilot?" she asked.

"He's both an expert pilot and experienced. For that reason I'm confident he'll be here shortly." Saif's attempt to comfort her was interrupted by a cheer from a nearby room. "Let's hope this is good news."

A communications engineer entered the room and saluted Saif. "Sir, Commander Malik does not seem to be using his standard call sign, but we achieved contact with a craft. Can you confirm his mission call sign?"

"I certainly can." Saif followed the young engineer to the communications room, which was packed with excited men climbing over each other.

"Officer present," shouted one of the soldiers.

"As you were," said Saif. "Engineer, show me your efforts."

"Sir, we have rerouted our northern communications stacks and doubled the reception intensity on the southern ones. We were able to pick up one craft, but the identification information from it was only partial. If we have Commander Malik's full code we can confirm it's him."

"He is Quebec-Romeo-Nine-Charlie-Oscar-Mike-Zero-Nine-Five."

The engineer performed a quick calculation and entered the results into his computer. "We've got a sixty-seven-percent match on that, sir. Chances are it's him. He's not far away."

"Officer present," shouted one of the soldiers.

General Ayden entered the room, followed by Elissa.

The flight controller was looking intently at his screen. "They're down," he said.

A shocked expression appeared on Elissa's face. "What?"

"That means they've landed safely," Saif explained. "They'll be in here in a matter of moments."

Saif watched the data roll up the screens. He smiled as he saw the various messages flying between the upper echelons of command. He loved the way they tried to twist events so it all seemed to be just miscommunication. And they were always so polite to each other.

Someone would say it was all just a big misunderstanding. Then the other side would say it could happen to anyone. And everyone knew exactly what had happened and it would be remembered. All dealings out here were done like this, Saif knew, from the smallest transaction at the local shop to the global marketplace. It was enough to drive any logical man mad.

A cheer erupted from the building's main room. Everyone dashed out from the communications room to see what the commotion was. Malik and Alex had arrived. They both looked exhausted, but in good spirits.

Elissa dashed up to Malik and gave him a desperate hug, which lasted a long time. He hugged her back and eventually lifted her off the ground. She giggled. He placed her down gently and they stood together holding hands.

"Many apologies for our lack of communications," Malik said. "The sand got the better of the equipment. We had to come in by sight alone, and you can guess how difficult that was."

"Just in case you can't guess, it was medal-awardingly difficult," Alex said, "and I'm going to need a large drink to calm my nerves."

"Commander, Saif has brought some most welcome news," Major Isifan said.

Malik turned to Saif.

"Yes, Commander, I picked up news on the home channel that the prime minister has been negotiating with the Saudis, and they will support us."

"Ah, the only force more deadly and insane than the Iranians."

"Well, Iran has backed down from their—what they are now describing as—training sessions," Saif said. "The conflict is over."

Malik let out a huge sigh and looked visibly relieved. He turned to Alex. "We did it, old friend. We did it."

"Who are you calling old? Does that mean more drinks, and soon?"

"You said at the ball you weren't drinking. That reminds me, how did you go with your lady from the other night? Did you stop being an idiot?"

"I don't want to talk about it."

"You continued to be an idiot," said Malik.

"She spoke at me for some time," said Alex. "I'm not sure what she said, because it didn't make any sense."

"That means she's in love and she doesn't know how to express it," Najla explained to Alex. "She's reaching out for help."

"Are you star-crossed lovers with a desire that can never be?" Elissa clutched her hands to her chest.

"No," said Alex after a considerable pause. "She's amazingly annoying, talks too much, and is always in trouble. Yet I yearn for her so much it hurts, and I long to hear her voice. For me the world is a dark and empty place without her, and I would do anything for her."

Najla and Elissa let out a collective sigh. Abdul Aziz rolled his eyes.

"Did you ever tell her how you felt?" asked Elissa.

"I wrote her a song."

Najla and Elissa let out a collective sigh.

"But I never heard anything from her. Maybe she didn't like the song. To me she's like a melody that's sweetly sung in tune, with the occasional flat note, and a big crescendo at the end. And at various points throughout."

"You must go to her. Tell her how you feel," Elissa said.

Najla placed her hand on his arm. "A woman like her may not truly understand what she has in you. A man who speaks like that is rare. I am immensely jealous of her. For me, please go to her before it's too late. We do not live forever, and time spent without love can never be reclaimed. Please go."

Alex nodded and sighed deeply. "All right. I'll go back to see her after the drink to steady my nerves and possibly gain courage to talk to her once more."

"Do it now," said Najla. "Sometimes we need to do crazy things for those we love."

Alex turned and left the room. The women watched him go with smiles on their faces. The men started planning the imminent celebrations for the victory.

"Why don't you do that?" Najla gave Abdul Aziz a hefty shove, disturbing him from his negotiations. He gave her a fierce stare. "Why don't you yearn for me and long to hear my voice?"

"You never leave me alone for long enough … and I can hear you a mile away."

CHAPTER 26

PARTY LIKE IT'S 1999

*O*ur noble and courageous Commander Malik has declared: Mission Accomplished. The Iranian forces have been immobilized and no longer possess a threat to the State of Qatar. Commander Malik invites every man to celebrate in the victory. Each man has earned a place at the relaxed gathering and should feel proud in all that we have accomplished.

There will also be a special toast to celebrate Commander Malik's new marriage. The recreation hall will be converted for the function, which will run from 21:00 until 01:30. The State of Qatar congratulates all men and the great wisdom and bravery of Commander Malik.

"Nice invitation," said Saif. "It's says you're noble and courageous. Have they met you?"

Malik laughed. The letter had come from the prime minister. A private letter for Malik had also accompanied it, thanking him profusely for his efforts in bringing the plan to fruition, and telling him that it would not be forgotten if ever there was a time when he needed assistance.

He hadn't shown the letter to anyone, but it had lifted him, and he walked with a renewed spring in his step.

"He's noble and courageous to me," squeaked Elissa. "And that's all that matters."

Malik and Elissa smiled at each other. Saif tried not to vomit.

They walked toward the recreation hall, Elissa and Malik hand in hand. It was early and the noise was already noticeable outside. The storm had nearly passed over but the air was still heavy with dust and sand, giving an eerie glow to the fading light of the day. Some of the men had spilled out of the building and were being generally boisterous.

They entered the hall, and all the men stood to attention. Malik made his way through and joined Abdul Aziz at the front. He gave a small speech, reiterating the points made by the prime minister, and added his own appreciation for everything that the men had accomplished.

Abdul Aziz stepped up and led a series of toasts to the emir, the country, their hosts, Malik, and Malik and Elissa. Malik was beginning to fatigue after the long day. With some of the men already getting rowdy, and with his own objective in mind for the night, he called Saif over.

"Captain Saif, please keep a careful eye on the soldiers tonight. They've been through a tense time, so they'll want to relax a lot tonight. We're not on home territory so I'm okay with being a little bit lenient with the rules and expectations, but make sure some level of restraint is exercised. If the party gets too wild, don't hesitate to shut it down."

"Abdul Aziz has issued orders on what to do. But I'll see to it and keep an eye on it as well."

"He's a good man," Malik said. "I feel he should join in the partying sometimes. He's very serious all the time, but we would be lost without his experience."

"I wish I had your confidence in him. I understand he's experienced, but I'm uncomfortable when he's near."

"Abdul Aziz is simply a hardened soldier, forged solid by battle.

You'll be the same when you're his age. Goodnight, Saif. We'll need to meet early tomorrow morning and prepare a debriefing for the prime minister. He'll want details. Maybe if you have some time tonight you can think about the report."

Malik handed Saif a laptop bag. Saif looked inside. It contained a computer and a distressing amount of paper. He slung the bag over his shoulder.

Malik turned to Elissa, who was looking very excited and was furiously tweeting her followers.

He grabbed her hand and looked into her face. "Come with me, my love. It's time we became man and wife. Bring your high-heeled shoes."

The nearby men smirked, but said nothing out of respect for their leader.

Saif gave a broad grin and saluted his commander. "Don't do anything I wouldn't do."

"You've been in America for years. I believe there is nothing you haven't done." Malik turned to leave, then turned back to Saif. "Or posted on YouTube. Goodnight, all."

He whisked the light frame of Elissa off the floor and carried her in his arms out the door. She draped her arms around his neck and kissed his face. They weren't at home so it was acceptable to act a little different.

"Now that the wedding's over and all pressures of work have relented," said Malik, "we can have the pleasure of becoming a proper man and wife. Brace yourself, Elissa."

Saif watched the two of them go. He made his way through to the officer's area at the rear of the recreation hall. It was a smallish room and quietish. The men outside were considerably louder now that Malik had gone.

Saif commandeered a trestle table to use as a desk. He opened the bag, emptied out the paperwork, and turned his attention to the monumental task of writing. He hated reports. If he was back home he could pay someone to do it, like in school. Maybe even offshore it to India, to one of those technical-writing warehouses where they churned out this kind of stuff for peanuts. Maybe there was one on the Internet he could cut and paste.

He opened the laptop and started to type. A shadow loomed over him.

"Hello, Abdul Aziz," said Saif. "Is it time for us to patrol the perimeter?" He didn't look up.

"Not yet, Lieutenant. It's not even ten o'clock. The general got rid of us early tonight so he could be with Elissa."

"Yeah, I saw them go."

"I can't blame him. He hasn't spent the night with her yet, and she's beautiful enough to be a wife of the emir," said Abdul Aziz. Saif noticed his voice was quite leery. "If she was Turkish she might end up in the harem, right, fellas?" He looked over at his local guests, and they smiled back.

"Yes, she's nice," Saif responded. He closed the laptop and turned his attention to his fellow officer.

Abdul Aziz had brought a couple of local NCOs with him. They looked a bit suspect to Saif. Their uniforms were fairly casual, and their personal grooming could have been improved.

"And I bet she's good in bed, too. She'll ride him raw," said Abdul Aziz. He had a lecherous smile on his face.

"Yes, she's young and enthusiastic," Saif said.

"And such pretty eyes. Like an invitation."

"Yes, she's pretty. But she's modest and ladylike too."

"And when she speaks, doesn't her voice stir up passion?"

"She's really nice, it's true, but I'm not sure we should be speaking like this. Who are these soldiers, Abdul Aziz?"

"Ah, these are some friendly Turks. They're officers here at the base. This is Lieutenant Tanzer and Lieutenant Kasim."

The two soldiers nodded their respect to Saif.

"Well, good luck to him tonight in bed," said Abdul Aziz.

"Hopefully Malik's heart will hold out. And other parts of him. Come with us, Captain. I've got a jug of wine, and these two Turkish soldiers want to drink a toast to the old dog."

"Not tonight, Abdul Aziz. I'm not much of a drinker. And I've got this stup—challenging report to finish. I need to focus on this, but thank you for the offer."

"Oh, come join the men. They already see you as a stuck-up American."

The two Turkish officers sniggered.

"Spending some time with them will gain you some respect," Abdul Aziz continued. "Just one glass. I'll do most of the drinking for you." He gave the young officer a punch on the shoulder.

"I should really focus on my work," said Saif. "I've got to get it finished tonight."

"What are you talking about, man? Tonight is for celebrating. The men are waiting."

"Oh, all right. I'll have one, and one only."

Saif rose from the table and the men walked back out to the party, which was in full swing. Abdul Aziz winked to Kasim as they walked past.

"I'll do it, but I don't like it," said Saif.

"No need to get too uptight. I'm sure I can find you a light Budweiser, an Efes, or a horrible Fosters. Leave it to me. I'll get you something not too strong."

Abdul Aziz sauntered off to the makeshift bar and ordered some drinks. He returned with a handful of cans. "Have a Fosters. Australia is known for its beer. I've got you a glass. Officers should not drink out of cans."

Kasim cracked open a can and passed it to Abdul Aziz. He poured the drink into a large glass, and surreptitiously slipped a small tablet into the foaming liquid. The head of the beer frothed excessively and ended up so high that no barman would have owned up to the appalling pour.

"How big are these glasses?" Saif asked. "I only wanted a small drink."

Abdul Aziz passed Saif the frothy glass. "See?" he said. "It doesn't even take up all the glass."

Saif took a sip from the large glass. Some men nearby cheered and one slapped him on the back.

Saif frowned and peered into the glass. "It's awful. Do Australians really drink this stuff?"

"No, not that I've seen. It seems to be a practical joke from them to the rest of the world."

Saif took another sip and grimaced. "I prefer Buds from when I was in America."

Kasim leant over to Abdul Aziz. "What was the pill?" he asked.

"It was a terexal," Abdul Aziz whispered. "By the time he gets to the bottom of the glass he'll be as argumentative and eager to fight as a little dog. And he'll look incredibly drunk to everyone."

Abdul Aziz kept the stewards busy making sure that each man had a full glass all the time. He needed to do something while Saif was drinking, to allow time for the tablet to take effect. He climbed up on a table and shouted to the assembled men until he got their attention.

"We're all having a drink, having a laugh," he said, and the crowd roared its appreciation. "A good time, right?" He paused then bellowed, "That's why the West must die."

There was silence.

"I was just joking," said Abdul Aziz. "As you were, men."

Noise roared in to fill the sudden silence vacuum.

"Let me make this totally clear so there can be no misunderstanding," said Abdul Aziz. "There will not, under any circumstances, be any singing at all. And especially no dancing. We all know what happened last time Kasim danced. They still talk about it in the wastelands of the Russian steppes. So, Kasim, there will be no dancing. All right?"

Kasim raised his glass and nodded. The men cheered. From the corner of the room, a young soldier appeared with an oud. He was strumming a popular singalong song designed for men of a rowdy nature.

"Remember, everyone," said Abdul Aziz. "No singing. Or dancing."

He led the crowd of men through the bawdy song. They all sang along, but as they didn't know the song that well each man sang his own line and his own tune, until it got to the chorus, when there was a loud cacophony of expletives and innuendo.

"That's enough, you bunch of reprobates."

The men cheered.

Abdul Aziz raised his glass to the men, took several large mouthfuls to further cheering, bowed and stepped down from the table. The crowd turned inwards and the men dissolved into their personal groups, taking blurry, low-resolution photos of each other on their cell phones.

"Nice song," said Saif. "That would be banned in America. You can't be rude about any race or gender without express written permission from those who you wish to insult."

"I learned it in England, where they have a talent for drinking and singing when things have gone well," Abdul Aziz explained. "And fighting when things go wrong. Or well, too."

"It sounds more like a rugby song than a military one," Saif said, holding his head in his hands. "My head feels very light."

He sat down on a trestle table. "I must stop this drinking and get back to my work. Gentlemen, thank you for the drink. I hope you have a very enjoyable evening. I need to leave now. I don't want anyone thinking I'm drunk. That would be such a disgrace on my rank and country. This is my right hand, and this is my left hand. I'm not drunk. I can stand well enough, and I can speak just fine. Do I appear drunk?" He looked imploringly at Tanzer.

"You're fine," Tanzer said. He appeared slightly more respectable than either Kasim or Abdul Aziz, so there was an added level of believability to his statement.

"Yes, thank you. So don't think that I'm drunk, because I've only had one drunk, er, drink. I really don't feel well. I'd better go …" Saif lurched a little awkwardly off to the latrine.

"I'm off to the comms room to confirm all is still quiet," said Abdul Aziz. "The men might like a show of appreciation up there. Tanzer, come with me." He signaled his fellow solider to follow. "They'd definitely like to see an old war dog like you up there. You can regale them with some of your old stories."

The two officers strolled out of the rowdy mess hall.

"Did you see the young officer who just left?" Abdul Aziz asked Tanzer.

"He's new, isn't he? The West Point graduate you were talking about?"

"Saif's a good soldier, good enough to be the emir's right-hand man. But he has a serious weakness. It's too bad. I'm worried that Malik trusts him too much, and it'll be bad for Qatar eventually."

"Is he often like that?"

"He drinks like this every night before he goes to sleep. He'd stay up all night and all day if he didn't drink himself to sleep."

"We should tell him," said Tanzer. "He clearly looks out of control, which is against Malik's direct orders. Maybe Malik's good nature stops him from seeing it, and focuses on Saif's virtues rather than those aspects that could draw controversy. *We* wouldn't be allowed to act like that."

CHAPTER 27

TUB THUMPING

Saif returned from the latrine. He glanced around, looking for Abdul Aziz and the others. He saw Kasim and made his way over. Kasim looked him up and down, with his contempt clearly visible.

"Do you know where the others are?" Saif asked.

"Leave me alone, drunken fool," Kasim said.

"Drunk! I'm no such thing. I've only had one drink."

"One drink. Hah! A child could drink more than you and still be more sober. You cannot hold your liquor, officer." Kasim gave Saif a subtle push. No one else saw it.

"Hey, don't push me."

"I didn't touch him," Kasim said to the watching men. "Don't blame me if you can't stand up straight," he said to Saif.

"What's going on? My head feels so strange. I don't like this, appearing like a fool."

"What did you call me?" Kasmin leapt up from his seat and stood several inches away. He raised his voice so all those nearby could clearly hear him. "I asked you what you called me."

"I didn't call you anything. Please just back down." Saif pushed him away.

"How dare you push me," Kasim shouted. "You are guests on our soil."

Everyone turned to look.

Saif pushed Kasim away again. Kasim fell over theatrically, crashing into a trestle table and scattering glasses over the floor. Several men formed a circle around the two men.

"Right, that's it," said Kasim. "You are no guest of mine."

Kasim took a swing at Saif, who was incapable of blocking the punch and it landed on his jaw. Saif spun around and fell on to his hands and knees.

"He dares to fight me," said Kasim, "yet he fights like a girl. Is this what they teach you in America? Did you only learn with the ladies rather than the real men of war?"

Saif was furious. He jumped up to his feet and swung wildly.

Kasim moved in close and blocked. "I bet your mother taught you how to fight," he whispered. "Did she fight when you slept with her? Because she didn't when I did."

Saif went crimson with rage. Kasim dropped his guard, as agreed, and Saif's punch landed on his chin. Kasim dropped theatrically to the floor, appearing to be unconscious. Saif's shocked expression was quickly replaced by a horrified one as he looked at his hands and the fallen officer on the floor.

Abdul Aziz rushed into the room and stepped into the situation.

"People let's be calm about this," he said. "Obviously our young recruit is a little worse for wear. I deeply apologize on his and our behalf, and hope that you can be gracious enough to allow this minor disagreement to be forgotten. He will be disciplined accordingly. Kasim, can you forgive us?"

He extended his hand and glared at the man. Kasim took the hand and Abdul Aziz lifted him up.

"All right," said Kasim. "But I'll expect a full apology when he can remember who he is, or was."

. . .

"Saif, how could you do this? You of all people." Malik paced around his office. He had been woken by a junior soldier and been summoned to deal with the situation.

"Sir, I'm so sorry," said Saif, "but I promise you it was only one drink. One glass, and that was all. I've never behaved that way before. And the things Kasim was saying were obscene."

"But everyone says you started it. You were pushing him around. You took a swing at him. There's only one thing I can do. And I am so furious. You're our shining light for the future and you've let me down badly. I could smooth the ruffled Turkish feathers, but I personally feel you should be taught a very severe lesson. My disappointment runs deep. You are hereby taken off active duty. You are to return to Qatar immediately, and to take the rank of sergeant."

Saif's face fell.

"I'm sorry," Malik said. "Actually, I'm not sorry. I'm furious. Furious with you, and with myself. I've obviously misjudged your ability and responsibility."

Saif lowered his head in shame.

"Go and pack your things, and check in with admin to arrange the first flight back to Doha. You are dismissed."

Saif saluted, turned and left the room. He closed the door behind him but held on to the door handle. He paused and his shoulders briefly shook. He released the door handle and dejectedly made his way back to his quarters.

From the shadows Abdul Aziz watched him walk away. He took his cell out of his pocket. He flicked through the recent texts. He had received a message from one of his less scrupulous men, stating that Elissa was in the officers' garden.

He made his way through the complex to the gardens in search of her. He slowed his walk to an easy stroll. He put his hands in his pockets and a look of thoughtful concern on his face. He wandered among the manicured walks until he found her.

"Abdul Aziz," she exclaimed.

"Why, young Elissa. What a surprise finding you here. You look sad. Is everything all right?"

"Malik seems cross at something. When he's not happy I feel like I'm not performing my duties correctly."

Abdul Aziz leaned against the wall, extracted a cigarette from his top pocket, lit it and puffed serenely on it. "I assume you haven't heard the latest news." He paused and looked over at her. "Saif was caught up in an altercation with a local NCO. That's why he's angry. It's nothing to do with you."

"OMG." She placed her hands dramatically on each side of her face. "I can't believe it. Saif, in a fight. Poor Saif."

"I'm not too sure who this NCO is, but I think he's a bit untrustworthy and a troublemaker, and Saif has been a little hard done by. He is young. You know what it's like when people won't see you for the adult you are. Maybe you can say something to Malik. Yes, he is young, but we all need the occasional second chance."

"I don't know, I don't think I should get involved."

"We should all do what we can to help solve this situation. If you talk to Malik and get him to change his mind, I'm certain he'll be happy again."

"You think so?" She looked expectantly up at the old soldier.

"I am certain." He smiled at her.

"Okay."

Elissa knocked and entered the room. She bowed her head and spoke softly. "Malik, is it true? Are you sending Saif home?"

"Yes, I'm very unhappy about the situation, and I feel betrayed by him." He was brisk with his response until he noticed Elissa's expression and softened. "Of all people, and of all places."

"But are you not being a little rash? Surely, in all your stories I've heard of similar situations. And this never happened to you. Your superior always stood by you, even if the facts were a little confused. Maybe rethink it, for me. Saif is one of us."

"All right, give me some time. He still needs to go back home. But maybe I have over reacted. I don't know this Kasim. He could be a troublemaker, and he seems to have disappeared, which is highly suspicious. Maybe I should get Abdul Aziz to look into it. I'm sure he can ferret out the truth."

"Oh, thank you, Malik. I believe you've made a wise decision." She kissed him and went out to text her three hundred and fifty friends about the excitement of the last hour. There weren't enough emoticons to express how she felt. She considered repeating some of them a dozen times or so.

Abdul Aziz knocked on Malik's door and entered. He marched into the room and saluted.

"Abdul Aziz, at ease. At last a sensible head to talk to. I had forgotten how emotional the young are."

"I'm sure you have it all under control now, like the true commander you are."

"Yes, well, I've been persuaded to rethink my reactions. How well do you know this Kasim?"

"For quite some years."

"Has he ever been a troublemaker? Is there any way he could have caused this deliberately?"

"Well, anything is possible. I haven't heard of him causing trouble before, but there's always a first time." He paused. "I'm sure you know best, Commander."

"What are you implying?"

"Well, why are you changing your mind?"

"Elissa persuaded me to reassess."

"Oh."

"You look concerned. Tell me your thoughts."

"Elissa was talking about Saif a lot. She seemed very keen to talk to you about him. Did they … know each other before?"

"No. Why?"

"Oh, it's probably nothing. She was talking rather … affectionately about him. I thought they might have had some … young romance in the past. As I said, it's nothing to worry about. I'm probably reading too much into things. You know how it is with the youngsters."

"I think perhaps we should all go home."

CHAPTER 28

RUNAWAY

The windows were rolled down and we were both singing "Daisy, Daisy" loudly. The car was swinging from one side of the road to the other, with the headlights dancing through the dusty fog. The visibility was marginally better, but Damien assured me the worst of it was not over, and there was a second, even bigger wave due through later tomorrow. Until then, the sky would remain heavy and vision low while the dust and sand hung in the air, slowly settling down over everything and into everywhere.

"The sand destroys everything," he said. "And what it don't destroy it reclaims. The wind roars in like the breath of the gods and unsettles the sand lying in its ancient bed. In these desert countries, it makes the sand dunes creep over the desert, burying everything— *everything*—in their path. And it's all lost forever, and from out that shadow that lies floating on the floor, shall be lifted ..." he paused and looked at me.

"All right, you can say it. But only this once."

And we both chorused "Nevermore!"

He both howled with laughter, perhaps me even more so.

There was a beep from underneath the passenger seat. Damien fished around and extracted the culprit.

"My phone," I cheeped.

He flicked it open. "On its last legs. Ain't gonna last the night."

"Crap. I can't recharge it. I've only got the car charger, which is back in my case."

"I got a survival tip for you. If you got a dead battery and need to make a call you can use either a pear-tree leaf or a piece of paper, dependin' where you're abandoned. Neither is gonna give you much time, maybe a minute or two at best, but that might be enough one day."

"I'm guessing the pear leaf has some kind of high electrolyte content," I said, "but how's the paper going to put power into a cell battery?"

"All phones have a tiny battery for remembering the time and date and numbers. Take the battery out and cover the center pin with a piece of paper, but leave it sticking out the side. Put the battery back in. The system will short, transferring the power from the tiny battery to your cell battery. Pull out the paper and you're operational again for two minutes. Simple."

"That is very clever and technical for an artist."

I woke with a start. I caught the dying echoes of what sounded like metal being dragged over something hard. It reminded me of the sound my father made when sharpening his axe. There was always wood needing chopping, or chickens to be sacrificed to the great god of chicken sandwiches in the sky.

I was really tired; you could even say weak and weary. It had been a good night, and it hadn't ended in disaster. I took a quick look out the window. The night was dreary and it was well after midnight. Sun will probably be coming up soon, I thought.

I picked up the Lonely Planet guide to forgotten places and flicked through its pages. There was a loud thump outside my door, followed by heavy footsteps. It startled me. Then there was a loud bang outside the door, and the sound of footsteps receding.

Just some visitor, I thought, Damien, probably, on his way to the toilet.

Again, there was that scraping sound, metal on rock.

The room had cooled considerably during the early-morning hours, and I felt a chill for the first time in a week. The wind was beginning to pick up again outside. A big gust rolled by, and the sad, cheap curtains flapped in my face.

I had a bad feeling about this. I could feel my heartbeat beginning to race, so I repeated to myself that it was Damien. After all those drinks, he was tripping over and knocking against the door. That's all it was, and nothing more.

I stood up and paced to the door. I stared at it long and hard, wondering, fearing dark places in unknown countries. My mind was full of dark visions of tourists taken in the night by murderers too crazy to be in their own country, so they had come to a place where the heat and humidity would eventually drive everyone insane.

And now here I was, defenseless. And the silence lay unbroken, and the darkness gave no token. So I whispered to the darkness that lay beyond the door, "Damien." And an echo murmured it back, merely this and nothing more.

I turned my back to my door, with my imagination populating every dark corner with danger, and tried to settle my nerves. But, soon again, I heard the scraping sound, somewhat louder than before. Surely, I thought, It's coming from outside. The rusted sign on the post outside—that wasn't in here.

I glanced through the window once more to see if I could spot anything that could be making the mysterious sound. It was just the wind, as Damien had said, that blows forever more.

But there was no rusted sign swinging in the growing breeze. There was no sign of life out there, no rustling in the trees. There were no trees. I turned my back to the window, with the dread fear I had to face when I stepped out into the darkness of the corridor.

I opened the door and looked out into the corridor. It was empty.

I stepped out to get a better look down the dark passage. Behind me the door creaked and closed. I turned slowly. There was Ash, with a demented look on his face. In his hand was an axe. I couldn't help but notice that the edge, although very sharp, had bloodstains on it.

He swung, and I fell back, falling to the floor. The axe narrowly missed me and lodged itself into the wall. My senses seized the moment to catch up with events and I screamed. This appeared to enrage Ash. I scrambled to my feet and ran down the corridor. I was heading into a dead end.

A door opened and Damien appeared.

"Damien! Help me, *please*."

He was groggy and didn't see the axe coming. The side of the blade hit him in the head, and he collapsed straight to the floor. Blood instantly started pooling under his head.

Ash took another swing at me and the blade lodged into the door frame. As Ash turned sideways to wrench out the blade, I kicked at his leg. He went down on one knee and I took the opportunity to jump past him. For the first time he shouted as I disappeared down the stairs.

Those fricken stairs. I tripped and fell against the wall. I tumbled to the bottom, my head crashing into the wall, dazing me.

There was a hand around my wrist. "I got you, you harlot."

Harlot? Who says that anymore? My eyes focused and saw that it was Cheryl who had grabbed me. Hah, she can talk. I'll show her skinny teenage ass who's boss.

I kicked her knee, and she squealed and dropped to the floor, releasing me from her clutches. While she was down I kicked again into her head. It crashed into the opposite wall. I heard a shout from the top of the stairs. Ash said a whole lot worse than "harlot," and charged down.

I scrambled for the door, but it was locked and barred. Ash grabbed me from behind and flung me into the kitchen. I tumbled across the floor and crashed into the table and chairs, which scattered around the room. He ran in after me and swung down wildly. I rolled to the side and the axe swung past me and bounced off the floor.

He took aim again, but I was able to grasp a chair and swing it up to meet the axe midway. The axe bounced off the wood and clattered away over the floorboards. I clambered up from my knees and staggered toward the doorway. Ash grabbed my belt, hauled me back around, and I crashed into the old sink.

There was a chair next to my feet, and I lunged to pick it up. In one fluent movement Ash swooped down, picked up the axe and swung it down toward me. He narrowly missed me and the axe connected with the faucet, severing it from the wall. Water and mud sprayed over us.

I brought the chair around in a wide arc and managed to break it over Ash's head, knocking off his stupid cap. I noticed he had a huge bald patch, which he had been hiding. Busted!

He swayed and brought the axe in from the side. It hit my hand, and as the pain washed through my arms I dropped the chair. He had me backed into the corner, and there was no escape.

Cheryl turned on the light and came into the room. "Did you miss me, honey?" she hissed to Ash. She had blood on the side of her head, and her hair was matted.

"Aw, honey, are you okay?" he purred.

"Ain't got nothing that won't heal." Her voice was hoarse and strangely ancient.

Blood was trickling down his face. Cheryl noticed, and lapped it up in a long sensual lick, all the while staring at me.

"You didn't just … lick his face? Erg! Do you need the salt?"

She lifted up a set of handcuffs and swung them on her finger. "Let's lock her up in the basement out back with what's left of the others. I cleared some space for them and their parts when you sent them on that stupid diversion," she rasped. "I can't believe they was stupid enough. Let's chop 'em up slow."

"Nah. This one will just die, right here."

Ash wrapped his left hand around my throat and started to squeeze. He raised the axe above his head. There was a series of loud explosions. The wall next to me erupted and shards of wood flew everywhere. And there was blood.

Cheryl collapsed to the floor. Ash was distracted and looked down at his fallen angel. She was riddled with bullet holes. I kicked as hard as I could into his groin, and he let out a groan. His eyes crossed but he didn't let go. He didn't even flinch. Then there were men everywhere. The small room was full of military-looking guys with their heads wrapped in smaghs. All brandishing machine guns.

And they shot him. Just like that. One shot. No warning. He lay there as still as a corpse. The men leveled their machine guns at me. The only thing I could think to do was raise my hands slowly in the air. I stood there trembling, too scared to cry.

There were three in all, two smallish men and one huge one. The small, heavyset one at the front signaled with his gun for me to move to the doorway. I followed the instruction and made my way slowly out to the front room. The front door was open and outside there was a beat-up old four-wheel drive. Its engine was off but its headlights were on, and dimming in the night air.

The leader signaled for me to go outside. I hoped they didn't want to shoot me out there.

I stepped outside into the cool early morning. The others followed closely behind me.

Damien jumped out from behind the building. He charged and, wrapping his arms around the close-knit group, brought them to the ground. He started to swing a thick piece of wood into the men.

"Run, Ellen, run," he hollered.

I ran. I jumped into the rental. I fished out my keys, rammed them into the ignition, and fired the engine into life. I prepared to reverse the car into the men, to try and save Damien. But as I looked over my shoulder I saw one of them stand up and shoot Damien. His last word had been "Run."

I floored the gas pedal, and the rental, spraying sand and gravel over the men behind me, shot off toward the road. The horrible and bloodied apparition of Ash appeared in my headlights. I swung the wheel around violently, trying to avoid him. There was a thud from the passenger side of the car and I lost control.

The car spun around, flinging me sideways. My head crashed into the side pillion, stunning me. There was loud shouting behind me. I was disorientated, but managed to turn the car around and pressed the gas pedal again. The car lurched off down the road. I kept the pedal pressed hard down until my hands stopped shaking.

I couldn't see any lights behind me so my heart rate eased up, and sweat stopped gushing off my head into my eyes. And the sun rose before me.

I watched the sun slowly toil its way into the early morning sky as I sped across the landscape. I saw a sign indicating the Pamukkale hot springs. A tourist spot should mean people. Even if it was too early in the day for it to be open, surely someone would be there.

I pulled the car into the parking lot. I was the only one around, which was a bit of a shock. I had been hoping for someone, anyone, to be there, perhaps some crazy nature lover or Greenpeace freedom fighter who happened to carry an Uzi. This was one of the big tourist attractions. That meant people, and that meant safety.

Maybe it wasn't peak tourist season, I thought, but I couldn't drive on blindly forever; I needed to find someone else, some help. I needed height.

I grabbed my water bottle, and started the trek to the pools. There was a dusty, fading sign that informed visitors to the springs that the pools were white due to the calcium deposited by the waters, and people could bathe in the warm waters, which were once believed to have healing properties. Allegedly. I could sure use them now.

It was eerie being on my own. I hiked up the hills to the pools. It wasn't long before the sweat was beginning to form on my skin. At the high point I surveyed the panorama, looking for signs of life. There was no one for miles. The wind was blowing gently. I held out my arms, momentarily closed my eyes and cooled in the breeze. I took a couple of deep breaths to quiet my mind. That's when I heard the clicking of the guns.

Oh no, not again.

Someone grabbed me from behind and tried to force a bag over my head. I twisted away and kicked out, hoping to hurt something. I made contact, which was followed by some swearing. I quickly looked over my shoulder to see who my attackers were. There were two men from before, still with their heads concealed by checkered *smaghs*.

I ran across the rocky surface and dived behind a large collection of boulders. I knew they had guns, but I questioned whether they were prepared to use them. I guess it was all about what they wanted from me. Living hostages would get ransom. Dead ones, not so much. Even if they wanted to do one of those horrific Internet executions, they still needed me alive. I was going to go with the odds.

I jumped up and ran for it. The car was only a hundred yards away, and in the fog it would be hard to see me clearly. There was shouting, and there was shooting, which abruptly stopped.

I opened up the car door and jumped in. I fumbled with the keys, but managed to recover and slot them into the ignition. I started the car and put it in gear.

There was movement to my left, and the driver's window shattered. The attacker had smashed the butt of his machine gun through. The glass cascaded over me. He wheeled around and pointed the gun at me. I raised my shaking hands. He signaled for me to get out. I could only wonder what they wanted. If it was just money, then they had come to the right person. I'd give them everything, maybe even the penthouse overlooking the bay.

The man wrenched the door open and signaled for me to get out. I slowly extracted myself from the car. The man was huge and towered above me. He motioned for me to walk down to the road. There was the beat-up four-wheel drive, idling, with no one in it. Behind was another vehicle, a very new, black dual cab. It was running, too. The windows were up and I couldn't see who was inside.

My captor slung his gun over his shoulder, grabbed a piece of rope from the floor of the car, and tied my hands behind my back. He signaled for me to get into the back of the four-wheel drive.

The other two men arrived from the pools.

One man, the short stocky one, went over to the black truck. The other two stayed by me, watching me intently. The window slid down with motorized ease. I couldn't make out the man inside.

There was a quick exchange of words and the stocky man nodded. The hidden driver passed something out to the stocky man, who accepted it. He looked around to see if anyone was looking, then placed it in his pocket. The window slid back up, and the black vehicle gently purred away down the road.

The short man next to me watched me observing the others. "You don't seem scared," he said. He had a young voice.

"I'm used to it," I glibly replied.

The comment seemed to throw him, but only momentarily. "We'll give you something you're not used to. Welcome to Iran."

And in the dual cab, the dark man with the dark heart picked up his cell and dialed.

"It is done," he said.

Abdul Aziz was watching the Al Jazeera news. It had a late-breaking story on an American that had been kidnapped in Iran. The captors were making outrageous claims and demands. He smiled then turned off the display. The phone rang and he answered it.

"Abdul Aziz, who have you got involved in this situation?" came a terrified voice down the line. It was Sheikh Green, or Sheikh Aktah al-Jennah, as he was known when not hiding behind a mask. "They're madmen. They'll kill her. They've put her up on the Internet with a ransom of one hundred million dollars."

"What does it matter? Another loud-mouthed American gone. Who will miss her?"

"But this is murder and terrorism. We—well, I—didn't agree to any of this."

"Hold your courage. You have so much to gain. Isn't it all worth it for just one life of a person you've never known?"

"I'm very uncomfortable about this. I'd like to talk to the others to gauge their opinion."

"You will not do this."

"Don't tell me what to do. I am a sheikh."

"I know this. I also know where you live, where your children live, and where your wealth lies."

"Are you threatening me?"

"Yes, and you should be scared. I have men very close to you who only need a word from me to execute you and your family. Don't think for one moment that I didn't expect this from you and didn't plan for it. I've had people infiltrating your security for months. All of you are only as safe as I will let you be. And don't get any ideas about killing me either. If my men don't hear from me on a regular basis, they have their orders to exact revenge."

CHAPTER 29

WE ALL FALL DOWN

A bdul Aziz made his way toward Elissa's quarters. He had his usual array of locksmith's tools secreted in his pockets, and was going through the various possible items he could get his hands on for his plan to work. He needed something personal and important. He got to the door and saw it was ajar. He knew Elissa was out. He wondered who was in the room. His hand hesitated over the door handle.

Najla looked at the necklace. It was beautiful and undoubtedly cost tens of thousands. She stroked her hand over the ornate design. It had been a gift from Malik to Elissa, who always wore it. When she didn't it was locked away. It symbolized so much to both Malik and Elissa, such a simple thing that conveyed so much emotion and commitment. And on this rare occasion Elissa had left it out. Someone should put it back.

Najla picked it up and the gold called out to her.

She would borrow it, momentarily, to see how it felt. There couldn't be any harm in that. Just for a moment. She was sure that if Elissa had been here she would approve.

It must be wonderful to have a man who loved you so much he

wouldn't even pause to buy something so beautiful, she thought. There was a mirror next door. She went to her anteroom with the oversized Victorian mirror.

"Wife," Abdul Aziz commanded, "what are you doing here?"

"What are you doing here?" The confrontation startled her.

"It's none of your business."

"Well, this is none of your business." Najla placed the necklace behind her back.

"Everything you do is my business, especially if it involves you and a credit card."

"You handing over your precious credit card—that would be a first, offering up something so personally important."

"Woman, tell me what you're carrying." Abdul Aziz stood up and confronted his wife.

"Malik wants to have the necklace he gave to Elissa polished, so it will be ready for the awards presentation."

Abdul Aziz's eyes gleamed in the light. The cogs in his mind whirred as he suddenly saw an opportunity. "Why are you sneaking out with it?"

"I'm not sneaking out. I'm getting it past you and your interfering nose, as big as it is."

"As is your body, crone."

"Fool."

"Why didn't Malik ask me to do that?"

"He undoubtedly wanted it *done*, rather than forgotten about as soon as you got a phone call and were instantly distracted."

"Give it to me. I will do it."

"No. It's my responsibility."

"You know nothing of gold and jewels."

"This is true, as you have never bought me any. The only chance I get to see precious items is with friends. Then I feel like the pauper because you're too mean to dip your short fingers into your bottomless wallet."

"I don't waste money on frivolous items. There's a future to plan for. And if there's any justice in this world it will be without you."

"I often wish for the same."

"Give me the necklace."

She stared back, but reluctantly handed over the shining item. Abdul Aziz turned and left the room. Najla sat on her couch and stared vacantly at the wall, too numb to cry.

He sprinted across the courtyard. He couldn't believe his luck. He had been prepared to break into the safe to steal something like the necklace, but his foolish wife had saved him the time and effort, and handed it to him. Now time was of the essence.

Saif was being dressed down, first in front of the senior officers then with various government officials. It would give him ten to fifteen minutes to accomplish his task. Saif would undoubtedly feel sorry for himself and head straight back to his quarters. He hoped that Western harlot who was masquerading as a reputable woman would be there to console him. Then the deck of cards would fall.

Abdul Aziz wound his way through the various officers' quarters until he found Saif's. He took out a small toolkit consisting of various picks and keys. He tried a couple until he found a reasonable match, then fiddled until the key was fitting snuggly into the lock. The lock clicked into place on his second attempt and he opened the door.

The room was full of Americana memorabilia, with many pictures of Saif and his friends at famous monuments. He noticed one of Britney and Saif embracing in front of Abraham Lincoln by his bed, both with smiles threatening to stretch beyond their faces. He laid it face down and dropped the necklace under the bed.

His phone vibrated. He checked the display. Malik had summoned him.

He backed out of the room, making sure no one was watching, and ran back across the courtyard to Malik's office. He knocked, entered and saluted his superior.

"Abdul Aziz," Malik said when he entered the room. "I've been thinking about Elissa and … this Saif issue. Although I regret this process, I fear you may have a point. If only we could get him to confess one way or another. Of course, it goes without saying that I wish this to be a big misunderstanding. This whole incident is giving me a headache." He rubbed his temples. "It's enough to give me a seizure."

"I think I can get an answer for you, sir."

"Are you sure? It would be good to be able to put the issue to rest, if only in my own mind."

"I'll engage him in conversation. I'll call you and steer the discussion to the subject with you listening in. I'll then ask him the appropriate questions. With you not being there, I believe he'll be honest. Especially with me and my training."

"You want me to spy?"

"If it gets the result and eases your mind," said Abdul Aziz, "won't that be worth it?"

"Fine. But never tell another soul."

"If I go now, I believe I can intercept him after the meeting with the government officials, sir."

"Fine. Go. I'll await your call."

Abdul Aziz saluted, turned and marched out of the room. He ran across the courtyard again to the mission-debrief room. He paused to catch his breath. He listened at the door and heard the dull drone of politicians talking. He waited until the meeting concluded then moved to the side of the building out of sight. He watched the politicians leave and saw Saif dejectedly wander out behind them.

Abdul Aziz casually sauntered out from behind the building, placed a concerned expression on his face, and called out to Saif. "Captain Saif, you look distraught."

"Don't call me that. I don't feel worthy of the title at the moment. All in all, it's been a bad day."

"Come to the officers' mess. We can have a drink and you can cool your heels for a moment. Things won't seem so bad, given a bit of time."

The men entered the mess and sat at an empty table. Abdul Aziz placed his cell on the table, along with a selection of objects from his pockets. He snapped his fingers and a waiter mystically appeared from the shadows. He ordered two coffees. The waiter nodded and disappeared into the background.

Abdul Aziz subtly checked that Malik's number was selected and pressed his dial button.

"I wish I had your optimism for the future," said Saif. "I feel it'll take a very long time to recover from this setback. The other senior officers may never have complete trust in me again."

"I don't think you need to panic. I think some praise should be given to Elissa, who managed to persuade Malik to change his mind. Maybe you should spend some more time with her to give her some incentive."

Abdul Aziz rustled his keys next to the phone and lowered his voice. "If it was Britney, it would all be resolved by now." He stopped fiddling with his keys and winked.

Saif laughed. The waiter reappeared with the drinks. He took a sip from his cup and grimaced.

"Why can't we get a cappuccino machine?" said Abdul Aziz. "It's the officers' mess. There should be some standards. I can see that she's really fallen for you."

"Poor girl, I think she's fallen in love."

"Has she used the M-word?"

"Mortgage? Monopoly? Misogynistic bastard?"

"No, marriage. I think I've heard her say it. Do you think you will marry her?"

Saif laughed. "I don't think so. She isn't the right one. She's so intense. She's fun for the moment, but she's a typical soldier's wife. I can tell you that she gets up to all sorts of mischief in bed. I just can't see her being suitable for raising my children."

"I'm sure I've heard a rumor that she has said this."

"It would be her who started the rumor. I mean, she's nice and everything, and great in bed, but, well, she's so obsessive and needy at times. But for me she serves a need. It's a horrible thing to say, but I believe it's the truth."

"She's not all that bad, and there are certainly a lot worse. Don't be too hasty with your decision. You can be certain of one thing— she will support you now, when you need it the most."

"Abdul Aziz, again you are correct. You are a voice of reason amongst the maelstrom."

"Will you call her now? She may make you feel better."

"Maybe. I'll go back to my quarters and try and get my head straight."

"A wise idea."

Both men finished their coffee. Saif got up and nodded to Abdul Aziz.

Abdul Aziz watched him walk away until he was out of sight. He picked up his phone. "Malik, sir, are you there? I believe you have your answer. I am sorry."

The prime minister had returned to his office. The view over the Corniche and the bay was exceptional, but the monolith of paperwork on his desk blocked the view, depressing him. He wondered if he could outsource it to the subcontinent. He sat down, put on his reading glasses, and started from the top.

After half an hour the pile had shrunk by an inch, and the coffee machine had been working overtime. There was a knock on his office door. It hushed open over the thick carpet and his personal assistant, Rashid, entered.

"Prime Minister, sir, we have had news from Hammad Hospital. The first minister has been rushed there after a heart attack."

"Will he be all right?" The prime minister lowered his glasses and looked up from his immense piles of paperwork.

"He was in a meeting with some Westerners who called an ambulance straight away. It's touch and go. The car crash certainly weakened him. We can only hope he pulls through."

"Lucky he wasn't amongst his brethren. They would've let him die and claimed it was Allah's way. Then taken his wallet. How long will it be until he can resume his duties?"

Rashid hesitated. "It may be some time."

"Are you saying that we could take this opportunity to appoint a younger, and highly skilled, person who may take the chance to learn and contribute?"

"The opportunity has presented itself, sir. I leave the decision to you. But who would you choose?"

The prime minster smiled. He took out his phone and scrolled through the unending list of senior cabinet members.

"What we need, I believe, is some new blood. Someone with new ideas, who may even have been trained overseas. Not some old stalwart from the old families who refuses to see opportunity in change. And as it happens, I was publicly being disappointed with such a young man earlier today. Let's see if he's available." He typed a series of letters understandable only to the initiated and pressed Send. "I do hope he has some time available for us."

Saif opened the door to his quarters, and he and Britney stepped into his domain.

"Thanks for coming over, Britney. Today's been a very bad day, so your friendship is welcome."

"Abdul Aziz called me. He said you might need some support."

"He's a kind man. I feel I've misjudged him all this time."

"I'll take your mind off your troubles."

She ran her hands around to his back. She held him tightly and wrapped her legs around him. She gave him a passionate kiss. She put her legs down and rubbed her groin against his.

"You've been away a week," she said, "and baby is desperate for some lovin'. Things other than the heart have grown hungry while you've been away."

She turned and sauntered toward his bed. "Your place always reminds me of a college dorm. Remember the things we used to do in that room? All you need is a big US flag behind your bed. Or some football pennants."

"That wouldn't be allowed."

"But it would be funny."

"Not really."

Britney went over to the bed and jumped on it and bounced up and down. "You're not allowed to have a bed neater than mine." She rolled over and noticed the photo. "Hey, you knocked our photo over. Should I be suspicious?" She gave him a sly look.

"I don't know how that happened."

"Yeah, right. Did you bring some floozy back here and feel guilty?"

She giggled and placed it back upright. Light bounced off the glass and reflected off something under the bed.

"What's this?" She reached down and picked up the ornate necklace. "What the hell is this?" She sat upright and stared at the mass of jewels. "I know who this belongs to. What's it doing here?"

"I don't know how it got here."

"Well, it didn't just walk in on its own, did it?"

"You must believe me. I promise I don't know how it got here."

"This is Elissa's. There's no way she would be separated from it. Either you stole it or she left it here. So what was she doing in your bedroom? And why was our picture down?"

"I don't have an answer for you."

"I know you guys have a reputation, but I thought you were different."

Saif's phone beeped. He flicked it open to look at the message. He went pale. "I've been summoned to present myself to the prime minister. I have to go."

"Of course you do. You always have to go." She let the sarcasm sink into his conscience.

"I promise I don't know how it got here, and I'll find out as soon as I get back." He turned and left.

Britney sat down and stared vacantly at the wall, too numb to cry.

CHAPTER 30

TWISTING BY THE POOL

After ten minutes, Britney's fury had driven her across the courtyard to one of the few people who she could trust. She knocked on Malik's office door.

"Come," he replied.

She entered the room and marched up to his desk.

Malik jumped up from his chair as the young lady entered. "Britney, what can I do for you? Is all okay? You don't appear to be your usual effervescent self."

"Malik, I'm really concerned. I found Elissa's necklace in Saif's quarters. Is there any reason why it would be there?"

"Which one?"

"Your one. The one. The fabulous one that, at all times, she is either wearing or has locked up securely. This one." She took the necklace out of her pocket and placed it on his desk.

"This is the last straw. I heard earlier today, from Saif's own mouth, that they were having an affair, and this reinforces it. They laugh at us as though we are fools."

"I can't believe it. I would be able to tell. I would be able to smell her on him. Sorry, Malik, but I need to go. If it's true, I'll, well, I'll just … I need to think about this. It's so unlike him, and I've known him for many years. There were no hints, nothing. When did he even get the time? And really, would she accidentally leave this beneath his bed? Something doesn't add up."

"To me it all adds up," said Malik. "All the evidence has come together and shows the truth."

"I need everything out of my face for the moment so I can clear my thoughts. I'm sorry to have brought you such news, Malik, especially you of all people." She turned and left, doing her best not to burst into tears.

Malik picked up his receiver and called Elissa. "You must come now," he said. His voice was void of emotion.

He paced around the room, trying to keep the images of infidelity from his mind. It seemed like everyone close to him had betrayed him. Eventually there was a knock on his door.

Elissa made her way slowly across the room, with her head bowed. "Is everything all right, Malik? You sounded distant on the phone."

"Your necklace is on the desk. Do you know how I came by it?"

"No, Malik. Did you take it out of the safe?"

"No. I did not. Maybe you asked someone to take it somewhere. To clean it or something. And they lost it perchance."

"No, I promise."

"I'll tell you where it was found. It was found in Saif's quarters under his bed. Would you tell me how it got there?"

She looked down at the sparkling object, then up at Malik, not understanding what he was asking.

"How should I know?" said Elissa. "The last time I saw it, it was in the safe. I thought it was in the safe."

"This happens after your somewhat suspicious support of Saif a few days ago."

"Suspicious? I was doing what I thought was right."

"I've heard it from his own mouth. He mocked me, while boasting of his conquest of you."

Elissa stood in front of him with a stunned expression.

"How could you do this to me?" said Malik. "I have waited my whole life to find a special partner, and within days you have betrayed me. Go back to your home. You are no longer welcome here."

"Please—"

"No more. I cannot bear to hear your voice anymore. Please, be away from me. I need you out of my space until I can decide what course of action to take."

Saif entered the office of the prime minister, who was standing looking out his window over the water, his hands clasped behind his back.

"Captain Saif, thank you for joining me. You may sit if you wish, but I'm aware you soldier types often prefer to stand. So please do whichever one makes you comfortable."

"I would prefer to stand, sir."

"So be it."

The prime minister continued to peer out of his window. "I've been reading the report from this morning," he said. "You've acted well out of character. And it seems unlikely that you would be like this after only one drink."

"I have my suspicions, sir, but I need to look into it a bit further. I feel there's someone or maybe a group that would like to see the current status quo shaken up."

"I have a suspicion too, but I can't talk about it at the moment. But things have been done that cannot be undone."

"I'm sorry, sir, that I've shamed everyone. It was never my intention. This has had repercussions that have affected every part of my life."

"At least there's been a lesson in it for you. But unfortunately there's a state punishment on top of the military one. I need to be seen to punish you."

The prime minister turned to face the young officer. "You will be my liaison with the elders of the Advisory Council. That should give you enough of a headache to either make you give up drinking completely or make you an alcoholic. Kill or cure."

Abdul Aziz was taking a moment to get his breath back. He had been charging around the barracks all morning in the heat and it was beginning to get to him. He had picked up his Land Cruiser, put the air conditioner to maximum, and gone for a drive. He had received the news about the first minister, Dr. Hassah, while driving to the Four Seasons Hotel. He had turned around instantly and driven as fast as the traffic would allow him to pick up Adnan. This was it. The moment. The motley crew of useless old men had come through on their planned actions. They had stood up and seized the day.

"Adnan, this will be your moment," Abdul Aziz said. "I hope you're prepared to accept the great responsibility that comes with the position we're about to negotiate for you. You don't need to feel worried, as you'll have many friends who'll be able to offer you advice. Now is your time to be proud, but don't forget to be gracious."

The two men strode through the security scanners. Adnan surrendered his various phones and communication devices. Abdul Aziz simply waved security aside. He strode though the great chambers until he stood before the prime minister's immense doors. He checked to make sure Adnan hadn't got lost. He braced against the doors and flung them open as dramatically as he could, and both men stepped into the prime minister's lavish office.

"Prime Minister, may I beg you for a moment of your precious time?"

"Abdul Aziz, Adnan, what an unexpected surprise. Please, let me know what brings you to my doors."

"Adnan and I were driving nearby," Abdul Aziz said, "after Adnan had delivered a magnificent speech leading to an in-depth debate with the Advisory Council on some of the finer points of international trade and diplomacy, when we were notified of the terrible news.

Obviously our deepest wishes go out to the first minister and his family for a brisk recovery, and I think I can say, on behalf of the Advisory Council elders, that we would like Adnan to assist you in any of the ministerial responsibilities. Only until the first minister is fully recovered, of course, and is able to resume his duties."

"Abdul Aziz, you are one I can always rely on to appear when there's an issue that needs to be resolved, often before I even know myself what needs to be done. Your awareness and alacrity in these issues is truly a gift. As always, I appreciate your experienced and learned assistance, and advice in times of consequence. As always, you are correct with your eloquent discourse, and I should take immediate action …" The prime minister paused.

Abdul Aziz bowed. "Once again a wise dec—" Abdul Aziz managed to get out before the prime minister resumed his sentence.

"… except that I have already decided who will be the person to provide assistance to the ministerial duties."

Abdul Aziz was momentarily speechless. "I assume your decision was made in a rational state of mind, and wasn't a spur-of-the-moment decision based upon less than substantial advice."

"I made the decision; thereby it is the best decision."

"Of course, Prime Minister, your wisdom is unquestionable. May I be so bold as to ask who the worthy apprentice is?"

The prime minister snapped his fingers and Rashid stepped forward. "Saif al-Noor," he said.

"What? How can you appoint Saif after all he has done? Adnan is here and has the support of the elders. It would be a wise and applauded appointment."

"The decision has been made and I have deemed it so."

"I have the full backing of the elders. I will appeal directly to the emir."

"Appeal as much as you feel you have to. I have the full backing of the emir. He trusts me. Do you think he trusts you?"

Abdul Aziz was furious. He tried to hide his emotion, but his masterstroke had failed. He had devised a highly risky alternative plan, but it relied on idiots doing stupid things without his apparent involvement. He ushered his pawn out the doors and slammed them behind him.

The prime minister happily watched them depart. "That, Rashid, was a lot of fun," he said. "We need to do it more often. I loved Abdul Aziz's expression just before I told him I'd already decided. Do you think Adnan understood any of it?"

"I think it will be explained to him. He may not like it."

"I can't wait for Abdul Aziz to tell the elders. I may even turn up."

"Your Eminence, is that wise? The elders will be furious and may petition the emir."

"Not all of the elders, and certainly not all members of the Advisory Council, Rashid. Do you think these little dalliances these renegade power groups orchestrate occur without my full knowledge, and some subtle support as well? Our world is what we make it, and I make it so the power rests with the right people. We guide, we suggest, we divide, and we conquer. If there's one thing we've learnt over the centuries it's how to play this game."

There was a knock from a side door.

"Come," said the prime minister.

A timid-looking elderly man came into the room. He bowed before the prime minister.

"Rashid," said the prime minister, "I present to you Sheikh Aktah al-Jennah, AKA Sheikh Green. He's been supplying us with the information as it became available."

"I knew something was wrong, Prime Minister," said Sheikh Aktah, "when Abdul Aziz wanted to hurt individuals."

"Sheikh Aktah, you have been most loyal and helpful in this matter. The emir is preparing a special tribute for you and your family for your continued support of the stability of the state. Well done, Sheikh Aktah. Well done."

Sheikh Aktah bowed, turned, and left with a broad smile.

The prime minister waited until he had closed the door. "All in all, Rashid, today has not been a bad day. I think our new Advisory Council attaché has been a good choice. His frustration will provide us with many enjoyable hours, as it won't be us dealing with them. Saif will be an interesting man to watch. The military's been good for him. He's responded well to the discipline, but I feel his future doesn't lie there. We need his more lateral thinking within our politics."

He drummed his fingers on the table, lost in thought. He took a final pass over the papers in front of him and nodded at some internal decision.

"Please, Rashid," he said, "send instruction to Saif that the emir wishes him to accept the position immediately. Maybe you could casually let Saif know great things will be expected of him, so if he could start doing great things straightaway it would be appreciated."

"Would that be an instruction, Your Eminence?"

The prime minister smiled. "No, let's see how he responds. Let's see the making of the man."

CHAPTER 31

SAVE ME

A lex, did you have any success with your ladyfriend when you got back?" Saif had entered the room quietly. He looked pale.

Alex looked up from his paperwork and out the window over the dusty vision of the city. The sun reflected off his glasses. "No, she was gone. The concierge said she'd gone away but kept the room. He assumed she'd return at some time. Why?"

"An American's been reported missing in Turkey."

"Not another one. Can't they stay out of trouble?"

"An abandoned car was found out by the Pamukkale springs with a shattered window. The police say there were signs of a struggle."

"What's this got to do with us?"

"The police traced the details of the person who hired the car, and her last destination prior to Turkey was here."

"What are you saying?" Alex took off his glasses and folded them neatly into his pocket. He rose from his seat and stretched out his back.

"The person caught by suspected Iranian terrorists, known for executing their victims, was … Ellen Martin."

Alex's face went ashen, and his head spun. He staggered back against the wall.

"I knew you'd want to know. I can see that you needed to know. The group has posted the video on their website. They've given the American authorities twenty-four hours to pay one hundred million dollars to their cause. We know what that means. I'm sorry, Alex. The situation isn't good."

"What are the chances of the Iranian government allowing us in, or helping?"

Saif shook his head. "Between you and me, as men rather than officers, I'd say your best chance is with a small covert force. Most of the communications are still down. You know anyone like that?"

"Let's get this done right now." Alex grabbed his phone and dialed his team. "We're live. Get a helo from somewhere. Johnno needs to fly it as we're going in low. And Jake on weapons. No, only the two of them. Get them together and get them to me now."

There was a low muttering coming from his phone speaker.

"I don't care if nothing is prepared, make it happen now. I'm on my way." He disconnected the call.

Alex stood staring at the wall for a few moments, his face furrowed in concentration. He dialed another number. "Jess, it's me. Ellen's been captured by Iranian terrorists."

"Yes, hello to you too, brother," said Jessie.

She floored the accelerator and her Jeep barreled forward over the icy terrain of the frozen steppe. A burst of gunfire erupted from the car in front. An errant bullet caught the windscreen, causing it to crack. She shouted to the man behind her. "Just shoot him, Sergeant. Don't let him get away."

"Sorry, Ax," she said into the phone, "I'm in the middle of something here. Ellen? The Chicago chick? For crying out loud, Alex, let them have her."

"Jess, this is important. I need you."

There was a pause.

"Sorry, Alex, the line dropped out. What did you say?"

"I need you, and stop laughing."

"Hah! I've recorded you. I'm going to use it as my ringtone."

"You're still a cowface."

"Is it off reservation?" Jessie asked.

"Yes."

"Okay, I'll pull in some favors and be there as soon as I can. Have you got a transponder out there?"

"I can get one."

"Set it to your old agency frequency. Go get your uptown girlfriend and I'll catch up."

We had driven for hours. Roads had long gone. I guess where we were going we didn't need roads. We had driven for hours, bouncing our way to this derelict set of buildings, literally in the middle of nowhere. The midday sun glared down but the sandstorm took the edge off the oppressive atmosphere.

They pulled me out of the car and led me to this sorry excuse for a house, a combination of mud, stone, and concrete, with a couple of boarded-up windows.

They pushed me inside through the old wooden door. It was heavy but old, and warping under the extreme sun. Inside it was a concrete box. No light except what managed to force its way through the cracks. Sand covered the floor. There was no furniture. Exits were few. There was only one door apart from the entrance, which seemed to lead into a tiny alcove. I was unable to see what was in there.

The short, stocky one pointed his machine gun at me and signaled to me to sit down. I sat on the floor and examined the room carefully, looking for anything that I could use to escape.

I wondered what was in that little room off to the side. It had a door, and that could give me a moment of seclusion. I tried to think of what I could do away from prying eyes.

The pressure was getting to me outside and in. The bumping along dusty tracks hadn't helped. I realized I hadn't been to the toilet

for some time, and I was getting to the point of desperation. The
men were milling around, waiting for something, by the look of it.
The leader kept checking his phone. Phone. There may be a chance.

I shouted at them, but the word "toilet" and all the derivations I
could think of seemed lost on them. In the end I settled for crossing
my legs, and jumping up and down with a pained expression on my
face.

The elder man, who probably had his own bladder issues, seemed
to understand. He spoke to the younger one, who approached me
hesitantly. He waved his gun in the direction of a small room in the
corner of the building.

The door was warped and hardened from the eternal heat, which
meant it didn't close properly. The toilet was just a hole in the ground.
Should have practiced squats more, I thought. My hands were still
tied, which was going to make things difficult. I unbuttoned my pants
and pulled them down. I pulled out my cell and quickly fumbled it
open. I rested it in my panties as I struggled to get my wallet out. I
found an old receipt.

Then, because I was about to explode, I relaxed and was hit by a
moment of bliss as my bladder emptied. I placed the receipt over the
center pin inside the phone and replaced the battery.

I wasn't sure how much time I could buy from this trip to the
bathroom, but I knew I must have been pushing the boundary. On
cue, there was a loud banging on the door. I shouted out that I was
finishing, hoping the young guard would understand.

Hissam looked at his phone. He quickly flicked through the encoded
text. Eventually, with a grave face, he turned to the others. "We
execute the woman."

"Don't we wait?" Jeneah's youthful face radiated shock.

Only Farhan looked happy.

"Some Americans are preparing to come. I would guess we don't
have much time. Maybe an hour, maybe a few. But they will come.

Who knows what they'll bring. Jeneah, go to the roof and keep a lookout for anything."

"In this weather?" said Jeneah. "I won't be able to see anything until it's right on top of us."

"Maybe the storm will ease briefly and you'll see the demon beast approaching."

Jeneah gave Hissam a hesitant look. "You said we didn't have to kill her."

"The plan has changed. Americans are coming. I'm also not comfortable with the orders, but they are orders."

"So we get no money?" said Jeneah. "Imagine what we could achieve with even one-tenth of the ransom."

"I'll make sure we get something," said Hissam. "Check her. See if she has anything of value. I have a feeling this was always the plan. I think someone's making a fool out of us and the cause."

My thighs were burning. I struggled upright and pulled up my pants, which was a lot harder than pulling them down had been. I held my breath. I was investing everything in Damien being right about this trick. I ripped out the piece of paper and turned the phone over to turn it on. The door slammed open and the young guard stormed in.

Jeneah grabbed Ellen and dragged her back out into the main room. He felt her pockets for anything bulky. He found nothing. Then shock ran through him when he saw what was in her hand. He grabbed the cell phone from Ellen's clutches. Her wallet lying on the floor of the bathroom caught his eye. He scooped it up and presented the items to Hissam.

"A phone," said Hissam. "They can track that. No wonder they're coming." He quickly fumbled for the switch, held it down, and the phone beeped.

"No, Hissam," cried Jeneah.

The display lit up. A series of messages scrolled down its display. "It was off," Jeneah told Hissam. "You just turned it on."

"Got you," said General Ayden. "We did get that, didn't we?"

"Pretty close, General," said the communications officer. "As you saw, it was only on for a few seconds. We're triangulating it now."

"Good work, team. Let's hope we're in time."

Alex jumped into the passenger seat of the helicopter. Johnno was finishing up preflight checks. Jake was waiting by the aircraft with a spare helmet. He handed it to Alex, who wedged it on, jumped into the aircraft and strapped himself in. Each man was dressed in sand-camouflage uniform, with a light-armor Kevlar breastplate.

The earpiece in Alex's helmet buzzed and a voice spoke.

"Alex, I've got General Ayden on the line."

"Thanks, Si. Patch him through."

The line crackled and the deep tones of the general's voice echoed in Alex's helmet. "Captain."

"General Ayden."

"We have a rough locale. If you give us the IP of your aircraft I'm told we'll send through the dual X and Y coordinates."

"Johnno, do you know the aircraft IP?" hissed Alex.

"Of course. I've written it down here." Johnno indicated the IP numbers written above the radio unit.

Alex read out the list to the general, who relayed the numbers to his communications team. "Captain, they're sending them through now."

"Got them," shouted Johnny.

"Coordinates confirmed. Thanks, General."

"Good luck, Alex. We're all hoping for the best for you."

"Thanks, General. It's much appreciated. Okay, kick it, Jay."

"Make it so?" asked Johnno.

"Do I look like a seamstress? Just take off."

"Engaging primary thrusters."

"Stop messing around and get the stupid bird off the ground," Alex shouted.

The blades started rotating.

"Clear," shouted Johnno. He pulled back on the joystick and the helicopter lifted into the air. The navigation unit blinked, recalibrated, and started flashing. He tilted the stick and the craft headed east out over the gulf toward Iran. Within ninety minutes they were flying over the coast and headed inland.

"Jesus, look at the sky," said Jake. "Are we going in that?"

Alex looked up from the navigation unit. "Yup."

"Are we coming out of it as well?"

"You'll have to ask Jay that," said Alex.

"How many hours you done in a bird, Johnno?" Jake said.

"Hundreds," replied Johnno.

"How many in a huge sandstorm?"

"Don't sweat it. Top Gun was a true story about me."

"Do I need to remind you that movie was about jets rather than Blackbirds?" Jake gave Johnno a brief and enigmatic smile.

"Jay, what's the ETA?" Alex asked.

"Forty-five minutes."

The dust settled in around them and they wrapped their faces in the camouflaged scarves. Johnno sat in silence and stared intently into the distance. Jake was conducting an inventory in the back of the helicopter.

"Jake, have we got any firepower on this bird?" asked Alex.

"No."

"None?"

"Okay, we got a handful of small-caliber shells. I can load them but we're only going to get three or four shots. A couple of light pistols, which you can take." He threw them over to Alex. "We got lots of rounds for weapons we don't have. I said we didn't have anything prepped. Sorry. You'll have to use your wits and ingenuity."

"You're done for," said Johnno. He smiled at Alex and gave him a wink.

"Thanks for the vote of confidence, clown."

"The dust kills every sound," said Jake. "Even my own thoughts seem loud. Spooky stuff. They definitely won't hear us coming until it's too late."

"That's what I'm planning on," Alex said.

Time crawled. The men watched brief glimpses of the desolate landscape flicker past below. Johnno kept the helicopter low, and as far from civilization as he could safely navigate. The dust continued to thicken and visibility shrank. The storm had immobilized the country and left it deserted.

"I think we're near the potential location. Engage whisper mode," Alex commanded. He scanned as much of the plains ahead as he could see with his binoculars. It was a desolate place. Flat and dry. Vegetation was thin and tough. A few wild goats skittered away as the helicopter flew over them.

"There." Alex pointed to a small isolated hut set outside a very small village. There was an old, badly damaged four-wheel drive next to the hut that looked abandoned. There was no sign of life. As the helicopter flew in lower the dust blew around, reducing visibility even further.

"This is a joke," said Alex. "I can't see anything. I'm going to go in on foot. Jake, take over on surveillance. Use the infrared goggles. Chuck over the remotes."

Jake handed over a radio headset. Alex put the battery in his pocket and adjusted the new headset. He turned it on and the two men nodded to each other.

The helicopter lowered to a few meters off the ground. Alex shielded his eyes and quickly scanned the area. He jumped to the ground, rolled forward, and set off toward the hut.

"Johnno," he radioed to the helicopter, "what's the range of these headsets in a sandstorm?"

"Not far. If you're lucky maybe a hundred meters," crackled the reply. "I've never really tested them, or read the instruction manual."

"Jake, can you see anything alive?" asked Alex.

"No. No heat sources apparent," replied Jake.

There was a moment of absolute stillness, and everything slowed. The blades hushed through the air and the dust whirled in eddies. Johnno was looking up through the blades at the hazy sky, and Jake was scanning the nearby buildings.

The hair on the back of Alex's neck bristled. Ghostly lights danced over the ground. He could feel his heart beating through his light armor. He heard the metallic click.

"Cover!" he shouted. He dived to the ground and took shelter behind an old, dying tree.

Gunfire exploded from somewhere out of view. Sparks flew off the helicopter as the bullets ricocheted off the metal. There was a loud clang and a sudden high-pitched squeal. The helicopter rocked to one side.

"We're hit," cried Johnno.

"Go, get out of here." Alex screamed into the mike, waving them away.

He wheeled around, trying to locate the attacker. The only place he could be was on top of the building. Why hadn't he seen him?

"Yes, Captain," said Johnno. "We'll sort something out and be back as soon as we can."

The helicopter soared into the sky and disappeared into the dust. The gunfire stopped, and Alex's headset went silent. Great, thought Alex. What do I do now?

The silence rolled over the building and calm settled over the area. He could hear two voices in the building, both fairly low, which indicated older soldiers. He thought about it and wondered whether they were soldiers or just a bunch of guys with some rudimentary training. If the latter was the case, that was one thing in his favor.

No further activity had been forthcoming since the helicopter left. Normally a patrol would have been sent out to scout around the building. To Alex, it appeared the Iranians didn't know he was here. He couldn't hear anyone moving. The area had returned to its eerie state.

But someone knew we were coming and told the Iranians, he thought. That someone was an insider. In fact, it had to be more than an insider. A trusted, senior person. Very few people had known they were coming.

Another question was jumping for attention. What was the benefit of stopping him? At the most fundamental level, he was saving a tourist. Okay, it was Ellen, but who wanted her out of the way that badly? Besides health and safety experts, of course, he thought to himself with a smile.

He checked over his weapons. Sand was notorious for destroying modern technology, and after he had crawled through the surrounding sand patches his pistols were full of the stuff. It would take too long to clean them out. Alex was effectively weaponless, now and in the immediate future. Now would be a great time for Jess to turn up with the cavalry, he thought.

He couldn't hear anything at all, other than the rasping of his own throat. He rewrapped the scarf around his face. He took off his sunglasses and wiped the dust out of his eyes. He blinked and tried to focus on the building. It turned out to be a futile effort, and he replaced his glasses.

The building was fifty meters away. The solitary window on the facing wall was boarded over, and it was impossible to tell if someone was looking through some invisible crack. He rolled over and crawled toward the building. He scuttled along until he reached the wall and sat up against it. He quickly glanced around the corner and spotted the door. The coast was clear. He hustled down the side of the building and crouched next to the door. His options were limited.

"Men, pray to your chosen god," he whispered. "It's just as well you have exceptional breasts, Ellen."

He stood up, took a couple of steps back, charged, and kicked as hard as he could into the door.

CHAPTER 32

RING RING

How long has it been since the phone was turned on?" asked Hissam.

"You turned it on about forty minutes ago," said Farhan.

"It's best if we get going as soon as we can. I haven't received any further instructions, so I'm making the decision to move on."

"Do we kill her now, Hissam?" asked Farhan.

"No. Get everything ready first. We don't want her blood over everything. It'll be the last thing we do before leaving. Is the blade sharp? If not, sharpen it now. We don't need you only cutting halfway through."

Farhan unsheathed the long sword. He took a piece of soapstone out of his pocket and started to drag it slowly along the blade. The scraping echoed around the room. He appeared to be enjoying himself.

Hissam collected their belongings, packed, and made ready to go. He looked at the woman tied in the corner. She looked terrified. She kept bursting into tears, and then stopping.

There was a sudden burst of gunfire from the roof. Everyone looked up.

"They can't be here already," shouted Hissam.

They could hear the bullets bouncing off something metallic. Hissam and Farhan dived to the floor.

"Why aren't they firing back?" shouted Farhan above the noise.

Hissam shook his head. He could make out the dull sound of a helicopter, but it was too quiet to be close. "Maybe they didn't see us."

"I told you Jeneah was too inexperienced to bring along," said Farhan. "He's a boy. If he brings them here because of his stupidity, I'll kill him myself."

Hissam shushed Farhan. They all listened intently. There was a loud clang followed by a high-pitched squealing. Hissam clenched his fist and smiled.

The helicopter sounds diminished into silence.

"See, Farhan," said Hissam. "Jeneah has protected us and turned the mighty demon from the West away."

Farhan looked at him suspiciously. "We'll see."

Silence had returned outside.

Hissam took a camera from his bag. "Now is the time. Kill her and let's be gone from this place."

Farhan walked over to the woman huddling in the corner. He grabbed her and dragged her into the middle of the room. Hissam started to record the proceedings. The woman started to scream and struggle, but Farhan's strength was too great. He grabbed his sword but the woman twisted out of his clutches.

"Hissam," he said, "I need your help. She's too lively for me with only one free hand."

Hissam sighed and stopped his recording. "I think I have a camera stand somewhere."

"Forget the recording, just kill her."

"We need the evidence to thrust in the face of the Western demons."

"Just *shoot* the stupid bitch."

Then the door exploded off its hinges. The dust settled and there stood Alex, haloed by the empty doorway.

"Alex, help me," I cried.

He bounded into the room. Hissam was unable to reach for his gun, so he took a wild swing at Alex. Hissam was no brawler, but he managed to swing into the side of Alex's face. The punch skewed Alex's sunglasses, and left him peering over the rims. Alex glared back unflinchingly under the feeble attack. He swung at Hissam and knocked him across the room. Hissam clattered into some derelict furniture, which crumpled under his weight.

Farhan rounded on Alex and swung wildly with the sword. Alex ducked expertly out of the way. Farhan overbalanced and fell past him. Alex took the opportunity to pick up the camera stand. It was a heavy steel tube. The two parried and traded blows with each other. Farhan was a tall, strong man, and had the advantage of height, but I could see that Alex was even stronger than he had been before.

The two stayed locked in a deadly dance of sword and steel. Farhan tried a feint from the left and a lunge from the right, but Alex anticipated the move, dodged to the left, and brought the steel pole down on Farhan's wrist. Farhan screamed in pain and dropped the sword. Alex kicked it away.

Farhan dived desperately for his gun lying under the bags. Alex punched heavily into his side as he went past, knocking the Iranian to the ground.

Jeneah appeared in the doorway. He saw the fallen bodies. He saw Alex reaching for me. He fired his machine gun into the room. I cowered on the floor and screamed. The bullets thudded into the walls behind us.

And into Alex.

He stood there, in that moment, looking at me, motionless and shocked. I reached for him, but it felt like he was falling away from me down a dark tunnel. I tried to call out to him, but no sound came out. All was muffled, and all was dark except the moment between us.

Alex wheeled around and collapsed on the floor. My hearing

returned and I could hear myself screaming, crying out in anguish. Jeneah stood in the doorway, hopping from foot to foot. He was sweating profusely, and looked scared. He entered the room and stared at the devastation. He looked at his fallen comrades and then at Alex. He raised his gun to shoot at him.

I screamed out and he lowered the gun. He went over to tend to his friends.

"Alex, you came for me." I kissed Alex's forehead.

He was lying still on the floor with his eyes closed. "Yes, I wanted to ask you out on a date," he murmured.

"What?"

CHAPTER 33

GRENADE

I went to find you in your hotel room—"

"Suite."

"It is, and I wanted to work things out. There had to be a way. But you weren't there."

"Sorry, Alex, I needed to get away."

"Anyway, I came to find you. I would have preferred it, on the whole, if you'd gone to the Maldives."

"Yes, I concede that it may have been a safer option. Certainly with fewer bullets."

"You couldn't stay out of trouble for just a few days?"

"I'm sorry, Alex, I really am. I never meant for this to happen, especially for you to get hurt—again. There's been enough of that. You should've stayed home and met someone who can cook and iron without blowing up the apartment block."

"That's a nice attitude. No wonder you're intolerable."

"For god's sake Alex, what do you want from me? I've said sorry until all my breath's been sucked from my body. I don't know what you want. I just want you to forgive me."

He laughed and winced.

"You're forgiven," he said. "Now kiss me. And don't ever leave me again for as long as we live." He closed his eyes and lay there with a smile on his face.

"Was that it? Was that all I had to do? You could've saved a lot of time and trouble if you'd said that last week."

He didn't respond. He lay motionless on the stone floor. I couldn't even see him breathing.

I was kneeling in front of the men with my arms still tied behind my back. Alex was prone on the floor. He was losing blood quickly from the bullet wounds and looked pale. I leaned forward and kissed him on his lips.

I looked over at Farhan with his sword, then at Hissam, then back to Alex. "I commit to you for the rest of my life. And I think that is a commitment I can keep."

The Iranians stood by and watched. They were men with a cause. There was no bargaining.

"Are you prepared to make peace with your maker?" Hissam said.

"I'm not afraid," I said. "I have something you can't take."

"Now you die."

Hissam nodded to Farhan, who raised his sword above his head. He took a deep breath to concentrate his strength. His muscles tensed. I felt numb before them. I tried to find some solace in the fact that Alex and I were together for our final moments. I closed my eyes, and with my lip trembling, I waited.

The wall exploded, and bricks and concrete flew everywhere. Through the dust strode a female soldier. She threw down the rocket launcher and ripped off the surveillance headset. I recognized her from the faded newspaper clipping. Jessie. In the background another helicopter hovered two meters off the ground, sleek, black and silent.

Farhan, who was closest to the wall, received the brunt of the explosion. The flying debris rained down around him and he crashed to the floor.

"Not today, fellas," said Jessie.

With absolute fury in her eyes, she leapt at the remaining men. Within moments they lay unconscious on the floor. They hadn't even had time to react.

Jessie knelt down next to her brother. She examined his injuries.

"Sergeant!" she shouted. "Bullet wounds in both legs and one arm, Several in breastplate, lodged in Kevlar. The bruising's going to be bad, and he's going to be in a lot of pain, but his chest is all right."

She looked up at me and scowled.

"Administer an adrenaline shot immediately," she told the sergeant.

A soldier hurried over and kneeled down next to her. He took a short, flat cylinder out of his medipack. He twisted off the top and jabbed the exposed needle into Alex's neck. There was a sudden intake of air as Alex gasped and spasmed back into consciousness. He swore.

"Lucky you're fat, and in our armor," Jessie said.

"In war there is no 'our' anymore, Cowface."

"Jeez, Alex, we could've been in Fiji." Jessie examined her brother's body. "It's bad, but you'll survive." She gave him a gentle pat on the shoulder.

"Could you have left it any later?" Alex said.

"Do you know how hard it was to get this mission happening? I'm telling you, no nice girl should have to do some of the things I've had to do for a man, unless she fancied him. But that's another story."

"Lucky for us you're not a nice girl."

"I can still leave. Officially I'm not here." Jessie caught the eye of one of her soldiers and signaled him over. "Get him out of here, Sergeant. My brother will live to annoy me another day."

Another soldier bustled in with a stretcher. He put it down next to Alex, and the two soldiers manhandled him on. They lifted the stretcher and made their way out through the rubble to the helicopter.

"He saved me again," I said to Jessie. "How can you ever repay someone like that?"

Jessie shrugged. She was idly wrapping up some unused bandages. "You could argue that I saved you. I'd hate to call you ungrateful."

"But he chose to come. He didn't need to, especially after the Past."

"I think you're looking at it all wrong. Alex has been waiting all this time for you to save him. The past is a horrible place to get trapped in. Trust me, I know. Tragedy can do that to you."

"What's the difference between me apologizing to Alex, and me asking for forgiveness from him?"

"You've got a lot to learn about Alex. Forgiving you is about him letting go of the past. He's never liked being tied down to things. Forgiving is his way of letting go."

"But that's stupid."

"Well, he is male. Who knows how they think. Look, I was there when he hunted down the guys who killed our parents. Jeez, I remember as if it was yesterday. He just stood there with them cowering against the wall. He had them in his sights; he had his finger on the trigger. Then he said in his stupid, deep voice, 'It's over.' He could've killed them, he had every right to, but in his mind he forgave them. Then he turned and left."

"What kind of a person can do that?"

Jessie shrugged. "Someone who's a pain in the ass, that's who. Stupid goody two-shoes big brother. He needed to let them live so he could be better than them." Jessie grinned. "But I didn't need to be better."

"You killed them?"

"Oh honey, I killed them all, with them begging for their lives, crying for their mothers. I looked into their pitiful eyes and watched their despicable little existences drain away. They took away the most important things in my life, and I made them pay dearly for it. Don't forget I'm the angry one. I still need to find a way to make my peace like the stupid show-off did. Being all righteous and everything, forgiving them. He's such a pain."

"But you're here."

"Don't talk to me about it." She sighed. "No one hurts my brother and gets away with it. I don't have much family left. That reminds me, you, enough is enough. If you dare hurt him again, I will hunt you down and I'll … I'll … do something horrible to you. And trust me, I'm prepared to do some pretty horrible things."

I looked down, not really knowing what to say. "What happens now? Will he be all right?"

"On the outside he will. The rest is up to you. Anyway, I'm taking Goofy back to the US base in Qatar. You'll have to wait."

"Why can't I go with him?"

"There's limited space and I'm not sure if I like you yet after the way you treated him. Don't panic. Alex's crew is not too far away. They landed to make some emergency repairs, but they'll be here in about thirty minutes."

Jessie stood there, a fierce figure in the half-light. She stared at me, her hands on her hips. "You know what your problem is? You need to change your engine."

"My engine?"

"Yes, the thing within you that drives your ambitions. If you're not happy, you need to twist it, or let it twist into something that will allow you to be happy. Ask yourself, really ask yourself, if you're happy with your life. And if not, what you can do about it. Understand?"

I nodded. "Sorta."

"Good. And when you do, let me know how you did it. We could all use a bit of a change in our headspace."

The soldiers had loaded Alex into the helicopter and were awaiting instruction. Jessie turned and shouted a sentence of abuse, with the occasional verb thrown in. It seemed enough of a command for the men to act. With everyone aboard but me, Jessie did a final scan around the site.

"Half an hour, you said. Are you sure?" I asked.

"Yeah, why not. If you want." Jessie headed off to the helicopter. As she was about to jump aboard, she turned. "Hey, we have something in common now. We can be BFFs. Let's do lunch. We can talk about boys and stuff. Call me."

She formed her thumb and little finger into the mock phone and wiggled it. She jumped onto the Blackbird's runner, turned, and sat down on the cargo bay, letting her feet dangle over the edge. She gave the signal for take-off. Her face was without expression; her eyes hidden behind the dark glasses. She stared at me as the helicopter lifted off. She finally gave a short wave, a brief smile, and looked away into the distance.

The helicopter drifted away into the dusty sky.

CHAPTER 34

WICKED GAME

Adnan was red with anger. "What just happened there?" he said. "I followed all your instructions and here I am, not the deputy prime minister. I've lost a lot over this dream of yours. What have you to say?"

Abdul Aziz contemplated shooting him. It would get rid of so many issues in one go. If he could make it to the border and escape into the wastelands of the neighboring deserts, he might get away with it. But there was too much invested. Time for plan B.

"Sheikh, it was your position." Abdul Aziz was also red with anger. "What are you going to do about it? If I were you I wouldn't take this lying down like some exhausted whore. Be a man. Stand up and fight for what's yours."

"How do I do that?"

"Confront the man, and take what is yours. Tell him to stand down. You are a sheikh. You cannot be told what to do or what not to do. This is your land. It's your destiny. Seize the day. He'll be back at his quarters now at the barracks. A real man would go down and take what's his. What do you choose to do?"

Adnan slapped his hand down on the hood of the Land Cruiser. "Let's do it. Take me there, Abdul Aziz."

They climbed into the car and Abdul Aziz sped to the barracks. Not wanting the rage within Adnan to diminish, on the way he kept him riled about all the things that had been unfairly taken away from him. As a final stab into his crescendoing vehemence, Abdul Aziz reminded Adnan of his feelings for Elissa, who was now having an all-but-proven affair with Saif. Abdul Aziz wondered if Adnan would explode, and whom he could get to clean up the mess.

"You do realize," he said to Adnan, "that if something were to happen to him they'd have no choice but to give you your rightful position. I want you to remember that. Go to his barracks. Draw him out into the main quadrangle."

They got out of the car. Adnan waddled off toward the general living quarters.

Abdul Aziz dashed to the officers' mess, quickly organized two coffees, and carefully poured a fine brown powder into the left one.

The waiter asked what the powder was.

"Amyl nitrite mixed with crack and gun powder. I've used it in battle. All you know is rage. You hate everything. I used it in the early days of the second Liberian civil war. On the Johnny Mad Dog, a man becomes almost feral, committing acts of pillage and rape, with scant regard for even his own life." He winked at the confused waiter and left the building.

He walked over to Malik's office, and entered.

"Commander Malik, I've brought you a coffee. I wanted to see how you are faring."

Abdul Aziz placed the left cup near Malik, and the right one next to the guest's chair. He slumped down into the chair, quickly picked up his unpolluted cup, and started drinking.

"Thank you, Abdul Aziz. You've been a tower of strength for me over these last weeks. I must remember this when it comes time for promotions."

Malik took a sip. He looked into the cup. "Do you think they'll ever get the hang of making a decent coffee?"

Abdul Aziz laughed dutifully for his commander. "How are you feeling now, Commander?"

"I'm still very angry at everyone, but I'm trying to divide the emotion between what's personal and what's professional. I'm not allowed to take any action based on personal reasons. It all has to be within the expectations of the army. Do I punish Saif because he has offended me, or let him go because he's a good soldier and a damn fine pilot?"

"I'm sure you'll do what's required." Abdul Aziz took another sip from his coffee and watched Malik carefully. "Do you hear shouting?"

Both men rose out of their seats.

Malik went to the door and pulled it open. "I do."

"We should check it out."

Abdul Aziz could already see the drug taking effect. Sweat was beginning to form on Malik's brow, even though the air conditioning made the room cool, and his face was beginning to flush.

"If it's some of my men," said Malik, "I'll make them very sorry. I'm feeling very angry at the moment."

The two officers emerged into the quadrangle, where a boisterous scene involving a soldier and a civilian was quickly evolving into a spectator sport. Junior officers starved of entertainment filled the quadrangle.

The soldier was Saif.

"It is Saif again," Abdul Aziz said. "This man is no end of trouble. Who is the civilian? Is that Adnan?"

The two moved closer to intervene.

"What on earth is he doing here?" Malik said.

"How dare you. You have no right to take that position. It was mine. It was my destiny." Adnan was shouting into the face of Saif.

Abdul Aziz leant over to Malik and whispered, "I'll go behind Adnan. I'll restrain him if he does anything foolish." Malik nodded.

"And look who has appeared on the other side of the group next to Saif. It is Elissa."

Malik was starting to fume. He was clenching his jaw and grinding his teeth.

"I didn't decide it. It was the prime minister's decision. I didn't even want it. He made me do it," Saif said, shying away from the verbal onslaught.

"You lie," Abdul Aziz said to Saif. "You twist everything for your own gain. You don't deserve any of it."

He maneuvered behind Adnan and whispered, "Remember, he had Elissa. He took her from you. He rode her raw, indulging in many deviancies under your very nose."

Adnan flailed at Saif. But Saif easily ducked out of the way. He turned and flung his arms around the young officer and tried to drag him to the ground.

Abdul Aziz sighed. It was going to end badly unless he intervened. He stepped forward. "Let's break it up," he roared to the soldiers.

"Saif!" Elissa cried. She ran up to him to offer her assistance.

Abdul Aziz slipped a small pistol from beneath his shirt and fired it three times into the stomach of Adnan. He dropped the gun at the feet of Elissa.

"Elissa, what have you done," he cried. He glanced at Malik and could see the man was near the edge. "You've shot a man in defense of your lover, Saif."

"What?" she shrieked. "That is way the most stupid and unbelievable thing I've ever heard. Totally untrue."

"Do not deny it, woman. Your lies are not wanted here. Isn't that right, Malik?" He looked toward the commander.

The crowd turned to look at the man. Many were surprised by the apparition. Malik was bright red, his body slightly hunched. He staggered forward into the group.

"You stand there defending him again. You fallen … haven't … lying." Malik was having trouble forming his sentences. He struggled to say something, but all that would come was a series of animalistic grunts. He swayed violently.

"What are you saying? Malik, what's the matter with you?" Elissa cried.

In Malik's mind he saw the scantily clad woman, teasing him. Laughing at him. Laughing at his age, and his diminishing virility. And she spread her legs for the young men while laughing at him. Dishing out her sexuality to any who would take it. Enjoying it, and hating him.

"Malik doesn't look right," one soldier observed.

"Malik, please listen to me," said Elissa. "You're not well. You need to chill out."

Malik staggered around with sweat pouring off all parts of him. In his mind Elissa spat on him and his fury escalated. In front of everyone she taunted him, she belittled him. The drug had taken full effect and all he saw was a sea of red.

He heard his own voice say, "You betrayed me, you whore."

"I promise you with absolutely all of my life and heart I did not."

"The necklace," he stuttered.

There was a gunshot.

Saif pulled Elissa to the side, and the bullet burned through his left arm. He cried out in pain. Elissa screamed and drew her hands away from him as he fell to his knees. She reached out to Malik, both palms stretching out. She stepped toward him. He faltered and slowly lowered his gun.

Elissa rushed forward and threw herself around him. "I promise you with every fiber of my body that I don't know how the necklace got there." Tears were running down her face. "Please see reason."

There was a voice from the back. "He got the necklace from me and took it somewhere." It was Najla and she was pointing at Abdul Aziz.

"You lie, woman," said Abdul Aziz. "These are more words that spew from your mouth with no thought behind them."

"This is where your derision ends," said Najla, "and it ends right now. Don't think I don't see how you act when you think I'm not looking. Where is the man within you? You are no lord, no king. There is not one bone of benevolence in your body. Your selfishness undermines your authority to me. You, husband, should be my lord, my life, my head, my protector, my provider, the one who cares for me. Where is that man who thinks of something other than himself?"

She clutched her hands to her chest. "I'm ashamed that you're so foolish as to fight when you should be pleading on your knees for love, that you seek authority, supremacy, and power when you pledged to serve, love, and obey. But now I see you for what you are. Kneel before me and surrender your pride, since it has brought nothing but misery."

She extended her arm toward him with her palm facing upward. She beckoned him to her. "As a gesture of my loyalty, my hand is held out for you if you care to take it, and I offer you redemption. May it bring you salvation. I saw you take the necklace, husband. And where did you hide it?"

The group collectively held their breath.

Abdul Aziz put his hands over his ears and bent forward like he was in pain. "I can't take it any longer. You speak until all the air is sucked out of me. The ground is littered with the hind legs of donkeys. For once and all, shut up," he roared.

Abdul Aziz leapt for the pistol still lying on the ground. He scooped it up and shot a bullet into Najla. The body collapsed to the ground.

"You just shot your wife," one soldier said.

"It was a crime of passion," he replied. "Or a crime of sanity."

Malik turned to face Abdul Aziz. "It was you all along. Look at the carnage you've created. You have torn us all apart, and for what?" The color had drained from Malik's face. He felt faint and detached from reality. His face spasmed through a series of contortions.

"Don't listen to the ramblings of an insane old crone," said Abdul Aziz. "Malik, we've known each other for decades. You know you can trust me."

But Malik wasn't listening. The chemicals in his head refused to let anything in. He raised his shaking gun and fired at Abdul Aziz. The bullet went wide, and Abdul Aziz went pale.

"My head. The pain. I can't endure this." Malik dropped to his knees and turned the gun on himself. He was shaking but looked resolute.

There was a scream from Elissa.

The punch came in swiftly from behind. Malik collapsed forward, deaf to the violent thoughts in his head.

Saif stood behind Malik, shaking the pain out of his hand. "The heat gets to every man, no matter how noble," he said prophetically.

"That wasn't only heat," said one of the soldiers. "He's been drugged. I've seen it before out in the West African states."

"Who said that? You, soldier? Go to Commander Malik's office and see if there's any evidence that he's been drugged. If you find nothing, then go to his quarters. Search until you find the evidence."

Saif indicated another two men. "You two step up and detain Lieutenant Abdul Aziz."

Abdul Aziz stepped away from the soldiers. He suddenly felt the weight of all the planning fall heavily on his shoulders. Decades of planning and scheming had taken their toll on his heart and mind, and now it showed.

"Very well," he said. "The game ends as I am weary of it. Now." He indicated Malik.

"Why is he hunching over like that?" one soldier said to another. "And why did he say 'now' weirdly?"

"Shh," said another. "This is the big bad-guy monologue, where he tells us why he did it."

"You mean he had a plan? He's not going down without a speech?"

"Shh."

"It wasn't very good," said the first. "It was a bit old fashioned. I mean, who does a monologue anymore? Even at the Oscars they usher you offstage if you go on for more than thirty seconds. He forgets we're children of the Playstation generation. Excuse me while I check my emails."

"… the sun it shines, but not for us," Abdul Aziz said. "We, as proud Bedouins, conquered the planet, but have hung up our arms and forsaken our heritage. Westerners foresaw that the meek would inherit the earth, and it has come to pass. The weak run the world and the strong have been cast out as light entertainment. Our elders have fled as we have failed them. And this is what we have become? War's grim visage has smoothed its wrinkled brow …"

"Sounds like something from Led Zeppelin," said the second soldier to the first with a nudge.

Abdul Aziz was still talking. "And our leaders are led a merry dance for the whore that is the capitalist West to the lascivious pleasing of Pan's flute. If greed has been the tune of life, they have indeed played on."

Two guards came up and grabbed Abdul Aziz's arms. He shook them off.

"I haven't finished yet," Abdul Aziz said. "But I, with a malformed self-portrait in my attic; I, with a beaten passport, and a desperate allegiance for the country I love; I, did all of this for you. And where is my reward? Where is my share? I have done what has been asked when all the while the dogs of war bark and howl at me and linger on into the darkness to eternally remind me what I am. I have spied from the shadows under a merciless sun for you, until it deformed my spirit and faith. I did this for you, for all of you. All I wanted was to be one of you, and you never once graced me with a hand of friendship. So if you will not allow me to be your friend I choose to become your nemesis. Dangerous plots I have laid—"

"An admission," said Saif. "That's all we need. Take him away, men."

"No wait," said Abdul Aziz. "There is more."

"We live in a new world. Less is more," Saif said. "Lock him up and throw away the key. Maybe that will shut him up."

"Elissa, see to your husband," said Saif. "I feel he will need you now more than ever. Someone get stretchers for our fallen people. Let's see if we can at least save their bodies, even if their minds have been lost in the madness of the day. Oh, and can someone get me a doctor."

CHAPTER 35

LOVE IS A BATTLEFIELD

The plane touched down. Time was ticking away. It had been thirteen days and sixteen hours. The contract conditions had to be met within the next few hours or things would get messy.

Hinde had bailed because of the unsettled nature of the region, as he had said, but I guessed it was the weather. The man couldn't stand sweating, and dust was *waaaay* out. He would rather die than get one of his seven-thousand-dollar suits dirty. Or so I believed. So it was up to me to be the official dignitary from the company.

The power! Cue the maniacal laugh.

I presented my passport to the immigration officer. His scanner beeped as he read my passport. The officer looked over his shoulder to his supervisor and waved him over. The supervisor looked at the message flashing on the display.

The supervisor ushered me aside. "The emir would like to speak with you," he said. "You are expected immediately."

He led me to a waiting escort.

"The department of foreign affairs will be keeping your passport until they're ready for you to leave," said the supervisor. With my passport in hand he turned and left.

I turned to my escort. He motioned for me to follow. We walked through the various locals and tourists, past the anemic tourist shops desperate to claim the last notes of whatever currency the travelers carried, and waited by the luggage reclaim. The conveyor belt sprang into life and a solitary case emerged. It was mine. It came halfway around and the conveyor belt stopped. I could get used to this kind of convenience.

I lugged my new suitcase off the carousel and made for the screening area. My escort steered me past the security workers and he waved them away. Hah. I could use that level of authority when facing the infantile morons at the TSA who decided that any halfway decent-looking girl is an obvious terrorist threat to the country and needs to be violated by those horrific nude body scanners.

I'd only had a lightning stop in Istanbul before jumping on the plane back to Doha. Alex's team had landed on a helipad at the international airport, and I zoomed round the airport's duty free, abusing my credit card until it was warm to the touch, and racking up enough frequent-flyer miles in the process for a summer getaway to Hawaii, or new curling tongs.

My escort ushered me out to the VIP area, where a car, a stretch limo, was waiting. Oscars, here I come. He opened the door and I entered. He loaded my suitcase into the trunk and we were gone.

I flipped open my phone and switched it on. I surfed through the seemingly never-ending stream of text messages demanding this and that, alternating between work and my mother. There was a lone message from David. That was something I needed to address right away. It made me nervous. But I doubted whether it was worse than being kidnapped and nearly executed. I wished I could do it face-to-face.

I selected his number and dialed. My heart bounced around in my mouth. Maybe if I offered to buy him a Mercedes. Maybe that would help.

He answered the phone. Of course it was the middle of the night, which added to the insult. I explained. I apologized. I complimented.

I apologized. I cried a bit. I apologized. I hung up. I stared out the window.

I should have bought him the Mercedes. It would have been easier.

I'd got the guys to check out the hostel, to see if anyone had survived. I was worried about Damien and hoped he would not be nevermore. They had found him and he was alive. Just.

My phone rang, jolting me back to the present.

"Who's David?"

"Jessie, is that you? How did you get my number?"

"Yeah, who's David? The guy you were just talking to."

"He was the guy I was engaged to."

"Past tense?"

"Yes."

"Good. Just checking to make sure you got back safe. We can see you've landed in Doha."

"Are you spying on me?"

"I'm a spy. What do you expect?"

"Is Alex all right?"

"Yeah, he'll live."

"Where is he?"

"Down at the US base. They've probably used him as an excuse to smuggle in a hundred rashers of bacon. Hey, speaking of food, down near the souks I know a place that does an excellent sandwich. And it's cheap, too."

"Can't we go to the Ritz? I hear they do a great high tea."

"I'm a government worker, I can't afford that."

"Maybe this once I'll pay, since you saved us and everything."

"Okay, but I'll have to sign a gifts-and-gratuity waiver and an affidavit that you're not trying to influence the votes or actions of a government employee."

"That's a lot of paperwork."

"Tell me about it. You should see how much we have to fill out if we kill someone. Unless it's a Russian, of course. Anyway, go visit my brother."

"I will, straight after I meet the king and save the country. Is there anything I can take to Alex. Anything I can do for him?"

"Go flash him your boobs or something. He'll like that. You know how he is, a simple man with simple needs."

"I'll see you at lunch." I hoped it wasn't possible for spies to tell if someone was blushing over a phone line.

"Great. Don't forget to do your top up."

"Miss Ellen, this is your destination," the driver said.

We entered through the service gates at the rear of the palace grounds. We went through many security checks.

The door was opened, revealing the prime minister. He was dressed in a simple business suit that looked slightly crumpled, like he had been in it for a long time. He looked exhausted. He offered me his hand, which I gladly took. He smiled and I wondered if I could hug him. He was the first mentally stable, happy and reliable person I'd seen in what felt like ages.

"Are you all right after your ordeal?" he said.

"I will be. I'm still a little shaken at the moment, but nothing's broken or gouged, for once."

"Are you sure? You look pale."

"It's just the shock. I'll get over it. I have in the past. One thing I've learned is how to endure. And it helps if you have a bona fide hero around to help."

"Mr. Alex has been most helpful to both of us over the last week," he said. "We should not forget that. If there's anything I can do to assist you, please don't hesitate to let me know. But at this moment we have a very pressing matter. The emir has agreed to give you five minutes to discuss the contract. If he likes you, it could stretch to seven. All you need is his approval, which he will show by signing this document."

Hussein handed me a solitary sheet of paper. It had about two lines of text on it. I guessed the rest of the space was for his signature.

"That's not long. Can a rational decision be made in such a short time?"

"We shall see. But I have complete faith in him. He has never let the country down. He's a wise and adroit man. All you need to know is that the funds are ready. The various procedures have been followed, agreements have been signed and everything is ready to go ahead. We only received final approval from the IMF and Ex-Im China several hours ago. There were many questions we had to answer. The Chinese seem to be suspicious of us, for some reason. But I spoke to them and they became happy. I have flown many miles over the last week, making lots of new friends."

"You have a talent for assuring people around you." I gave him a smile.

"Thank you. But I prefer it when I like them." He gave me a smile in return. It made me want to hug him. I guessed he was doing his thing again. The man was formidable.

"I believe this will be the last time we meet," he said. "I wish you all the best, and I hope your life is full of happiness and prosperity."

"The last time? That is sad news," I said. "You have been very kind to me and I will miss you."

"Perhaps we may cross paths again if you come to our humble country on further matters of state. Or if you stay close to Mr. Alex, well, who knows." He smiled and opened a grand set of doors. He bowed, turned and left.

I entered the emir's domain with my solitary piece of paper, and it humbled me. The room was epic in both size and detail. Scattered around the walls were some stern-looking guards with sharp and alert eyes, not threatening but obviously present.

And there in the center of the room was the emir. He sat on a wide, low seat that curved up at the edges. There was a large, ornate desk on his left. I could see that when sitting at it he would be able to look over the city and bay. Maybe it was a reminder of what he was trying to achieve. He was talking to a tanned man in a dress-military uniform standing stiffly before him. I guessed his origin as Pakistan. The emir made a shooing motion. The soldier turned and left through a smaller door.

The emir turned to me and beckoned me closer. His face and eyes were soft. He was a large man, and well dressed in the traditional robes of royalty, much like the various pictures of him scattered around the city. There were no other chairs in the room. I guessed he didn't want people to get too comfortable in his presence.

The sky was a dull blue, and the early-morning sun shone through the large windows.

"Ms. Ellen, I am pleased to meet you. We don't have much time, but I hope to be of assistance to you."

"Emir, sir, Your Eminence, Grace, Your Worship ... I, that is, do you ... have you been told about this contract?"

"Yes."

"I don't understand. This is a bad contract. Why are you so keen for it to be honored?"

"The plutonium is more important to us than the money. Even if it was worthless it's still worth more than what we have paid. There are many questionable people around here who would kill, bribe, or coerce for it."

The emir looked out the window. He seemed to be lost in thought for a moment. Then he turned back to me.

"I won't give in to these people," he said. "It's safe with my men and me. I would worry if the West had it. Because the West is unlikely to use it, Western governments believe others are unlikely to use it either. We know otherwise."

"Being slightly cynical, I might also think that you're wishing to keep it away from a nearby hostile country that has an inclination to use such materials against you."

The emir smiled and moved in his seat. "I have my own dream," he said. "How many times have you been told that energy is the future? Imagine living in a world where you didn't work for money, but for energy. We talk about billions of euros, dollars, petrodollars, but show me where they are. They don't actually exist. It is only the concept. We are never going to agree on a global currency, other than the mighty megawatt. We will have great global power grids where we can roll around the energy to where it's needed at the time."

"Surely that's a flight of fancy," I said. "It would take an eternity to build the infrastructure."

"But in today's world show me where the money is. Money is only a dream, and a dangerous one that can easily collapse on itself. We already trade in petrodollars. There are not enough of them in the world to cover the amount of the transactions."

"I'm aware of the dream," I said, "but your world is proof that the dream can achieve so much as long as we all believe in it together."

"We are a fractured world separated by distance, beliefs, and language," the emir said, "but we are healing. Each country in the Middle East has its own currency. We are working toward a unified one, but of course we cannot agree. We want an Arab euro. Then how long will it be before it merges with the European euro? Eventually all currencies will become one."

"But that may take centuries."

The emir shrugged. "Perhaps, but it will happen. It has to happen. Corporatization and globalization are unstoppable. And once we are trading in a unified world currency, it can be based on anything. The experts say it will be based on energy. I am aligning with that idea. If it works our country will be in a very stable position. If not, then we still have plenty of money. But I eat into your valuable time."

At 7:45 A.M. GMT on September 15, 2008, Lehman Brothers Holdings Inc. filed for Chapter 11 bankruptcy protection, and the economic storm hit.

The emir looked at the large clock behind me. The hand moved to quarter of the hour.

"It is time, Ms. Ellen," he said. "What do you choose to do?"

"You know, ten years ago, maybe even ten days ago, I would easily have known what to do. There would've been no hesitation in my mind. But sometimes twenty-four hours is a long time, especially in politics. My job is to enforce this contract one way or another, but—"

The emir held up his hand. "Let's pause this chain of thought for a moment so we can assess the situation. If we leave things as they are, the shares in the plutonium will become worthless. If we forfeit the contract we have to surrender two blocks from the gasfield. Is that correct?"

"I'm sorry, but that's what the contract says. Your ministers knew that."

We sat in silence for a while. I became aware of the ticking of the large clock, the short, sharp sounds throbbing in my head. The emir looked at me earnestly.

"There is a way out," I said.

"Yes?"

"The contract will be invalid if it hasn't been signed by an appropriate and authorized person. If you say the prime minister did not hold that position at the time and was not authorized to sign on behalf of the state—"

The emir raised his hand. "The prime minister and I have been friends and allies for a very long time. He stood by me in 1995. He will be my prime minister until he decides he no longer wants to be."

"Or if I said that I had quit the company before I got here it will be a null contract. It might as well have been signed by Mickey Mouse."

"What will happen to you?"

"Oh, I guess I'll just lose my job. No biggie. I may have to sell my Lexus."

"But it is a contract. We should respect it," the emir said.

"A contract is just words on a page. We decide if they mean anything or not."

"We have a saying: 'It is written.' For us, if someone has gone to the effort of writing something down then it is important. We have to be responsible with our words. If we say them we need to stand by them."

"I understand, but sometimes we need to reassess what has been written and come up with a version two or an amendment. We like amendments in America. Times change. We need to change with them, which is giving me—at this rather inopportune moment—a personal revelation. If we refuse to change we only end up hurting ourselves."

"Believe me," Ms. Ellen, "we know plenty about change."

"It was my job to make you default. In the future nothing will be worth as much as energy. Either way, the result for me isn't good."

"Won't your company try and fight it?"

"Perhaps. But international contract law is slow, expensive, convoluted, and amazingly dull. Simon Hinde might forget if you buy him one of those big yachts. Maybe he might pursue it, *pacta sunt servanda* and all. Maybe you can fight back with Consideration, stating that Hinde willfully entered into a contract knowing he was going to exchange something valueless. But then maybe someone could make a statement at the European Court of Justice outlining several ethically vague recent changes lobbied by a certain US law firm in an area they immediately profited from. After that, maybe Hinde will take the boat."

"So, Ms. Ellen Martin, what have you chosen to do?"

"I'm sorry, Your Eminence, I know the plutonium is what you want, but I can't do it to you. It's wrong."

"Would you believe it's not the worst contract we've had? During the fifties and sixties we didn't understand the world of international contract law and it hurt us badly. But we learned, and now we have a much better understanding. We know the risks and, more importantly, we can take the risks and treat them as business decisions rather than guesswork and gambling."

"So, in our special, agreed time machine, which has placed us exactly two weeks ago, I quit from Cowley and Tate. The contract is now void." I tore up the sheet of paper. "Buy it tomorrow, it will be on sale."

I gave the emir a smile. I would never know if he could tell, but I felt all those questionable acts I had had to perform for Hinde lift off my shoulders. I felt redeemed.

"You are a strong and brave woman. You remind me of Sheikha Mozah, my wife. She has many ideals and is very loud with them. But she knows where we need to go for our people to survive into the future. So, like her, I trust you. Even though you seem to be as mad as a bag of cats. Both of you."

The emir rose to his feet and motioned toward the door. "Help me, Ms. Martin." He waved me over.

How do you carry an emir? I stood next to him. Many of the youthful men at the edge of the room tensed and all slowly moved closer. The emir did some obscure regal signal and they stepped away, although they still seemed tense.

"You know," the emir said, "a bad contract wouldn't really affect us. There's more gas than we can get out in a thousand years. One minor hiccup would hardly matter in the long run. I fear it has cost you your job."

"I'll sort it out. After all, it's not the worst day of my life."

"And that noble hero of yours?"

"You've heard about him? It may be *his* worst day."

"Hopefully nothing is broken," the emir said.

I understood that he didn't mean bones. "He's pretty resilient."

"He's not as resilient as you think. You need to be with him."

I laughed.

"He needs the balance that only you can bring."

I laughed louder.

"It's true. He yearns to have a simple life. I will make some calls. But for now you should go. I understand he's at the military base."

We had reached the door. Sheikha Mozah was there. The emir reached out for his wife, and she took his arm. She nodded at me and I nodded back. I'm not sure what it meant, but she was a queen. A real queen. Okay, princess, but that's just a technicality. A queen! Of a whole country.

"Ma'am." I curtseyed.

She offered her arm.

"Isn't this what the men do?" I said.

"Let's not get caught up in gender," she said. "We are who we are."

The emir sighed in resignation. We leaned together and kissed three times on the cheek. I curtseyed again because some things need to be done. I then skipped out the door to laughter coming from the two royals.

And secreted in a rundown shack on the Turkish border sat Kasim, brooding in his poverty. Malik had issued a search and detain—or execute if the Saudis found him first. Kasim couldn't, for the first time, buy his freedom. He had nothing except the clothes on his back.

But he knew two names. Alex and Jessie, the American siblings with an agency or military background. He knew what the woman looked like. He'd had a good look at her face and wouldn't be forgetting it for a long time. He also had some contacts in the right place that could help locate the two of them.

He sat and planned his revenge against them for reducing his life to this. Jessie had his key with his riches on it, and he was going to get it back and make them both pay. He watched a bloated cockroach lumber across the floor. He slammed his boot down on it and twisted.

The sun set and the darkness wrapped around him, leaving his eyes glinting in the gloom.

CHAPTER 36

THE END

I can see one thing isn't broken," I said.

Alex was conscious now. He looked up at me and smiled. He stroked his hand under my chin. He pulled my face to his. His clothes had been ragged and filthy, and so the only sensible thing to do had been to take them all off and let his body breathe. Then it seemed to be unfair if he was the only one naked so I'd taken all mine off as well.

I took him in my hand and straddled his body. I steered him toward me.

"I allow you to touch me," I said, grasping and guiding his hands.

He entered me slowly and filled me. I closed my eyes and bathed in the sensations sweeping through my body.

We lay for a long time wrapped around each other in the dirt, dust and pain. We lay there until all those things went away and it was just us—the only two people in the world. I felt vulnerable, powerful, warm, elated, sleazy, drunk, hungry, peaceful, content, violent, and totally out of control. There was probably another million more things I felt, but that's our little secret.

So in a hospital room, on a bed in the middle of absolutely

nowhere, I finally got the opportunity to open my heart and give in to my desires. It was about love; and it was about time. It had been absolutely fantastic. Alex had both his hands wrapped around my heart and I was the happiest I had ever been. My mind was at peace.

I woke up at six. He was safe and stable now. His wounds were tended and he was going to be all right. I got up from the bed, sat down on the little chair and looked at him. It would be unlikely I would ever meet a person like him again. He was absolutely everything I could want or need. He was wild and untamed, yet fiercely loyal and protective. I believed he would defend what he cared for to the bitter end. He was a savior; he had saved me in so many ways. But Ax and I were so different in absolutely every possible way. How was this ever going to work?

I looked at our clothes strewn around the room. Someone should do something about it.

I packed everything away. There was so much to do, so much to think about. I had to make sure Ax was going to be all right. I had to go back home. There was no getting around that. I had to face Hinde. I had to face the authorities in both countries. Someone was going to be in an apocalyptic amount of trouble. I hoped it wasn't me. I was going to have to tell my mother I'd met someone amazing, and then ...

But right now they could all wait. I lay next to Ax, with my hand resting on his chest. I could feel his heart beating. For now it was our world.

It was six-thirty. I walked away. Because that's what I do.

I'm Ellen Martin.

CHAPTER 37

THE END 2

Then I turned around and went back.

EPILOGUE

Why did I go back? I went back because Jessie was right. It was time for Ellen Martin to change.

The engine disappeared from my life. It twisted and found a new way to live, now its own master. And it left me free. Change can be scary, maybe the scariest thing of all, but it has to happen. Otherwise we don't live.

And maybe I couldn't do any better and Alex couldn't do any worse, so where we met in the middle, it sort of worked out.

And maybe Alex wasn't destined for a future in the suburbs, but really, was I? Perhaps there was a point where we could meet, where he took something from me and I took something from him.

I'm Ellen Martin.

But I want to be Ellen Heart.

Or perhaps Ellen-heart-Alex.

Yeah, so I lost my job. I guess no one will ever offer me a job again. I may, one day, even have to resort to being a consultant. Oh, the humanity!

Well, maybe not. Alex sold his security business to a prince in Abu Dhabi for twenty million. Everyone thought it was a steal, but after the crash, everything was cheaper, including this tropical island he bought. And this is where we met. I had to admit it was way cooler than the suburbs.

"Ax? Ax, could you sunscreen my back?"

He came bounding out of the surf and made his way up the beach. I loved that swimsuit.

I once thought my work was everything that defined me. What was I if I gave it up? It turned out the answer was happy.

I rolled over. "Thanks, loverboy."

Don't miss Mark Lingane's earlier novels.
Available in both paperback and e-book format.

Partly comedic, partly sci-fi/fantasy, entirely detective, film-noir,
genre-busting debut novel. In *Beyond Belief*, Joshua Richards
takes on reality in a fight to the death.

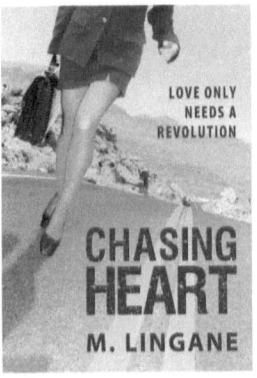

A fun and pacey read full of adventure, danger and
laughs, *Chasing Heart* is where it all started to go
wrong for Ellen Martin.

For more information on past and future publications, visit:
Mark-mywords.co